# MAGGIE'S TURN

# OTHER TITLES BY DEANNA LYNN SLETTEN

# MAGGIE'S TURN

## DEANNA LYNN SLETTEN

LAKE UNION
PUBLISHING

Published by Lake Union Publishing, Seattle

www.apub.com

Amazon, the Amazon logo, and Lake Union Publishing are trademarks of Amazon.com, Inc., or its affiliates.

ISBN-13: 9781503944350
ISBN-10: 1503944352

Cover design by Kerri Resnick
Cover concept by Deborah Bradseth of Tugboat Design

Printed in the United States of America

# CHAPTER ONE

It had been a hectic Monday morning at the Harrison household. Especially for Maggie. Her nineteen-year-old son, Kyle, had overslept, which meant he was late showering and would be tardy to one of the four college courses he was intent on failing. Because he was running behind, her fourteen-year-old daughter, Kaia, was also late getting ready for school. That meant Maggie's husband, Andrew, had to rush to shower for work. And, of course, Maggie then had to rush, too, since she was always the last one in the family to use the bathroom.

Kaia was pouting and stomping around because she'd wanted to get to school early to "hang" with her friends. Kyle rolled his eyes as he went out the door to his rusted pickup truck, muttering that it didn't matter if he made it to class or not. And Andrew ran through his schedule with Maggie before he rushed out the door to work.

"Remember, I have a seven o'clock meeting tonight—make sure dinner is on time so I'm not late," he instructed Maggie and was gone a second later.

All Maggie had time for was one long sigh as she slipped a light sweater on, pulled on khaki pants, grabbed her red coat and purse, then ran out the door, hoping Kaia wouldn't be late for school.

Maggie stole a glance at her sulking daughter as she maneuvered her minivan through the morning traffic. Kaia was a pretty girl, with long, thick auburn hair and brilliant-blue eyes. Her clear skin was still lightly tanned from summer vacation. *She'd be even prettier if she'd smile once in a while.* Maggie couldn't remember the last time she'd seen Kaia smile. Or joke, tease, or giggle. Much less laugh. It seemed as though she'd gone from a happy, young girl to a sulking teenager in the blink of an eye. But Maggie couldn't complain. Despite Kaia's constant irritation with her, she was a good student, had nice friends, and wasn't a troublemaker. Maggie knew she was fortunate. Both of her children had turned out to be decent people, even if they were a little confused about life. But who wasn't confused at their ages? Being fourteen or nineteen wasn't easy. Though Maggie tried to be understanding and give both Kyle and Kaia room to figure out their own lives, doing so was difficult sometimes. Kyle had gone from being a high-school honors graduate to a flunking college student, and he didn't seem to care one bit. He enjoyed his part-time job at the local motorcycle shop more than he did college. Evidently, earning seven-fifty an hour was fine with him. He had no financial obligations other than keeping gas in his pickup and going out with friends. Maggie sometimes wondered how he thought he'd make it on his own without a decent education, but she forced herself not to obsess over it. She had so many other things she could choose to worry about.

The northern Minnesota town of Woodroe was small—only twenty thousand people—yet the morning traffic was heavy as everyone rushed off to school and work. Maggie sighed again as she followed the parade of parents in minivans and SUVs rushing to drop their children off. It was only the third week of school, and she was already weary of the morning traffic in and out of the middle-school parking lot. Maggie had always maintained that parents in minivans and SUVs were the worst drivers on the planet. She found herself in near accidents at least three times daily upon entering or driving through the parking lot. Everyone had somewhere better to be and needed to get there faster than the next person. It was the same old story, year after year.

Maggie waited her turn to drop Kaia off at the front entrance. Country music blared from the minivan's speakers—Kaia's choice. Maggie always let her choose the music when they rode together. It was easier than fighting about the radio. Maggie could pop in the CD of her choice on her way home.

"I'm sorry we couldn't get here earlier," Maggie said as they pulled up in front of the school and stopped.

"Whatever." Kaia gathered her book bag and tennis racket. "Remind Dad to pick me up after tennis practice tonight" were her last words before she slammed the van's door and stormed off. She didn't even give her mother time to say good-bye.

Maggie tried not to take Kaia's rudeness personally, but her heart felt heavy as she switched AM on the stereo to CD and listened to Bob Seger sing "Roll Me Away," a song about escaping down a Western highway. Maggie had bought the CD on a whim two weeks ago, remembering how much she'd loved listening to Seger in the years before marriage, before kids—before life took control of her instead of the other way around. His music had a freeing effect on her, and she'd been listening to the CD continuously for the past two weeks.

Maggie dutifully followed the line of cars out of the parking lot to go home. She was relieved she didn't have to work today. Three days a week, she worked at a group home with developmentally challenged adults. She found it gratifying working with the residents, but it was exhausting to meet their needs all day, then go home to care for her family. Lately, she'd felt overwhelmed by it all—home, work, Andrew, and the kids. There never seemed to be a break in everyone's needs and wants.

Maggie glanced at her camera and laptop in the backseat—she took them with her everywhere—and smiled. She loved photographing Kyle's and Kaia's sporting events, school activities, and even her friends at the group home. Sometimes, her photos made it into the local paper. She'd been an art major in college and had fallen in love with photography. That was the one thing that made Maggie happy in between all the must-dos. She just wished she had more time to devote to taking photos . . .

Once, a long time ago, Maggie had dreamt of becoming a professional photographer and owning her own shop, where she could sell photos and artwork by local artists. When she and Andrew were newlyweds, they'd talked about this often, and he had said that once they were settled and had some money, it might be a possibility. But the years went by, and Maggie became so immersed in the children's lives, and in Andrew's, that her dreams had been put on the back burner, long forgotten. As Maggie sat in traffic behind other parents leaving Kaia's middle school, she thought about her old dreams and wondered if they would ever come true.

As the music played and traffic crawled along, her thoughts drifted back to the morning rush at home. Andrew hadn't kissed her good-bye. Not even a peck on the cheek. When was the last time he had really kissed her? She couldn't remember. Was it a year ago, two years ago? The heaviness in her chest swelled. Their relationship had changed greatly in the twenty-three years they'd been married. She remembered when they had first started dating in college, in Seattle. Andrew had moved there for school because he'd wanted to experience something different from his small-town upbringing. Maggie's father had been stationed at a military base there.

Andrew had been a junior and a communications major, and Maggie had been a freshman majoring in art. They'd met when they took a photography class together. He was quiet and serious in those early days, but Maggie's impulsive nature had brought out

4

his fun side. She had spent her youth being the dependable, responsible one, but in college, she had shed her old persona to become the carefree girl she'd always wanted to be. Even though they were opposites, something about Andrew had drawn her to him. Maybe it had been his boyish good looks or the charming smile that she was sometimes able to coax from him. She wasn't sure, but there had been something about him that made Maggie believe there was more to him than hard work and good grades.

With Andrew, Maggie had planned trips on a whim. She dragged him along with her, camera in hand, to rocky cliffs, sandy beaches, and lush, green parks on Puget Sound. Sometimes, they drove to Lake Tahoe for long weekends, enjoying its beauty. They'd married after Andrew graduated, and Maggie quit school to follow him to Minnesota. She made him promise on the day they married that they would always allow a little wanderlust in their lives, no matter how conventional they became. And she'd believed him when he'd said they would.

Maggie stopped at the red light, where she was to turn north to go home. She hit the Back button on the stereo to replay "Roll Me Away." She didn't switch her right blinker on to signal her turn. She just sat there, looking straight ahead. The lane she was in headed west, just as Bob did in the song. West, across the plains, over the mountains, to the ocean. She glanced again at her camera in the backseat. *Wouldn't it be fun to drive in a different direction and take a few photos? Just a few miles, not too far, not for too long.* Her heavy heart lightened at the thought, and a smile lit up her blue eyes. *North or west?* One direction meant home; the other, adventure. *North or west?*

When the light changed to green, Maggie turned up the stereo, smiled wide, and said out loud to no one but herself, "Roll me away." And she rolled clean out of sight.

It was just after five o'clock in the evening when Andrew Harrison stepped through the back door of the family's 1890s Victorian home with Kaia close on his heels. He'd planned on taking a quick shower before he ate dinner and then headed off to the county planning committee meeting he was expected at by seven.

Andrew was a busy man. He worked full-time as the marketing manager at Woodroe Communications, the local television and Internet provider. In addition, he served on several boards and committees in the area. The contacts he made at these meetings were important to his job, and his community-service work looked good for the company. Besides, he loved the town they lived in, and he enjoyed being a part of the many decisions made about Woodroe's growth and development. Plus, he also had a bigger goal in mind: he wanted to become mayor of Woodroe someday, just as his father had been. Many of the people he volunteered with believed he could accomplish that goal in the next election.

Tonight, the planning committee would be discussing the possibility of developing a large parcel of land as a new upscale neighborhood, and Andrew was anxious to get to the meeting early to hear how some of the other members of the committee felt about the proposal. He hoped Maggie would have dinner ready on time so he could leave right afterward.

But when Andrew and Kaia stepped into the back entryway, he immediately sensed that something was wrong. Their German shepherd, Bear, slipped past them and was out the door in a hurry, as if no one had let him out all day. The kitchen was dark, with only the afternoon sunlight streaming in through the windows, and there was no aroma of food cooking in the oven or on the stove.

Andrew set down his briefcase and hung his coat on the rack by the door. He called out, "Maggie, we're home! What's for dinner?" to the silent house. Their two chubby cats, Jazzie and Ozzie, ambled lazily into the kitchen to see who was there. Maggie was nowhere in sight.

Andrew frowned as he looked around the kitchen and saw that the breakfast dishes were still sitting, unwashed, in the sink. It looked as if Maggie hadn't been home since this morning.

"Great," he said under his breath, running his hand through his thick, dark hair in frustration.

Kaia noticed her father's agitation. "Maybe Mom is at work and will be home soon," she offered, laying her backpack on the kitchen table. "Sometimes she picks up takeout if she works late."

"Did your mom work today?" Andrew asked. He didn't keep track of Maggie's work schedule and rarely asked her about it. She was usually home before he was, because she picked Kaia up from school except on tennis-practice nights.

"How would I know?" Kaia shot back. She walked past him and opened the refrigerator to rummage for a snack.

Andrew eyed Kaia for a moment but held his tongue. He hated her smart mouth, but Maggie always told him to be patient before he reacted. Besides, he was more annoyed with Maggie for not being home on time than with his daughter.

"I'm going to shower. If your mom comes home, remind her I have to leave soon," he told Kaia. She shrugged as she grabbed an apple from the bottom drawer of the refrigerator.

It was after six o'clock by the time Andrew came down from his shower, and Maggie still wasn't there. Kyle was home by then, and Andrew heard him ask Kaia where their mom was.

"Who knows," Kaia answered irritably, looking up from her algebra homework.

Now, Andrew was even more annoyed. He couldn't believe how irresponsible it was of Maggie not to be home.

"Maybe Mom's van broke down, and she's stranded," Kyle offered through a mouthful of chocolate-chip cookie. There were always homemade cookies in the house, and he usually went for those first when he was hungry.

Kyle's offhand remark caused Andrew to pause a moment and Kaia to look up from her homework. He hadn't considered that something might have happened to delay Maggie. He picked up his cell phone and dialed her number, although he realized that she'd have called him if she'd broken down.

The phone rang several times before his call went to voice mail. Andrew didn't bother to leave a message. He hung up and stared at the kids.

"I just got her voice mail," he reported. He wasn't overly worried yet. He knew that there were places in town where there was no phone reception.

The three of them continued staring at each other until Kaia broke the silence.

"Do you think Mom is okay?" she asked.

Andrew wasn't sure how to answer. Maggie was never late coming home. Not once in twenty-three years of marriage had he had cause to worry about where she was or what she was doing. He knew she couldn't say the same about him. But seeing the worried look in Kaia's eyes made him want to reassure her.

"I'm sure your mom is okay." He glanced at Kyle for support.

"Sure," Kyle agreed. "She might be in Walmart or at the grocery store. Cell reception is lousy in those places. Or she may have left her phone in the car. There could be a thousand reasons why she's not answering."

Andrew nodded, grateful to Kyle for trying to put his sister at ease. And who knows, maybe Kyle was exactly right?

Looking at his watch, Andrew realized it was getting late and he had to leave soon.

"Listen, kids, I have to go to my meeting." He pulled out his wallet and handed Kyle some money. "Kyle, why don't you take your sister out to eat? I'll leave my phone on so you can call me when your mother gets home, okay?"

Kaia didn't look pleased but kept silent. Kyle said they would call him.

By the time Andrew arrived at his meeting, he'd convinced himself that Maggie would be home any minute and there was nothing to worry about. The meeting held his attention, and for the next two hours, he thought only of property prices, taxes, and zoning permits. It wasn't until the meeting ended that he realized it was nine thirty, and Kyle hadn't called to say Maggie was home.

# CHAPTER TWO

Maggie hadn't planned on being gone for more than a couple of hours. As she'd driven west, toward Fargo, North Dakota, she'd stopped along the way to take pictures of sites that interested her. She stopped in a small town and took pictures of its old cemetery, where worn granite and marble headstones dating back to the early 1800s stood at attention. She snapped photos of abandoned barns and ramshackle farmhouses sitting in knee-high golden grass that swayed gently in the breeze. She took a picture of a grain elevator at work, and of a man off in the distance on his tractor, cutting hay. They were ordinary photos, but they depicted the reality of life on the plains. And that was what Maggie had always loved: using her camera's lens to capture simple moments in time that everyone could relate to. It had been so long since she'd done this, and she reveled in every picture she snapped, as if she were taking photos of great importance.

Before she knew it, two hours had flown by and Maggie was in Fargo. Without even thinking twice, she turned her van south on Interstate 29 and headed for Sioux Falls, South Dakota. Bob Seger continued singing his greatest hits over and over, and Maggie didn't grow tired of them. Bob was right—it felt so good to finally feel free. She was smiling again, singing along with the CD, feeling the weight of the world, her world, being lifted off her shoulders. The freedom was intoxicating. She felt silly and young again, just as she had years ago when these songs were new and she had so much to look forward to in her life.

Night was falling as she rolled into Sioux Falls, so Maggie pulled into a hotel at the edge of town and rented a room. She told herself she'd just take a few pictures of the falls in the morning, then turn around and drive home. She thought for a moment about calling Andrew to let him know where she was and that she'd be home the next day, but she couldn't bring herself to dial the number. Andrew would be angry, and all her carefree feelings would dissipate into thin air. How could she explain what she'd done? She hadn't planned this escape—it had just happened. Andrew wouldn't understand. And the kids? Kyle usually went for pizza with his friends, and surely, Andrew could make dinner for Kaia. Frankly, she felt she wouldn't even be missed. Andrew was always so busy, and the kids paid so little attention to her anymore. For just a few more hours, she wanted to enjoy the freedom she'd felt all day. So she pushed aside all thoughts of responsibility, family, and work obligations. Reality would be waiting for her when she returned tomorrow. It seemed that easy.

Andrew called the local sheriff's office that night to report Maggie missing. He knew Sheriff Derrick Weis well. They had graduated from high school together and volunteered as baseball coaches years ago, when Kyle played Little League. Luckily, Derrick was working the night shift, so Andrew was able to get through to him right away. Kaia and Kyle sat nearby, anxiously listening as their father explained that no one had seen Maggie since eight fifteen that morning.

The sheriff listened quietly until Andrew finished.

"I'm sorry to hear this," Derrick said. Andrew knew that Derrick and Maggie both volunteered in the schools, so he knew Maggie well.

"Are you sure she didn't go home for a while after dropping Kaia off?" Derrick asked. "Or maybe was around town shopping? Have you called any of her friends to check if they've seen her today?"

Andrew was at a loss for words. Maggie didn't really have any friends, or at least none that he knew of. There were the people she worked with at the group home and parents she volunteered with at school events, but he didn't think she ever saw any of them socially.

"Maggie doesn't go out with friends," he said, suddenly realizing how strange that must sound to Derrick. "She's either at work or at home."

"I see," Derrick replied, sounding surprised. "Well, if you can think of anyone she might have been in contact with, call them. That will help narrow down the search. Meanwhile, I can start by checking the accident reports and calling the local hospital."

Andrew took a breath. "I hadn't thought of her being in an accident," he told Derrick.

"I'm sorry to bring it up, but we have to check all possibilities."

"I understand." Andrew thought that in this small town, he'd have already heard if Maggie had been in an accident. But he appreciated Derrick looking into it.

"Maggie drives a silver Honda Odyssey, right?" Derrick asked. "Looks like this year's model."

Andrew frowned. "That's right. How do you know that?"

"I see her at school in the morning when she drops Kaia off and I'm dropping off our daughter. I've often wondered how you get off so lucky not having to drive Kaia in when you work only a block from school," Derrick said.

Andrew had never really thought about it that way. Maggie drove the kids to school. That was her job. "I have to be at work early," he explained, which he knew wasn't completely true; he chose to go into work an hour early each morning. His coworkers always teased him about being a workaholic, and even in college, he'd been pegged as an overachiever. He hated those labels. The last thing he wanted to do was justify his working habits to Derrick, too.

"I'll get this out to my deputies so they'll be on the lookout for Maggie's van," Derrick said. "I'll also pass around her description, and we'll do a quick sweep around town to see if anyone has seen her. And I'll send out an alert about Maggie's disappearance to neighboring towns. In the meantime, have a look around the house to see if anything's missing or out of place. You might also want to see if Maggie packed a bag. She may have stopped by the house sometime this morning, and it would be helpful to know if she had planned on leaving."

"Planned on leaving?" Andrew asked, his anger flaring. "Do you think she's left me? Why would she do that?"

"Now, don't get upset, Andrew. I'm not suggesting anything. It's just that sometimes when a spouse is missing, we find out that they left intentionally. It would be good to rule out that possibility before we file a report."

Andrew had heard enough. *Maggie leaving? How ridiculous.* She had no reason to leave him. As far as he was concerned, her life was perfect.

"Fine," he said tightly. "I'll take a look around. But I can assure you she didn't leave me."

"No doubt you're right," Derrick said. "But look around the house anyway, just to make sure nothing is out of place or missing. The kids must be upset, so why don't we wait until tomorrow for you to come by and fill out an official missing person report. I think you need to be with your family tonight."

Andrew thanked Derrick and hung up. He turned to face Kyle and Kaia, who were seated on the living-room sofa, looking pale and anxious.

"Did Mom leave us?" Kaia asked in a small voice, now sounding more like a lost child than an obnoxious teenager.

"Of course not," Andrew insisted.

"Then that means we have to assume something happened to her," Kyle said reluctantly. "That's not a great alternative, either."

Andrew's brow furrowed. He didn't know what to think, but he had to keep the kids calm.

"Listen, kids. All we can do right now is let the police do their job. There's still a chance your mom might come home tonight. Until then, let's not get upset, speculating about what may have happened."

Kaia narrowed her eyes at her father. "How can we *not* be upset? Mom's gone. Doesn't that mean anything to you?" she said sharply.

Andrew took a deep breath and stared at both his children before answering. He'd been trying to learn, through Maggie, to control his own reflex to yell back when the kids snapped at him. He wondered exactly when he'd lost control of them, or of their respect. It seemed they'd grown up so fast. At six foot two, Kyle was two inches taller than he was, and his oversized clothes hung loosely on his lean body. The two of them had the same brown eyes and dark, wavy hair, but Kyle's hair was longer and shaggier. Kyle also had a laid-back air about him, something Andrew had never had. Kaia, on the other hand, was intense and always pushing the envelope. She'd recently grown taller and was almost as tall as her mother. She had thick, auburn hair, completely the opposite of Maggie's fine, blond hair. Both kids were an interesting combination of their parents' genes, and Andrew had always been proud of them. But over the years, he seemed to have lost touch with them, and it had been a long time since he'd had to relate to either of them without Maggie as a mediator.

"Of course I care that your mother is missing," Andrew finally responded in a controlled voice. "I just don't want to get worked up about what we don't know yet."

Kaia rolled her eyes and threw herself against the back of the sofa with dramatic flair. Andrew realized that the night ahead would be tough.

After much arguing and protesting from Kaia, both kids had finally gone to bed. Andrew turned his attention to searching the house. His first problem was the luggage. He had no idea where Maggie stored it. He started in the basement but came up empty-handed. Climbing the stairs, he realized the basement wasn't the logical place to store luggage, because it would get damp and moldy there. Of course Maggie would have thought of that. Next, he tried the hall closet, which was too small to store anything except their coats and winter boots. Finally, he tried the closet under the staircase and hit pay dirt. There sat a complete three-piece set of black luggage along with several nylon duffel bags and a couple of large backpacks. But as Andrew stared at them, he realized he had no idea how much luggage they owned; even if a duffel bag was missing, he wouldn't know it.

Frustrated, he slammed the door and headed upstairs to see if any of Maggie's clothing was missing. But he realized, even before he entered their room, that he wouldn't have any idea if articles of Maggie's clothing were missing. He paid so little attention to what she wore. Besides, if any of her clothes were missing, they could easily be in the laundry or at the dry cleaner.

Their older home had only one small closet in the bedroom. Maggie used an antique wardrobe for her clothes. He opened its doors and glanced at the clothes hanging there—jeans, sweaters,

T-shirts, khakis, and dress pants—then looked at the shoes and inspected the two drawers below. Everything looked neat and orderly. He saw no gaping holes to suggest she'd packed anything.

Andrew shut the doors and sat on the bed that he and Maggie had shared for twenty-three years. He gazed around the room. Everything looked exactly as it always did. Her jewelry box sat on the dresser, undisturbed, as did the glass dish beside it filled with earrings and rings. The checkbook they shared for family bills lay there, too. Nothing was awry. Andrew breathed out a frustrated sigh. Not only because he had no idea where Maggie was but also because he didn't know as much about their daily life together as he should have.

# CHAPTER THREE

When morning broke, the pull west was so strong that Maggie ignored her resolution to return home and continued on her impromptu trip. Going home meant facing reality, and after the stress of the past two years, Maggie could no longer face the heartbreak and disappointment that lay behind her. Her subconscious took center stage and urged her forward, blocking her visceral need to worry about everyone but herself. Whether she completely understood it or not, Maggie needed this escape, or else she'd lose herself completely.

Maggie explored downtown Sioux Falls and relished the simple pleasure of taking photos of the many sculptures strategically placed on the downtown sidewalks. After that, she went to Falls Park and immersed herself in the beauty of the falls, taking multiple photos of the water as it splashed over the rocks. The morning sun shone bright overhead, and the Big Sioux River sparkled as the fall leaves rustled in the breeze. Maggie was entranced by it all, the simple feeling of just being there, free to do as she pleased.

Maggie stopped at a discount store on her way out of town and purchased a few personal necessities and a change of clothes. Then she drove the van west on Interstate 90, with no idea whatsoever of where she was headed, only that she needed to continue on.

Around one o'clock in the afternoon, Maggie pulled into Deadwood, South Dakota. She had stopped in the small town of Wall, South Dakota, for only a short time to take photos of the famous Wall Drug Store and the long street of old-time buildings that made you feel like you'd just been transported back to the Old West. It was touristy but charming, and Maggie loved the simplicity of the log buildings and overhangs that shaded the sidewalks.

Maggie had noticed the turnoff for Mount Rushmore and almost taken it, but then thought better of the idea. It would be fun to see the monument again, but it was out-of-the-way and she just wanted to keep heading west.

Driving slowly down Main Street, Maggie absorbed the atmosphere of this once-famous Western town turned tourist trap. Maggie loved Deadwood. She, Andrew, and the kids had visited a couple of times on their way to Seattle to see her father and sister, but they'd never spent as much time exploring it as she would have liked. She didn't care that the town lived and breathed tourists. It still pulled you back to its lively, uncensored roots and made you feel as if you'd stepped into another era. She planned on taking her time, camera in hand, discovering every inch of it.

Wanting to enjoy the mood of the town, she rented a room at the historic Bullock Hotel, right on Main Street—a charming three-story brick building with rooms that were plush and inviting, and even had their own ghost who might haunt you at no extra charge. Maggie found this delightful and exciting, and settled right in.

The day was warm and sunny, so she set out to explore on foot. After picking up several brochures from the front desk, she wandered through the many casinos, saloons, and shops, taking pictures of whatever caught her eye and luxuriating in not having a schedule to dictate her every move. Just before three o'clock, she headed into Old Saloon #10, the site of the famous shooting of Wild Bill Hickok in 1876. The saloon boasted in its brochure "Wild Bill Shot Daily," so she found a seat in the dark saloon at one of its high, rough wooden tables, ordered a Diet Coke, and settled in for the show.

By three o'clock, the place had filled with tourists. A gentleman appeared dressed to the nines as the famous James Butler Hickok, alias Wild Bill, and began telling his life story to the fascinated crowd. Speaking with a soft Southern drawl, he strutted back and forth in front of his audience, describing the events that led to his untimely demise. Then, after choosing three members from the audience to portray his fellow card players, the four sat at a table and played out the final minutes of his life.

Maggie took several pictures of the man who called himself Wild Bill. His brown hair was long and wavy under his hat, and his mustache hung down on each side of his mouth in true Hickok fashion. His eyes sparkled with mischief. She thought he had an interesting face, so she took several close-ups in the darkened room.

At the end of the short reenactment, he ended up on the sawdust floor with a "bullet" in the head, holding in his hand the infamous "aces and eights." After the gun had fired and the audience finished cheering, good ol' Bill rose from the dead to thank everyone for coming. He reminded them that they replayed the show several times a day, then he disappeared into the back room from where he'd come.

Maggie was sifting through the brochures to decide where she might want to eat a late lunch when a deep, male voice made her glance up in surprise.

"Did you enjoy the show, ma'am?"

Maggie found herself gazing into the eyes of Wild Bill. Still in costume, he smiled at her while brushing off the sawdust that clung to his long black jacket.

"Can't say I've seen a better shooting recently," she told him. His face was just as interesting up close. Lightly tanned with the beginnings of crow's-feet framing brown eyes that sparkled when they caught the light. Mischievous maybe. Downright dangerous for certain. His smile, however, was warm and inviting, not the least bit dangerous.

"I couldn't help but notice you were taking pictures earlier. That's a nice camera you have there," he said, nodding toward her camera on the table.

"Thank you," Maggie said. She wondered what old Bill was up to. Maybe he needed a few copies of the pictures for his wall.

"Do you take photos for a living?"

Maggie laughed. "Heavens no. I'd like to, even hoped to one day, but that's not in the cards anymore, I'm afraid."

Wild Bill cocked his head and wrinkled his brow. "Why?"

This caught Maggie off guard. "Well, um . . ."

"Can I buy you a drink?" he asked, interrupting her. "Or do you have a husband and family waiting for you somewhere?"

*Husband and family waiting for me somewhere?* Maggie sat there a moment, wondering why he'd ask this question. "No. No one is waiting for me right now," she said carefully. *Drinks with Wild Bill? This should be interesting.*

"Well then," he said as he slid up onto one of the high stools and waved the waitress over. "What can I get you?"

Maggie looked at the empty glass in front of her. "Diet Coke."

Bill smiled up at the waitress. "Two Diet Cokes, please, Missy," he said, handing her two wooden tokens. He looked back at Maggie. "I hate to come off looking cheap, but they give me dozens of those drink tokens to pass out to the guests, so I might as well use them."

Maggie grinned mischievously. "Wild Bill drinks Diet Coke?"

Bill laughed. "I'm sure I'm a disgrace to the real Bill Hickok, but I have a show later, and I like being sober so I don't fall down for real."

Maggie smiled. It wasn't like her to sit with a strange man in a bar, but he seemed friendly enough. She relaxed and decided to enjoy his company.

"How long have you been getting shot here, Bill?" she asked him as the waitress delivered their sodas.

Bill grinned. "First off, my real name is Robert. Robert Prescott. But you can call me Bob."

Maggie nearly choked on the sip of soda she'd taken. First Bob Seger, now another Bob. What a strange coincidence.

"I prefer Wild Bill, if you don't mind," she said after clearing her throat. "You're certainly dressed for the part."

Bill looked at her curiously over his glass, but nodded. "Whatever the lady prefers. And what shall I call you?"

Maggie grinned. "Calamity Jane seems appropriate. Don't you think?"

Bill smiled. "Okay, Calamity Jane it is." He raised his glass to toast her. She touched hers to his and they both laughed.

"Well, Calamity, getting back to your question, I've been getting shot here since June. As Bob, I'm just a mild-mannered eighth-grade history teacher in Salt Lake City. I've always wanted to try my hand at acting, and my favorite time period is the Old West, so I signed on to play Bill for the saloon and for other events in town. I find it much more interesting reenacting history than just talking about it."

"School must have started by now in Salt Lake City. Why are you still here?" Maggie asked, interested in this faux outlaw's story.

Bill twisted one end of his long mustache between his fingers. "I was having such a fun time playing Wild Bill, I decided to take a year off from teaching and continue through the winter. After twelve years of teaching, I was ready for a change."

Maggie nodded, understanding perfectly how change was needed sometimes. Hadn't she just turned her world upside down in only one day?

"Before I ask about your story, Calamity, I have another question. Can I buy you a late lunch? I'm famished and would enjoy some company with my meal for a change."

Maggie thought a moment, but could read nothing more into his invitation other than sharing a meal. And she was starved, too. She agreed, and the two of them stepped out into the bright sunshine and strolled up Main Street to the Midnight Star casino. Bill assured Maggie that Diamond Lil's, the bar and grill upstairs, served a delicious lunch. And she'd also enjoy the movie memorabilia displayed there.

Maggie found it amusing that no one looked twice at Bill's costume while they were walking up the street. And the hostess at Diamond Lil's merely smiled and said, "Howdy, Mr. Hickok." She seated them at a table by a window facing Main Street. Apparently, people in Deadwood didn't think too much of long-dead gunmen turning up on their streets or in their eating establishments.

After ordering cheeseburgers and fries, Maggie and Wild Bill wandered the room to look at the movie costumes that hung in glass display cases on the walls. Wild Bill explained that actor Kevin Costner owned the Midnight Star, so the costumes and posters were from the many movies he'd made over the years.

They laughed at the plastic-handled pistols displayed with his clothes from *Silverado*.

"Do you think he really used those toy guns?" Maggie asked, surprised at how cheap they looked.

Wild Bill grinned and shrugged.

As they walked through the restaurant, they shared which movies they had seen and talked about which costumes had impressed them most. They agreed that those from *Dances with Wolves* and *Robin Hood* were their favorites. When their food was ready, they sat and enjoyed it as they talked about their lives before coming to Deadwood.

"Your turn, Calamity," Bill said between bites. "What brings you here alone without that family of yours that I know you have?"

"Is it that obvious?" Maggie asked, frowning at the fact he could tell she had a family at home. "Do I look that settled?

"No, ma'am. As a matter of fact, you're quite the looker. But I see a ring on your finger, and you're dressed like every other middle-school mom I've ever known, so that gives you away." He winked at her, teasing, and Maggie actually blushed at his words.

"I'm sort of taking a much-needed vacation by myself," she told him, wondering if it sounded as bad as she thought.

"Ah, burnout, right?"

Maggie's eyebrows rose. She thought she must look really old and haggard if he could tell just by looking at her. He wouldn't be far off, either. She felt that way.

Bill only smiled and shook his head. "Nothing to be ashamed of. We all get burned out now and then. Heck, I used to wonder what kept some of those mothers going at the school. They'd have two or three kids in different schools, running from one to another, volunteering their time plus working, plus running a home—not to mention driving kids to sports and music lessons. Who wouldn't burn out and run away?"

*"Run away."* That stung. Maggie sat quietly, considering what she'd done. She hadn't planned on leaving. It had just happened. And now, only a day later, she was sitting in a bar with a strange man in a strange town. What had seemed so innocent just seconds ago now seemed like something only a terrible person would do.

"Hey, Calamity," Bill said in a soft voice. "Did I say something to upset you?"

Maggie looked up into Bill's warm brown eyes.

"You must think I'm a terrible person. I walked out on my family. How could I do such a thing?" She lowered her eyes to the table and stared at her half-eaten meal.

Bill reached over and gently touched her cheek, drawing her eyes back to his.

"Actually, Calamity, I think you're one brave woman. It's not just anyone who can see what they need to do to survive and grab it. You did what you had to do, and who knows where it will lead you. At least you didn't stay behind to confront your other option— going crazy." Bill smiled at her. "You'll go home a better person, better wife, and better mother for having had the guts to escape for a while. And you *will* go home, Calamity. Make no mistake about it. But only when you're ready. Up here," he said, touching the side of her head, "and here." He pointed to her heart.

Maggie stared at him a moment, taking in everything he'd said. A small smile spread across her face.

"That's pretty deep for a gunman-slash-lawman of the West," she said.

Bill laughed. "Pretty deep for a history teacher, too," he added. His eyes suddenly lit up. "Say, I have tomorrow off, and the weather's beautiful," he said, glancing out the window. "Have you ever had the privilege of riding up the mountains to Rushmore on a hog?"

"A hog?" Maggie repeated, laughing. *Heavens no!* "Why, Bill Hickok, I'd expect you to ride up the mountain on a horse, not a motorcycle."

"Well, I believe that if Wild Bill were alive today, he'd ride a motorcycle. But not just any cycle, mind you. A Harley-Davidson.

How'd you like to ride up with me tomorrow, Calamity? I promise you, it'll be a blast."

Maggie thought a moment as she looked into his eyes, considering his invitation. It was absurd, of course, completely ridiculous to consider going into the mountains on a Harley with a complete stranger. It was exactly the type of thing that the old Maggie would have never considered doing. Which was precisely why she knew it was the right thing for her to do now.

"How do I know you're not a serial killer who lures women up the mountain and disposes of them there?" Maggie asked, half teasing, half serious.

Bill smiled. "I can give you references. Just ask the local sheriff if I'm trustworthy."

Maggie took a deep breath as she formed her next words. "I'm not looking to start anything," she said. "If I say yes, we go only as friends."

Bill nodded in agreement. "Your honor is safe with me, Calamity," he said with a thick Southern drawl.

Maggie relaxed and agreed, and they made plans for him to pick her up at her hotel the following morning.

As they stepped outside into the late-afternoon sunshine, Bill took off his hat and tipped his head while bowing slightly. "Until tomorrow," he said. He turned to walk down the street toward Old Saloon #10. Only a few paces away, he stopped, turned, and called her name.

"Calamity Jane!"

Maggie turned, too, and looked at him.

"It's cold in the early morning. Be sure to dress warmly and wear your leathers." With another tip of his hat, Bill turned and ambled on down the street.

Maggie gazed after him, her brow furrowed. Tourists brushed past her, but she didn't pay attention to them as she pondered what Bill had said.

"My leathers?" she whispered to herself. Then a big smile spread across her face as she realized what Bill meant. "Whatever you say, Wild Bill!" she exclaimed as a woman passed her and frowned. Maggie spun around and headed back up the street toward a specific shop she'd passed earlier.

# CHAPTER FOUR

Andrew was already waiting for Derrick Weis when the sheriff entered the station at eight thirty the next morning. Derrick frowned and shook Andrew's hand in greeting. "Still no sign of Maggie, I take it?" he asked. Andrew nodded.

The two men walked into Derrick's small, cluttered office, and Andrew dropped heavily into the faux-leather chair opposite Derrick's desk. Andrew was dressed in a suit, as usual, but he felt tired and nervous. He kept running his hand through his hair and was having trouble sitting still in his seat.

Derrick studied him but didn't say anything.

Uncomfortable under Derrick's stare, Andrew finally spoke, his voice sounding less confident than usual. "So what do we do now?"

Derrick pulled a sheet of paper from his desk drawer to take notes. "We need to file a missing person report and get this information out officially. Tell me everything you know."

Andrew explained again that Kaia was the last person to see Maggie; he didn't think she'd come home after dropping Kaia off at school, and he hadn't noticed any missing clothes or luggage. He was sure she hadn't packed anything. He gave Derrick the name and phone number of Maggie's workplace—he'd written it on a piece of paper, because he didn't know it by heart since he never called or visited Maggie at work. Then Andrew filled out a form describing physical information about Maggie. Height, weight. *How the hell should I know?* Blue eyes, blond hair. *Yes, real blond, not bottled.* What had she last been wearing?

"How would I know that?" Andrew blurted out, pointing to the question. "Who pays attention to clothes?"

Derrick's eyes scanned Andrew. "Looks like you pay a lot of attention to your own clothes."

"What's that have to do with it?" Andrew insisted, and then he caught the look of disapproval in Derrick's eyes. Andrew knew he was losing control. He was already on edge because of Maggie's disappearance and from the fight he'd had with Kaia this morning. She had insisted on staying home from school, but he'd made her go anyway.

"You can't do anything for your mom here," he'd told Kaia, who replied by glaring at him and calling him an insensitive jerk. And now Derrick was looking at him with that same disapproving stare.

"I suppose you remember what your wife wore this morning," Andrew shot back.

"My wife is a nurse. She wore white this morning," Derrick replied calmly.

"That's not fair," Andrew countered. "Your wife wears a uniform, like you do. Of course you remember what she wore."

Derrick conceded with a nod. "At least try to remember everything you can. Every little detail counts."

Andrew stared back at the sheet of paper. He closed his eyes and tried to imagine yesterday morning when he'd last seen Maggie. He'd been preoccupied with his own daily schedule. Noticing his wife's outfit, or even how she looked in it, wasn't something he'd thought to do. Besides, it seemed as though she wore the same thing every day. A T-shirt or sweater, jeans or khaki pants. He had no idea which of any of those she'd been wearing yesterday.

Finally, Andrew gave up. He finished filling out the form and handed it back to Derrick.

Derrick looked it over a minute before returning his gaze to Andrew. "Is there anything else I should know?" he asked, his tone steady.

Andrew glared at Derrick. "What do you mean?"

"Did anything happen between the two of you to make Maggie leave? Did you have a fight recently? Are there problems with the children?"

"No, of course not," Andrew answered quickly.

Andrew ran a hand through his hair again, took a deep breath, and let it out slowly in an effort to relax. He didn't understand why he was being so defensive—it wasn't as if he were guilty of something. He didn't like people prying into his personal life, and he felt as if Derrick was pointing a finger at him for Maggie's disappearance. He knew that if he didn't calm down, he'd look guilty as hell over something he didn't do. Slowly, he lifted his eyes. Derrick stared back at him, frowning.

"Listen, Derrick," Andrew said, his tone calmer. "This has been tough. Sorry for snapping at you."

Derrick nodded. "I understand. I really don't want to pry, but anything you can tell me may help us find Maggie."

Andrew nodded. "Maggie and I were . . . *are* fine," he said, quickly correcting his slip into the past tense. "At least as far as I know. I mean, hey, every couple has their problems, right? We're no different from anyone else." Andrew wasn't about to share the details of his marriage with Derrick. It wasn't any of his business, and he didn't believe it would help them find Maggie anyway. But the look in Derrick's eyes told him that Derrick maybe knew more about him and Maggie than he was letting on.

"We'll do our best to find her, Andrew," Derrick said. "Just let us know if you hear anything. The sooner we have information, the better."

Andrew nodded as he stood and then left Derrick's office. His heart pounded as he walked out to his car. Where could she be? He'd watched enough crime shows to know that if Maggie didn't show up soon, the chances of finding her would get slimmer with each passing day.

Andrew went to work as usual but couldn't keep his mind on anything except Maggie's disappearance. He didn't mention it to his coworkers, and he hoped she'd be found before they learned she'd been missing. The way Derrick had looked at him this morning, as if he were to blame for Maggie's disappearance, had aggravated him. He hadn't done anything wrong—he was innocent. He'd just been going about his business when, all of a sudden, she was gone. It made no sense at all. Yet Derrick's question, *"Did anything happen between the two of you to make Maggie leave?"* hung heavily in the air.

*No marriage is perfect*, he told himself. They had their problems. But that was no different from anyone else, right? Yet deep down, he knew that if Maggie had left on her own, he was partly to blame.

Just before school let out, Andrew left the office. Andrew's job included securing new advertising from clients, so it wasn't unusual for him to come and go from the office. He was thankful he didn't have to explain his absence as he picked up Kaia that afternoon.

From the moment Andrew picked her up at school, Kaia insisted relentlessly that Andrew should go look for Maggie. When Andrew tried to explain how illogical searching for Maggie would be since he had no idea where to begin looking, she accused him again of not caring that her mom was missing. Andrew didn't really want to go around asking questions, letting the entire town know Maggie was missing. It would've been embarrassing to him, especially if she'd left on her own. He didn't want to have to explain to everyone he knew why his wife would leave him if that was the case. "Just let the police do their job," he finally told Kaia, but she disagreed. The tension between father and daughter grew by the minute, making Andrew feel weary.

When Kyle finally came home, Andrew decided it was time to discuss what they were going to do. Without Maggie around, they needed to come up with a plan to take care of the things she usually did.

"Listen," he told the kids after they'd all finished picking at the pizza Kyle had brought home for dinner. "Until Mom comes home, I'm going to need you both to help out around here."

Kaia shook her head and snorted. "You make it sound like Mom's on vacation or something."

"Kaia, enough, okay?" Andrew said, trying hard not to lose patience with her. He turned to his son. "Kyle, I'm going to need you to drive Kaia to school in the mornings, and we'll take turns picking her up."

Kyle frowned. "No can do, Dad. I have to be in class by eight, and the college is on the opposite side of town from the middle school. I'd have to drop her off by seven thirty to make it."

"Then do it," Andrew said.

"No way," Kaia said. "I'm not sitting around school for an hour before it starts."

"Listen, Kaia, you have to give in a little here. I simply cannot drive you. I need to get to work on time."

"Your office doesn't open until nine o'clock," Kaia shot back. "You can drop me off and still have plenty of time to get to work. It's only a block away."

The frustration of the day's events finally caught up with Andrew. "I'm not arguing with you anymore, Kaia," he bellowed. "If you don't want Kyle to take you to school, then you can ride the bus."

"What?" Kaia asked, stunned.

"You heard me. Ride the bus. Your mother may have had the time to spoil you, but I have to earn a living so you can have all those things that you think you can't live without. From now on, you can ride the bus."

Kaia stood, fists clenched, her eyes spitting fire. But Andrew held his ground, arms crossed, matching her stare. Kyle shifted his gaze between the two of them. Kaia turned on her heel and ran up to her room, slamming her door so hard the pictures on the walls of the dining room shook.

Kyle took a deep breath.

Andrew stood there, a smug smile replacing his anger from only moments ago. *Round one won.*

"Hey, Dad?" Kyle said tentatively. "Maybe it's not such a good idea to let Kaia ride the bus."

Andrew glanced at him. "She'll live," he said tersely.

Kyle shrugged and headed up to his room.

# CHAPTER FIVE

As Maggie settled in for the night at the Bullock Hotel, she enjoyed the peace and quiet of having the large room all to herself. She loved the Victorian decor, the thick flowered comforter on the queen-size bed, and the antique oak wardrobe where she'd hung her new purchases. After leaving Wild Bill, she'd spent the rest of the after-noon shopping, picking up more personal necessities and a couple of nonessential items that would be suitable to wear on her ride tomorrow. It had been years since she'd spent so much time doing exactly as she pleased, and she felt relaxed and happy.

Maggie left the television volume on low as she brushed her teeth and got ready for bed. Slipping into new pajamas she'd just purchased, she snuggled into the cushy bed, using both large pil-lows for herself. She picked up the TV remote, poised to turn it off when a photo appeared on-screen. It was a picture of a middle-aged woman with the word *Missing* printed underneath it.

Fear suddenly overtook her. The photo wasn't of her, but what if Andrew had reported her missing? The idea had never even occurred to her until now, and she admonished herself for not calling her family sooner, a rare lapse in her good judgment. She grabbed her cell phone and turned it on. How could she have been so selfish?

It was so unlike her. Of course they'd wonder where she was. She'd been so caught up in her unplanned escape that she'd forgotten everyone but herself. She quickly punched in the number for home.

Andrew answered on the second ring. "Hello."

"Hi, Andrew."

"Maggie." Andrew gave a relieved sigh. "Where are you? Are you okay? We've been trying to find you."

His questions came all in a rush, and Maggie felt deeply guilty as she heard the concern in her husband's voice. She took a deep breath, controlling her own emotions as she answered.

"I'm fine. Everything is okay," she told him. "I'm sorry I worried everyone. I should have called sooner."

"That's an understatement," Andrew said, the concern now gone and replaced by a tone Maggie knew all too well—sarcasm.

Maggie tensed. Nothing had changed.

"You had the kids worried," Andrew continued tightly. "Where the hell are you?"

Again, guilt flooded through her at the mention of the kids, but Maggie hesitated before answering him. She didn't want to reveal where she was. Andrew's tone had brought back all the unhappiness she'd felt over the past few years. He sounded like the same old Andrew—more annoyed with her than concerned. She couldn't go back to that. In that instant, she realized she needed more time.

"I'm sorry," she said again, almost automatically. Gone was the carefree woman who had driven away yesterday, on a whim, from her problems. Back was the old Maggie, feeling small and lacking control of her own life.

"When are you coming home?" Andrew asked, his voice insistent.

Maggie sat on the bed in her room, looking at the furniture from a time long past, a time when life was simpler, less complicated. She couldn't go home yet—that she knew for certain. The kids would be fine without her for a while. Kyle was an adult, even if he didn't always act like one, and Kaia was as strong-willed as her father. Besides, it was time for Andrew to step up and spend time with his children.

"Maggie," Andrew said, sounding irritated.

"I don't know," Maggie answered. "I only know that I'm not coming home yet."

There was a long pause at the other end as Maggie waited for Andrew's response. Everything suddenly became clear to her. She needed time away, time to rejuvenate after the past two years, and time to sort out her life after twenty-three years of marriage. Why else would she have driven off without a second thought? Self-preservation. Her mind, body, and soul had finally said *enough*, and she planned to listen to them more closely now.

"Maggie, what is this all about?" Andrew asked.

Maggie sighed. How could she explain to someone who thought the world should run on a timely, orderly schedule that she just couldn't do it anymore? His world consisted of *his* job, *his* meetings, and *his* activities. He expected his daily schedule to dictate the lives around him. Wasn't that why Maggie worked part-time instead of pursuing her own dream job? To be there for him? To cook his dinner so he could go to his meetings? To run the house and oversee the children? No, he just wouldn't understand.

Maggie didn't want to get into a fight about their many problems tonight. Andrew was angry enough as it was. "I just need some time to myself. I need to get away for a while. That's all."

Andrew snorted. "Time to yourself? Get away for a while? Isn't it enough that you've been back and forth to Seattle several times these past two years? How much time away do you need?"

Maggie cringed. How could he consider what she'd gone through the past two years as time off?

"That's not fair, and you know it," she said sharply. "I was handling family matters then. I wasn't on vacation."

"Well, you need to handle family matters here. The kids need someone home, and you know how busy I am with work and my other commitments. So it's time to turn yourself around and head back here from wherever you are," Andrew insisted.

Maggie sighed and shook her head. Sighing seemed to come naturally to her when she talked to her husband. "The kids will be fine. They're old enough to take care of themselves as long as you pay some attention to what they're doing. And I know you're quite capable of taking care of things around the house. I'm just not ready to come home yet, Andrew."

Another long pause hung in the air as Maggie waited for Andrew's response.

"If you won't come back on your own, I can stop you, you know," Andrew finally said. "I can cancel the credit cards and close the checking account. Without money, you'll have to turn around and come back."

Maggie shook her head sadly. Money was always a big issue with Andrew. "I have my own money, remember? My own checking account and my own credit card. You were the one who insisted we separate our money a few years ago when you accused me of wasting it on unnecessary stuff for the kids. The family checkbook is on the dresser, where it always is when I'm not using it. I'm only spending what I've earned, not *your* money. Besides, there's the money my dad left me, too, so there's not much you can do."

In the ensuing silence, Maggie thought back to that day when Andrew insisted they have separate accounts. Kyle was ten years old, and she'd bought him a pair of cowboy boots that he'd begged her for. They weren't expensive boots, just cheap knockoffs, but Andrew was furious that she'd spent money on boots that Kyle would outgrow in a matter of months. When she'd reminded him that she earned money for the family, too, he'd become indignant and told her if she wanted to waste her "little paycheck" on junk, that was her business, but she wasn't to waste the family money. She opened her own account the next day, and their shared account was used only for household bills, necessary clothing and items for the kids, and groceries.

"Maggie, is this your revenge for what happened last year?" Andrew asked in a softer tone.

Maggie drew a sharp breath. She hadn't expected this, not in this tone, not at all. Revenge? Is that what her running away was all about? She hadn't really thought of her escape like that, but maybe it was.

"I don't know," she replied honestly. "I hadn't thought of it that way. Maybe. I really can't say."

"I thought we were past that," Andrew said, sounding irritated again. "I thought we were okay now."

Okay? Did he really believe after all she'd been through—*they'd* been through—everything was okay? She realized at that moment just how disconnected he'd been from her all along.

"Everything isn't *okay*, Andrew. I need some time to figure out why I'm not okay." She sat in silence for a moment, collecting her thoughts, but when there was no response on the other end of the line, she decided they'd said enough for one night.

"Tell the kids I love them, and I'll be home soon. I'll call you again and let you know where I am. Good-bye, Andrew."

The connection clicked off before Andrew could say another word. He lay quietly on the bed for a moment, digesting all that Maggie had said. His eyes went to the checkbook on the top of their dresser. The money threat hadn't worked, but she couldn't possibly have enough money in her own account to gallivant around the country for very long. Or could she? He was shocked to realize he had no idea how much money she earned—even more so when he racked his brain and realized that he'd never even asked her how much money her dad had left her. He'd figured it hadn't been very much and hadn't given the amount another thought. Now, he wished he'd paid more attention to the family finances. He knew how much he earned, but he'd left the bill paying to Maggie. Anything extra she bought came out of her checking account. Maggie also took care of the taxes each year. He'd been so wrapped up in his own ambitions, he hadn't paid attention to details.

As he lay alone on their bed in the dark, quiet house, he wondered exactly where he'd gone wrong.

Maggie lay in her hotel-room bed, fuming. Her conversation with Andrew had brought back all the emotions of the past two years. If she had needed a good reason for fleeing, he had given it to her by making those stupid remarks and reminding her of his past behavior.

How could he possibly have insinuated her trips to Seattle were vacations? If he thought planning funerals and attending to family matters were vacations, he was an insensitive jerk.

Maggie's thoughts drifted back over the past two years. Her father had been very ill for a long time. He had breathing difficulties, a result of being a two-pack-a-day smoker for his entire adult life. Her sister, Amy, was still living in Seattle near their father, and, being single, she was able to spend time caring for him. Maggie did what she could from a distance, but she knew it wasn't nearly enough and always felt guilty about being absent. But she had her own family to care for and couldn't run back and forth across the country to be there. It wasn't until her father was dying from emphysema that she made the trip there to help Amy and spend the final days with her dad. It had been a heartbreaking three weeks, watching him slowly fade away. Maggie then helped Amy go through his belongings and sell the house he'd lived in since he'd been stationed there years before. Amy didn't want the house and all its responsibilities, which turned out to be a smart choice since a year later, she was diagnosed with breast cancer and couldn't have looked after it.

Maggie's second trip was even worse than the first. This time, she watched her sister die and had to pack up Amy's apartment all by herself. Andrew hadn't offered to join her or help her on either trip. He was too busy with work and his committee responsibilities, and he thought it best for her to go alone. At the time, Maggie tried not to resent his absence. She also tried to justify to herself that it was best for the family that he stay behind. As time went by, she realized that he hadn't accompanied her to Seattle out of selfishness, and it upset her that she'd let him get away with it. Her disgust for him grew deeper when she'd learned what he'd been doing while she was away.

Maggie brushed that depressing thought away. She focused instead on tomorrow's ride to Rushmore with Wild Bill. She wasn't going to let Andrew ruin her fun. He'd already done enough to make her feel miserable, and she wasn't going to let him spoil her newfound happiness anymore.

# CHAPTER SIX

It had never occurred to Maggie to argue with the men in her life. It wasn't that she had no backbone—she'd just never seen the need to use conflict to get her way. She resolved conflicts by either agreeing or quietly going about her business and doing things her way. Conflict was too hard to live with, anger too strong an emotion for her to deal with.

It had started when she was a small child. Her father was in the navy, a lifer, and he expected his home life to run as orderly as his work did. His word was law, and Maggie and her younger sister, Amy, would have never thought to question his authority. Not that he was unkind in any way. He adored his daughters, and even on his small salary, he spoiled them whenever he could. But his disapproval would have devastated them, so they sought to make life at home run as seamlessly as they could. Besides, there had been enough conflict, fighting, and tears in the household before their mother left them to last Maggie a lifetime.

The first five years of Maggie's life had been a roller coaster of emotions, and she was still deeply scarred by her mother's constant complaints and fits of tears. Her mother had grown to hate being a navy wife. She hated moving from base to base, hated the low income and the strict rules and expectations. So one night, when Maggie was five and Amy was three, their mother disappeared from the base housing where they lived in Florida, leaving no note, no explanation, and no good-byes. After finding out his wife had left him, Maggie's father never spoke of her again. The girls followed suit, but the pain of their mother's absence had remained with them throughout their lives. The family eventually moved on, first to a base in Texas, next to one in Southern California, then finally returning home to Seattle. Five years after her mother left, they learned that she'd died in a car accident in Florida.

From the day her mother abandoned them, five-year-old Maggie set out to make sure her father and sister were happy. Even though her father hired a woman to come in to watch the girls and do housework, Maggie soon took over as much of her father's and sister's care as she could. She became the nurturer, the good daughter, the good sister, the good student—and eventually, the good wife and mother. And she'd been doing it ever since.

Her years in college had freed her of all her responsibilities, and she'd enjoyed shedding her caretaker persona for a more carefree lifestyle. Andrew had fallen in love with the devil-may-care Maggie, but somehow, after they'd married, she'd slowly turned back into the pleaser.

At first, Andrew seemed to appreciate Maggie's willingness to please, but slowly things changed. Through the years, he'd started taking advantage of her willingness to take on all the household and child-rearing responsibilities. After a time, he just checked out of their lives completely, always too busy with work or commitments to spend time with his family. Maggie realized she may have been partially to blame for this happening. She'd let it happen rather than confronting him as soon as she'd noticed what he was doing. Maybe, if she'd insisted he pay attention then, things between them would be different now. Or maybe not.

After a restless night, Maggie awoke early and was dressed and down on the sidewalk in front of the hotel just as Wild Bill rode up on his bike. Bill pulled off his helmet and let out a whistle when he saw Maggie.

"Why, Calamity Jane, don't you look a sight in all that leather?" he exclaimed, making Maggie actually blush. She had purchased the outfit the day before in one of the many leather shops on Main Street. She wore black-leather chaps over a pair of Levi's, a fitted leather jacket that zipped in front, and a pair of low-heeled ankle boots. It had cost her a small fortune, but she had so much fun buying the clothes, it was worth it. Never in her life had she thought she'd own riding leathers.

"You don't look too bad yourself, Wild Bill," Maggie told him. He was also dressed in black leather, but his was soft and worn from use. Like a pirate, he had a red bandanna tied over his long hair, to keep it out of his eyes and under his helmet. He looked dangerous and sexy—no one would ever have guessed he was a history teacher from Salt Lake City. His Harley-Davidson was a looker, too. All metallic black and silver chrome gleaming to perfection. The handlebars were long, and the leather seat was raised in back with a medium-length sissy bar attached. Black-leather saddlebags hung on each side near the back, decorated with silver tabs and black fringe.

"This is for you, m'lady," Bill said as he reached behind him and took an extra helmet off the sissy bar. Maggie accepted the helmet and slipped it on her head—a perfect fit. After stowing her camera in one of the saddlebags, she slid behind Bill on the raised seat, slipped her arms around his waist—the only place to hang on—and off they went.

The morning air was cool, as Bill had predicted. As they sped along Highway 385 toward Keystone, Maggie was happy she had the leathers on. They kept her warm as the bike maneuvered the curvy mountain road. She viewed the scenery through the helmet's tinted visor as if for the first time. She had visited Mount Rushmore years before with her father and sister, but a ride through the mountains in a station wagon didn't compare to this. The open air, the smell of pine trees, and the feel of the bike between her legs were exhilarating. She almost laughed at that last thought. But it was true. Hugging a man she barely knew and being pressed against his back as they sailed along an asphalt river made her feel alive again. Womanly, even in all this leather. The excitement of a new adventure and the allure of spending time with a man who actually wanted her company were invigorating. She felt refreshed and revived for the first time in years, and Maggie absorbed it all, hoping to retain this carefree feeling long after the ride was over.

As they continued up the mountain road, Maggie tried to imagine Andrew maneuvering this bike as she held on behind him. She couldn't. He had lost all sense of adventure years ago.

They passed under the arched wooden bridge that Maggie remembered from long ago. As they continued up along the curves, she caught a glimpse of Washington's stone profile high above on their right. She tapped Bill's shoulder, gesturing for him to pull over. He did, and she took several pictures of the president's profile and of the surrounding trees and valley below. Maggie was as excited as a child at Christmas, and Bill laughed at her obvious enthusiasm.

From there, they hopped on the bike and continued on to their destination. They pulled up to the gates, paid the entrance fee, and headed to the parking structure. Once parked and off the bike, Bill noticed the frown on Maggie's face as she lifted the helmet from her head and shook out her hair.

"Something the matter, Calamity?" he asked lightheartedly.

Maggie pursed her lips. "I don't remember having to pay to see the monument before," she said. Her eyes assessed the parking ramp. "There also wasn't a parking structure. The last time I was here, it was all outdoor parking."

Wild Bill hung his helmet over the handlebars and smiled. "You haven't been here in a long time, I take it. Wait till you see what else is new."

Maggie grunted.

Bill suggested they take their leathers off and stow them in the saddlebags since the day was warming up. Clad in a yellow T-shirt and jeans, her camera hanging from around her neck, Maggie walked with him toward the monument.

The day was absolutely gorgeous. The sun shone bright as a gentle breeze stirred the mountain air. The cooler temperatures had tipped the leaves with a hint of the approaching fall, giving onlookers a glimpse of the beautiful colors that would soon explode over the entire valley. Maggie reveled in the fresh mountain air and the clear blue sky as Bill led her up the stone steps toward the monument's entrance.

When they reached the top of the steps, Maggie stood and stared, amazed by what she was viewing. Bill hadn't been kidding when he'd said things had changed. The sight before her would have done a tourist trap like Disney World proud. But here, in the majestic quiet of the Black Hills, it seemed ostentatious and extreme. She turned to Bill, stunned.

"They've commercialized it," she whispered.

Bill looked at her, nodded slightly, and shrugged. She could tell by the resigned look in his eyes that he felt the same way she did. Giving her a small smile, he took her hand in his, and they walked up the stone path.

Where once there had been only a stone-lined viewing terrace and a single gift shop and restaurant, there was now a flag-lined walkway, immense viewing terrace, and an amphitheater. And as impressive as the Avenue of Flags and Grand View Terrace were, Maggie couldn't help but feel saddened by the extreme changes to this once quietly dignified monument. The changes proved to her, once again, that progress and change weren't always for the best.

It wasn't busy, unlike on summer days when tourists flocked everywhere for that one special picture of the monument. This left Maggie time and space to snap photos of the granite faces, undisturbed, against the rich blue-sky backdrop. She and Bill stood on the main terrace for a while, then, after a little exploring, they came upon the old viewing terrace.

"Now, this I remember," Maggie said appreciatively as she began snapping a whole new set of pictures. Bill watched her, amusement in his eyes.

"What?" Maggie asked when she noticed him grinning at her.

"I've never seen anyone appreciate a little sun and a view as much as you do," he told her. "It's nice for a change."

Maggie turned back to her picture taking, a smile on her lips.

Bill wandered up to the stone wall, pressed his palms against it, and stared up at the monument. Maggie watched him, and then began snapping pictures of him. Wild Bill, a national treasure in his own right, standing in awe of Mount Rushmore. It was a great portrait, and Maggie was elated at being here, with this man she barely knew yet knew so well already.

After a time, Bill offered Maggie his hand again, and they followed the Presidential Trail, another new feature Maggie hadn't experienced. The winding trail led them along a tree-lined path that allowed for different views of the monument. In one section of the trail, Maggie stood on a stone wall to get a great side view of the presidents. Some changes were actually nice, she decided. Finally, she stopped taking pictures and enjoyed the rest of the trail walk with Bill.

He bought her lunch at the restaurant, and they sat at a table by the window that overlooked the monument.

"So what do you think of our Mount Rushmore now?" Bill asked between bites of his burger.

Maggie smiled and reached across the table with her napkin to brush crumbs from his mustache. "I guess some change is okay," she relented. "The trail is beautiful."

"Change is inevitable," Bill said matter-of-factly. "It's a part of life."

"But not always a good part," Maggie added, her eyes distant.

"Tell me, Calamity Jane, what changes are you running away from?" Bill asked.

Maggie looked at him and sighed. "Honestly, I didn't even know I was running away until I found myself miles from home and not wanting to turn around and go back. I've been ignoring things that have happened over the years, putting them on the back burner, so to speak, for so long that I think my mind just had one too many problems to deal with and snapped." She gave a small, nervous laugh. "The worst part is, now that I've started this journey, I can't seem to stop. I have no idea what I'm doing here instead of being home doing what's expected of me. Yet now that I'm here, I know I can't go home until I figure out a few things."

Bill smiled and reached across the table, taking Maggie's hand in his. "Well, Calamity, whatever the reasons, I'm glad you're here."

Maggie returned his smile, feeling warmed by the fact that someone actually appreciated her company. She hadn't felt this way in a very long time.

The ride back to Deadwood was just as pleasant as the ride that morning had been. Maggie felt alive on the back of Bill's Harley. She couldn't believe how riding along the curvy mountain road could lift her spirits so high.

When they returned to Deadwood in the late afternoon, Bill surprised her by driving up to Mount Moriah Cemetery, which looked down on the town from a plateau in the mountains nearby. "The town has spruced up the cemetery recently, so I thought you might like to see it," he explained as they stepped off the bike and put their helmets away. They walked over to the graves of Wild Bill Hickok and Calamity Jane, and stood silently for a moment, the only two people there.

After a time, Maggie broke the stillness. "Doesn't it seem a little weird standing at your gravesite, Bill?" she asked, smirking.

Bill grinned. "I die daily," he said. "Seems only fitting to visit my grave every now and then."

Maggie shook her head and smiled. Their pretense of names should have worn thin by now, should have been downright annoying, but here, in this town that thrived on make-believe and tall tales, it seemed fitting.

As evening approached, Bill pulled up in front of Maggie's hotel and cut the engine. She stepped off the bike, handed Bill her helmet, and retrieved her camera from the saddlebag. Finally, standing there in her black leathers—feeling so comfortable, as if she dressed like this every day—she smiled at Bill for the last time.

"Thanks for the sightseeing tour, Bill. I had a great time."

Bill nodded, his helmet off and in his lap. "Pleasure's all mine, ma'am," he said, using his best Hickok accent. "Will I be seeing more of you in the next few days?" he asked hopefully. But Maggie shook her head.

"I'm leaving tomorrow," she said.

Bill's eyes showed disappointment. "Home, or farther west?"

"West, I think," Maggie answered. "I have some more thinking to do before heading home."

Bill nodded. Taking her hand again, he kissed it lightly in a most gentlemanly fashion. "It's been a pleasure, Miss Calamity," he said, smiling up at her.

Maggie looked into his soft brown eyes, feeling warmed by this stranger she felt she knew so well after only two days. She was going to miss Wild Bill, and that surprised her.

"It's Maggie," she told him.

His eyes danced as he looked her over with fresh eyes.

Still holding her hand, he winked at her. "Maggie. Now, that's a fine name. See ya, Maggie." He let go of her hand and pulled on his helmet.

Maggie waved as he drove down the street. "See ya, Bob," she said quietly, using his real name for the first time. Then she turned and walked into the hotel.

# CHAPTER SEVEN

Kaia and Kyle stared at their dad as he explained that he'd spoken with their mom the night before and she wasn't coming home yet. "She's fine, but just needs a little break from everything," Andrew said, by way of explanation. Kaia continued staring at him through narrowed eyes, as if trying to extract the real truth from his words.

*Maybe he killed her*, Kaia thought, *and disposed of the body*. His eyes were just a little bit shifty, after all, if you looked close enough. Just because everyone thought her dad was good-looking and personable didn't mean he didn't have it in him. Wasn't it always the least likely person who ended up disposing of his wife, or even his whole family? And he looked nervous, as if he wasn't telling the entire truth. And what about all the tension that had been in the house over the past year? Had he finally snapped and done her in? Her stare turned into a glare, and her father finally gave her a confused look.

"What?" Andrew asked.

Kaia snapped out of her murder fantasy and back to reality. "Nothing."

"Fine," he said. "Make sure you don't miss your bus."

Grudgingly, Kaia didn't miss her bus, but she fumed all the way to school thinking of a few murder plots of her own.

*Okay*, she thought as the bus rolled on and on, stop after stop. So her father probably didn't kill her mother, but what was this bit about needing a break? Why would her mother need a break? And how selfish of her, to take off and not tell anyone, leaving Kaia under the reign of her dad, who knew absolutely nothing about running a house or being with kids. The more Kaia thought about it, the angrier she became. "Well, maybe I need a *break*, too," she said under her breath. "What if I just stopped doing what I'm supposed to do and did whatever I felt like?"

Kaia liked her new way of thinking. She'd never skipped school before, but she knew a few kids who did, on occasion, and she knew she could hook up with them. By the time the school bus stopped in the school parking lot to unload, she was ready to put her plan in motion.

All day, Andrew's thoughts kept returning to his conversation with Maggie. What exactly had she meant, she needed more time? Time for what? He refused to believe that she'd even consider a divorce. Sure, they'd had a rough patch over the past year, but he'd fixed his mess and had thought they were over it. Or were they? Thinking about Maggie disrupted his work, which only aggravated him more.

Walking through the back door at the end of the day, he was nearly tripped by Bear as he rushed outside to do his business on the back lawn. From inside the house, Andrew heard a voice say, "You're supposed to put Bear on his leash, or he'll run all over the neighborhood." He poked his head around the corner and saw his daughter leaning over a book at the kitchen table and eating a banana.

"Why didn't you let Bear out when you came home?" he asked as he put his briefcase on the back counter.

Kaia rolled her eyes. "No one told me I had to," she said. "Am I supposed to do everything?"

Andrew wanted to ask exactly what she'd done since she'd come home, but refrained and headed out to the yard to catch Bear and put him on his leash.

Andrew changed into a sweatshirt and jeans. He tried calling Kyle several times to find out when he'd be home but gave up when he didn't answer. He suggested pizza to Kaia.

Kaia wrinkled her nose. "We've had junk food three nights in a row. Can't we have something good?"

"I thought teenagers liked junk food," Andrew said.

Kaia rolled her eyes in response.

Andrew inventoried the food in the refrigerator. There wasn't much. Apparently, Maggie hadn't stocked up before running away. It seemed to Andrew that was the least she could have done.

He settled on grilled cheese sandwiches and salad that hadn't gone brown yet. Kaia, at least, was agreeable to eating this, but she made sure to inform him that the milk was almost gone as well as the fresh fruit. He knew he'd have to make a trip to the grocery store soon.

Andrew cleaned up after dinner, threw some towels in the washing machine, and panicked when he saw the basket of clothes that needed washing. He knew that Maggie dried some items, hung others, and took some to the dry cleaner. But which ones? The pile that stared back at him looked more complicated than he thought it should.

The cats whined to be fed, Kaia whined that she needed help with an algebra problem, and the whining sound coming from the dryer frightened Andrew. The last thing he needed was for it to break down. Who did Maggie call for repairs? Oh God, he just wasn't cut out for this. And he blamed Maggie for going off and leaving him with all her unfinished work. It wasn't fair. Just as it hadn't been fair to wait for almost two days to call and tell him she was okay.

Earlier that day, he'd called Derrick to tell him he'd heard from Maggie and that she was fine. Not wanting to go into details, he'd lied and said that Maggie had a family emergency in Seattle and had left a note that somehow had fallen between the stove and the counter. It sounded legitimate to Andrew, but there had been a long pause on Derrick's end of the line that made Andrew nervous. He was certain Derrick didn't believe him, but the sheriff finally thanked him for calling and quietly hung up. Andrew felt like a criminal. And he hadn't done anything wrong. It was Maggie who'd run off, and Maggie who'd put him in the position of having to lie to his friend. He didn't care what had gone on between them in the past, she was being selfish and immature, and he was going to tell her that the next time she called.

Maggie sat on the bed in her hotel room, reflecting on her day with Wild Bill as she loaded the day's photos onto her computer. It had been an incredible day. She felt lighthearted and alive for the first time in months. The photos she'd taken had turned out beautifully, too. The sunny day, blue sky, and lush scenery had exploded with color in her pictures, and she was thrilled.

As Maggie continued to go through the photos, her mood slowly changed to melancholy. Wild Bill had been attentive to her the entire day. He'd listened intently when she spoke, and smiled warmly at her for no reason at all. And when he'd taken her hand during the trail walk, that had felt nice. It had been such an inno-cent gesture, but one she hadn't experienced in a long time.

When was the last time Andrew had held her hand or looked into her eyes with any hint of tenderness? He hadn't done either in a long time, and it filled her heart with sadness that they had lost the loving and affectionate feelings their marriage had been founded on. She didn't understand where those feelings had escaped to, or why. But she knew that those lost feelings were part of the reason for her sudden escape. She had to make sense of where their lives were now, and where they were headed. With a heart now so heavy compared to the happiness she'd felt only minutes before, Maggie dialed the number for home.

It was a few minutes past ten o'clock and Andrew was exhausted. He'd just finished folding one load of towels and had thrown another load into the dryer. On her way past the laundry room, Kaia glanced in to make sure he wasn't doing anything wrong and saw her jeans in a pile of clothes on the floor.

"Don't shrink my jeans," she warned in an ominous tone, to which Andrew replied with a sharp, "Then do them yourself." Kaia ignored him and headed off to bed.

Andrew had just thrown himself on his bed, contemplating how he'd fit grocery shopping into his day tomorrow, when the phone rang. He picked it up with a short and sour, "Yeah."

"Hi, Andrew. It's me."

Andrew sat up, taken aback by Maggie's melancholy tone. His initial reaction was to ask her if she was okay, but then he remembered how angry he'd been with her earlier that evening and stopped himself before expressing his concern. "Hello, Maggie."

"How are the kids?" Maggie asked.

"Smart-mouthed and absent, as usual," Andrew shot back. "Kaia does nothing around here to help out, and Kyle isn't even home yet. Since when is he allowed to be out all hours of the night without calling to let us know where he is?"

"He's almost twenty years old. Who did you check in with when you were twenty?"

"That was different. I was away at school. He's living at home and we're still paying his bills. He has a responsibility to follow our rules, not make up his own."

Maggie sighed. "I didn't call to argue. I just wanted to check on you and the kids, and make sure everything is okay."

"Well, everything is *not* okay, Maggie. You're off to God knows where, and I'm stuck here doing all your work. You need to come home. And if you don't, well, I'm not going to be held responsible for what happens to our marriage."

"You've never taken any responsibility for our marriage before," Maggie said calmly. "So why should I expect anything different now?"

The long pause hung heavily in the air as Andrew contemplated what Maggie had just said. Finally, in a calm, controlled voice, Andrew asked, "Maggie, how much longer do we have to keep going over the past? When will it finally be over?"

"When I'm finally over it, I guess," she said. "I just need more time."

"And what will that time do to us, to our family?" Andrew wanted to know. "We'll never be the same, will we?"

"I hope not," Maggie said quietly. "I hope we'll never go back to the way we've been these past few years." Without another word, she hung up the phone.

# CHAPTER EIGHT

It was Kaia's second day of going AWOL from school, and she didn't feel at all guilty about it. She'd simply stepped off the school bus, walked to the parking lot, and slid into Lance's car along with Allie and Jessie, her skipping buddies. They weren't actually good friends of hers, but she knew them from classes, and they were more than happy to include her as long as she helped pay for the gas. Yesterday, she'd had them drop her off at home before her dad got there, and she'd deleted the message from the school inquiring why she'd been absent. Her poor, clueless dad had no idea she'd been running around all day instead of sitting in class. It was so easy. She didn't know why she hadn't tried it before. Except if her mother were home, she'd know. She had a sixth sense about both Kaia and Kyle, and always seemed to know instantly if something was wrong. But her mother wasn't home, so it was working out perfectly. Why not take advantage of it?

They drove about fifty miles out of Woodroe to another small town where no one recognized them, and shopped at the mall and played at the arcade all day. Kaia sometimes helped at her mother's work during the summer, so she had a little money to spend. It wasn't until they passed the earring shop that Kaia got a great idea.

No, a *fabulous* idea. And with her new friends urging her on, she knew it was going to be the best idea she'd ever had.

Andrew was working on an advertising campaign to run on the local television station when the phone on his desk rang. Absently, he picked it up. "Hello, this is Andrew."

"Mr. Harrison?" the lady on the other end of the line asked tentatively. "I'm calling from Woodroe Middle School."

This got his attention. "Yes?"

"Mr. Harrison, I'm sorry to bother you at work, but I tried your wife at both home and work, and she wasn't at either place. I know I usually call her, but we had your number as an alternate, and I thought I should try you." She stopped, sounding unsure. Andrew didn't know why she was rambling on and wished she'd get to the point.

"Did something happen to Kaia?" he asked, starting to worry.

"That's why I'm calling," the lady told him. "She's absent from school today, and you didn't call in, so I thought I'd check on her."

"Absent?" Andrew asked, confused. And what was this call-in bit about? What was he supposed to call in for? "Are you sure you have the right student?" he asked. "Kaia was perfectly fine this morning and went to school."

"Did your wife drop her off?" the lady asked. "I know she always drives her to school."

Andrew frowned. What was it with everyone knowing about Maggie driving Kaia to school? Did everyone in town know what Maggie did? "No, Kaia took the bus today. But what does that have to do with anything? She's in school today. I'm sure of it. Just check again." He was getting irritated. Didn't this lady know he had important things to do?

"I'm sorry, Mr. Harrison," the lady said firmly. "But Kaia isn't in school today. She wasn't in school yesterday, either. Didn't you get the message I left yesterday at your home?"

"Message?" Andrew mumbled. "No, there was no message." He thought back to the night before, and his mind began to spin. Kaia was home before him. And yesterday morning, he'd left for work before it was time for Kaia to catch the bus. Was Kaia skipping? He really didn't think she would do such a thing, but who knew? Feeling like an idiot for not knowing where his own daughter was, he told the woman on the phone he'd get back to her and hung up. Grabbing his jacket, Andrew let the secretary know he was leaving for the day and took off for home.

Maggie was headed to Reno. She hadn't really known that's where she was going, but when she'd reached Salt Lake City, she had her choice of four directions: north to Idaho, south to Las Vegas, turn around and go home, or continue on Interstate 80 west to Reno. She knew no one in Idaho, didn't care for Las Vegas, and certainly wasn't going home. So, Reno it was.

She remembered the times she and Andrew had spent long weekends in the Reno-Tahoe area in their college days and how much fun they'd had. It was such a beautiful, romantic setting. She was excited to visit again.

While passing through Salt Lake City, Maggie stopped at turn-outs beside the highway a couple of times to take pictures of the Great Salt Lake. She planned on stopping at the Bonneville Salt Flats farther down the road and taking photos as well. She was having so much fun, just taking her time and enjoying the sites along the way, and she was looking forward to spending a few days in Reno. She was especially looking forward to driving up to Lake

Tahoe and taking pictures of the beautiful lake and the breathtaking views.

As she drove, a sense of peace fell over her. She didn't understand why, but she felt she was finally heading in the right direction after standing at a stalemate for years.

Kaia felt very pleased with herself. She had Lance drop her off down the road from her house so the neighbors would think she'd taken the bus home. Neighbors are sometimes nosy. They'd probably tell on her. As she stepped inside the back porch, she was surprised to see Bear lying quietly in his corner, not begging to be let out. She let him out anyway and put him on his leash. Better safe than sorry. She didn't want to be the one to clean up a puddle on the floor.

The house was dark. The late-afternoon sun had yet to find its way through the back windows. Kaia dropped her backpack on the kitchen floor and opened the refrigerator to grab a snack. She'd erase the school's message from the answering machine as soon as she had something to eat, and all would be right in the Harrison household. The piercing would be pretty tough to explain, but she had plenty of time to think up a good story before her dad came home.

She grabbed an apple and was just shutting the fridge door when a shadow at the kitchen table caught her eye. Kaia screamed and her apple dropped to the floor with a heavy thud.

"Hello, Kaia," Andrew said from his chair at the table. "Did you have a nice day?"

Kaia fell back against the counter, her heart beating wildly. "You scared me to death. What are you doing here?"

"I live here," her father said. "The question is: where have you been all day?"

Kaia stared at her dad as she struggled to come up with a reply. She figured she could still con her way out of trouble. "What do you mean? I was at school all day . . ." she began.

"Don't give me that," Andrew said angrily. "The school called me at work today. Apparently, you've been playing hooky for the past two days." He waited for a response from Kaia, but none came. "Well?" he asked, rising from the chair and stepping toward her.

Kaia didn't know what to say. Maybe the less said, the better. She kept the left side of her face turned away from her dad, knowing that if he saw the piercing, he'd really blow up. But he continued toward her until he was standing over her.

"Well?" he asked again. "What did you do that was more important than school? And who were you with? I hope you had a good time, because I had to miss half a day's work to come home and wait for you."

Kaia bristled. It was always about work with her dad. "You shouldn't have bothered," she bellowed. "You should have just stayed at work. I'm fine, as if you care."

"Don't turn this around on me," Andrew said. "You're in big trouble, young lady, and you were caught. I don't know what's gotten into you, but you're not going to be running around as you please as long as I'm in charge. Your mother may let you flit around . . ."

"Leave Mom out of this," Kaia hollered. "This wouldn't have happened if Mom was around. Mom cares what I do. She's not as selfish as you are."

Andrew stared hard at Kaia. "But your mother isn't here, is she? If she cares so much, why is she halfway across the country and not here?"

Shock filled Kaia's face. She saw her father's expression change from anger to surprise, as if he regretted the words that had come out of his mouth.

"Listen, Kaia. I didn't mean that. I know your mother cares about you. It just came out." He reached over the sink and switched on the light to brighten the dark kitchen. Kaia backed away, turning her face.

Andrew frowned. "Kaia, hey, it's okay," he said, drawing near her. "Let's talk about this calmly." He gently touched her shoulders and turned her toward him. Something on the left side of her face twinkled in the light.

"You pierced your eyebrow?" he asked. "You pierced your eyebrow?" he said again, loudly. Andrew backed away and fell into the chair he'd left only moments before. "Oh, God, what's next?"

The lights of Reno winked at Maggie as she drove toward the old downtown in search of a hotel. There were so many to choose from, tall towers lit up so brightly that the night sky was a rainbow of color. She followed the traffic through the famous Reno Arch that proclaimed "The Biggest Little City in the World," then took a left, heading up to Circus Circus. Since she knew that hotel and casino was family friendly, she felt safer staying there. Silly of her to think that, she knew, but she'd been family oriented for so long, she couldn't change that mindset.

The streets were bustling with people in the early evening. Even though late September usually meant fewer tourists in many places, Maggie knew that Reno never slowed down. People streamed by at every intersection, crossing to the next casino, all hoping for the next lucky win. The town was alive with activity, and Maggie felt her spirits rise again after her long drive.

She found her way to Circus Circus and obtained a room on the sixteenth floor, where the view of the city was absolutely incredible. She was just working up the courage to join the throngs of people on the street when her cell phone rang. Seeing that it was Andrew, she took a deep breath and answered.

"Hello."

"Maggie, you aren't going to believe what *your* daughter has done!" Andrew bellowed.

Andrew's tone immediately irritated her. *My daughter?* Yeah, as if he hadn't had any part in her creation. "What is it now, Andrew?" Maggie asked.

"Your daughter's been skipping school, that's what. For two days she was gallivanting around the countryside with kids she barely knows. What do you think of that?"

Truthfully, Maggie was surprised. She knew Kaia was headstrong and fiercely independent, but she'd never done anything as rebellious as skipping school. Kaia was a good student and hung out with decent kids. But under the circumstances, she wasn't entirely surprised that Kaia was acting out.

"Well?" Andrew demanded loudly, making Maggie pull the phone away from her ear and stare at it a moment. It seemed he said "Well" a lot.

"*Well*," Maggie replied, "I'm not sure what you want me to do about it. You're the one there. You need to handle it."

"Well," Andrew said snidely, "maybe if you were here, there'd be nothing to handle. Maybe if you were here doing your job, there wouldn't be a problem."

Maggie hated it when he said the kids were her job. The kids were his, too, though he'd never taken much day-to-day responsibility for them. Now, it was finally his turn to deal with them.

"Tell me, Andrew, how did she manage to skip school? If you were dropping her off and picking her up, there'd be no way for her to leave without you finding out right away."

"I wasn't dropping her off," he admitted. "She was taking the bus, which is exactly what she should have been doing all these years instead of being babied."

"That's the problem, then. If you drop her at school, she won't be able to take off. You'll know for sure she's in school. I know you have the time to do it, Andrew. You don't really have to be at work until nine o'clock. Would it kill you to take the time to drive your daughter to school?"

"Wait a minute," Andrew said. "Don't blame me for her bad behavior. It's not my fault she skipped school. I'm the one who is here, remember?"

Maggie wasn't about to let Andrew make her feel guilty. She already felt bad about leaving, but she refused to take the blame for everything.

"Kaia is a good kid and you know it," she said. "But sometimes good kids make poor choices. You can't blame me for this."

"Oh, but there's more," Andrew said angrily.

Maggie frowned. What else could have possibly happened that would make Andrew so upset?

"Your daughter pierced her eyebrow."

Maggie sat silently for a moment, letting his words sink in: *"Pierced her eyebrow."* That was it? All his anger was over a piercing? Of all the terrible things Kaia could have done, and he was mad about a piercing? Maggie couldn't help it when laughter escaped her lips.

"What are you laughing about?" Andrew demanded. "Did you hear me? She pierced her eyebrow. The one thing you told her she couldn't do."

Maggie laughed harder at his indignant tone. Even over the phone, she could sense that Andrew was fuming. Finally, she calmed down enough to reply, "Honestly, Andrew. If the worst things Kaia ever does in her teen years are skipping two days of school and piercing her eyebrow, then I will consider us lucky."

"What kind of attitude is that?" he insisted. "Don't you even care what the kids do anymore?"

Maggie turned sober. Of course she cared about the kids, but what Kaia had done wasn't the end of the world. "You know I love the kids. They've been everything to me these past nineteen years. But honestly, Kaia piercing her eyebrow isn't that earth shattering. If that's really what she wants, then fine. It's done. Ground her for skipping school and start driving her there, and you'll solve the problem of her ditching. Maybe, if you spend more time with her and Kyle, you'll find out that they're actually really good kids."

Andrew was quiet for several moments. Finally, he said, "What's gotten into you, Maggie? First you leave without telling anyone, then you act like what the kids do is no big deal. You aren't the same person you were only a few days ago. What exactly is going on?"

Maggie sat down on the bed and thought carefully about what Andrew had just asked. "You know what, Andrew? You're right. I'm not the same person I was a few days ago. You know why? Because somewhere along the way, I lost the person I used to be. I became what you wanted me to become and what the kids wanted me to become. And I lost me. You know what's gotten into me? My true self. For the first time in almost twenty years, I'm finally back to being my real self—and I'm enjoying it."

Andrew sighed. "Is this about finding yourself, Maggie? Are you having some sort of midlife crisis? Is that what this is all about?"

"You can call it whatever you wish, because I don't care what you think. I'm feeling good about myself for the first time in years, and I'm going to enjoy it. You had your fling. Now, it's my turn to have mine." Maggie hadn't meant to bring up his affair like that, but it just came out. Who was he to ridicule her for having a midlife crisis? At least she wasn't sleeping with someone while the whole town watched and whispered about it.

"It always comes down to that, doesn't it, Maggie?"

"Maybe it does, Andrew. Maybe it does." Maggie clicked the button to end the call.

# CHAPTER NINE

Andrew stared at his phone in disbelief after Maggie hung up on him. Kaia came into the room and asked him in a small voice, sounding contrite, "What did Mom say?" He really didn't know how to answer her. It seemed that Maggie couldn't care less that her daughter had pierced her eyebrow, so what was he supposed to do about it? He felt useless and inadequate, and he hated feeling that way.

At a loss as to what to say, he just quietly told Kaia to go to her room and do her homework while he made dinner, and that they'd talk later. But he never brought the subject up with her again. He wasn't used to handling problems with the kids, and he was too worn out to argue with Kaia again tonight. They ate dinner in silence, and she returned to her room while he washed the dishes.

Kyle didn't come home until after nine o'clock, but Andrew was too distracted to say anything about it. *One problem at a time*, he thought. After all, Maggie was right. Kyle was old enough to have a little freedom. Acknowledging that she was right was difficult for him. In fact, it had made him angry all over again.

Andrew decided he needed help if Kaia wouldn't be riding the bus. Sitting on his bed, he grabbed his phone and called his mother, who lived just a few miles away from their home. He felt he didn't have any other choice.

"Hello?" Marcia Harrison said. She still had a home landline but no caller ID, so she never knew who was calling before she answered.

"Hi, Mom. It's Andrew." The fact that Andrew had to identify himself said a lot about their relationship. He was an only child, so there was no one else who would be calling her "Mom." But with Marcia, everything had to be formal and proper, and she expected Andrew to announce who was calling.

"Andrew? It's late. Why are you calling me at this hour?"

"I'm sorry, Mom. I hope I didn't wake you," Andrew said. It was a little past nine o'clock, but he knew his mother went to bed early. Her days were packed with volunteering and attending local board and committee meetings, so she started her days with the rising sun.

"I was just going to bed. What is it you need?" Marcia was curt and to the point, which didn't go unnoticed by her son.

Andrew took a deep breath. He rarely asked his mother for favors, especially for help with the kids. Although she lived nearby, the kids only saw their grandmother three or four times a year, for holidays and birthdays. His mother had always had a busy schedule filled with volunteer work, but since his father had passed away ten years ago, she'd added even more activities to her load. Even at the age of sixty-nine, she showed no sign of slowing down.

"I have a favor to ask of you," Andrew began. He hesitated, not quite sure how to phrase the next few sentences. His mother could be very critical, and he didn't want to give her a reason to blame him for his predicament.

"Yes?" Marcia asked impatiently.

"Maggie had to go to Washington for some family matters, and I need help with Kaia," he said.

"What on earth is Margaret doing in Washington *again*? I thought all of her family was dead."

Andrew's jaw dropped open—he was stunned by his mother's harsh tone. "Well, her father and sister passed away, but her cousin, Cassie, and her family still live out there. She went to help her," he said. Clearly, he should have thought this through a little better.

"Whatever for? Can't her family do anything without her help?"

Andrew frowned. Even though he was angry with Maggie, he didn't like it when his mother criticized her. "Her family is very close, Mother," he said sharply, then caught himself and softened his tone. "Anyway, Maggie is gone for a week or two, and I was wondering if you would mind picking Kaia up from school three days a week and staying at the house with her until I come home from work." He figured he wasn't asking too much with only three days a week. The other two days, Kaia had tennis practice after school and he could pick her up on his way home.

Marcia let out a long, heavy sigh. "Andrew, you know I'm very busy with my volunteer and committee work—and that I don't have time to pick up Kaia, who's old enough to take the bus and stay home alone."

Biting the inside of his cheek, Andrew held back the sharp retort that threatened to spill from his lips. Yes, he knew all about his mother being too busy to spend time with family. Because she had always been so involved with community activities, he'd spent most days after school—and even many weeknights—alone at home when he was growing up. His father had been a loan officer at a local bank for thirty years. He had also volunteered for many organizations and served as mayor for several years, which meant he had rarely been home, either. So, while the entire town looked up to the Harrisons for giving their time selflessly to the community, he'd sat home alone, eaten cold dinners, and gone to sleep many nights in a quiet, empty house.

"Mother," he said gently, trying to brush aside his resentment of his lonely childhood, "I realize it may be an inconvenience, but I would appreciate your help. I never ask you to help with the children, but I'm asking now."

"Children?" Marcia huffed. "I'd hardly call Kaia a child. What is she now, thirteen? Fourteen? Kaia is old enough to stay home alone for a couple of hours after school. You did it when you were much younger than that. I can't ignore my responsibilities to babysit a grown girl. It's ridiculous."

Andrew sat silent, not trusting himself to speak. He'd never spoken harshly to his mother in his life, and he didn't have the energy to start now.

Marcia harrumphed. "And another thing, Andrew. You really need to rein in that wife of yours. My goodness, she's been flitting off to Seattle an awful lot the past couple of years, and here she is, gone again. That isn't very responsible of her."

Andrew bristled. "Her father and sister were sick and died, Mother," he said tightly, feeling the need to defend Maggie. "She wasn't taking a vacation. She was *helping* them."

"Be that as it may, she has enough to do here at home. It's late. I'm going to bed. Good night." Marcia hung up before Andrew could say good-bye.

Andrew sat, stunned, staring blankly at the opposite wall of the bedroom he and Maggie had shared. He hadn't expected much from his mother. After all, she'd never been especially involved with Kyle and Kaia, even when they were younger. And he knew she'd never really approved of Maggie, either—his mother had always considered her an outsider. But would it have killed her to help out even a little? Apparently so.

As Andrew sat there, his eyes focused on the framed family photos arranged on the bedroom wall. They were of all sizes, arranged in a circular pattern and displaying scenes from their life together.

There was one of Maggie and him clowning around on a beach when they were younger. One each of Kyle and Kaia as babies, a family Christmas photo in front of the tree, and a group photo with all four of them, plus Maggie's father and sister, taken when they'd visited Seattle years ago.

Andrew zeroed in on that photo. He'd always liked Maggie's dad. He had been a tough guy but fair, and there was never any doubt that he loved his two girls unconditionally. He'd also been good to Andrew, welcoming him into the family the very first time he'd visited when he and Maggie were in college. Maggie's family was the warm, caring family he'd never had growing up—and it was comforting to spend time with them. The three of them openly hugged each other, teased, and joked. That openness and warmth was one of the many things that had drawn Andrew to Maggie in the first place. With her, he was comfortable enough to express his feelings and desires without any fear of being ridiculed. Maggie made him feel loved for the first time in his life, and it had changed him. Moving back to Woodroe, and near his parents again, had taken away the carefree feelings he'd had during those college years with Maggie and her family. His parents had always had high expectations for him, and once again, he'd been pressured into being the dutiful son who tried hard to excel at everything. But at what cost?

Andrew stood and walked to the wall to get a closer look at the photos. He smiled slightly when he examined the one of him and Maggie in their early twenties. She had been pretty, carefree, and adventurous then. She'd taken him hiking along the trails of Mount Rainier, on ferry rides across Puget Sound, and as far away as Lake Tahoe—places where they could be together and she could take beautiful pictures. He hadn't been any more spontaneous when he was young than he was now, but he'd been open to following Maggie anywhere.

As he stared at the photo, his own reflection stared back at him from the glass. He looked tired; his brown eyes were dull, and there were creases around his eyes and mouth. Silver tipped his dark hair at the temples, and he saw strands of gray scattered among the black. The contrast between how he looked in the picture taken over twenty years ago and how he appeared now startled him. Until this minute, he'd thought of himself as *only* forty-five years old, but now he realized that even though he still thought of himself as young and vibrant, he really wasn't.

Andrew backed away from the photo so quickly, he hit the back of his knees on the bed and almost toppled over. He headed to the bathroom, quickly washed his face, and readied himself for bed, trying hard not to look too closely in the mirror.

He'd never been a vain man, but in his youth, women had looked at him twice, smiled, and winked. Back then, he'd been too shy to do anything about it. Maggie had been the one to bring him out of his shell. But after years of responsibility earning a living for his family, he'd begun to feel tired and old. When a pretty coworker started flirting with him last year, he'd felt alive again. And he'd liked how that felt. But in the end, it had only made him feel good in the moment.

How had he dared accuse Maggie of having a midlife crisis when he'd gone and had the most classic kind of all?

Andrew pushed those thoughts away as he crawled into bed and turned out the lights. But sleep eluded him. He couldn't help replaying the conversation with his mother in his head. It occurred to him that she had said almost the exact same words to him that he'd said to Maggie about her trips to Seattle over the past couple of years. He realized how terrible it must have sounded to Maggie when he accused her of taking vacations to Seattle while her father and sister were dying. *I sounded just like my mother*, he thought, horrified. In that instant, he understood how deeply painful his words must have felt to Maggie.

# CHAPTER TEN

Maggie's phone woke her up with a start. She grabbed it off the nightstand and fumbled to find the spot to swipe it in the dark hotel room. "Hello?" she said, glancing at the clock. It was only six in the morning.

"Mom?" asked the tentative voice on the other end. Maggie recognized Kaia's voice instantly and sat up in the bed.

"Kaia, honey. I'm so happy to hear from you. It's early. You must be getting ready for school. What's going on?"

"Mom, are you mad at me?"

Maggie frowned. "Mad at you? Oh, you mean about what your dad and I talked about yesterday."

"Yes. Dad never said anything more to me after you both talked. I figured you must be really mad."

Maggie reached over and snapped on the bedside light. "No, sweetie, I'm not mad at you. I am disappointed in you, though, for skipping school. You've never done anything like that before, and it surprised me."

"I'm sorry, Mom," Kaia said.

Maggie heard the sincerity in Kaia's voice. "Why did you do it? Did it have something to do with me leaving?"

Last night, Maggie had thought over what Kaia had done, and she couldn't help but feel she was to blame for her daughter's actions. After all, Kaia had always had her mother to depend on—and then one day, her mom disappeared. Maggie loved her children and had given them her full attention their whole lives. When she'd driven away, she hadn't meant to hurt them—but she was afraid that, unfortunately, she had.

"I don't know," Kaia said. "I was mad at you after you left, but I know now that what I did was stupid. It's just, well, Dad was being all weird about you leaving—and he was yelling at us and making all these new rules, and I just felt like I couldn't stand it."

"I'm sorry you were angry with me, Kaia. I didn't mean to upset you. But I'm glad to hear that you understand you did the wrong thing. Your dad is having a rough time right now. He's not used to having so much responsibility at home, and I'm sure it's making him crazy. You just have to give him a break, okay? If something is upsetting you, talk to him instead of acting out. He will listen if you give him a chance." Maggie could practically hear Kaia's eye-roll over the distance, and that made her smile.

"Okay, Mom," Kaia finally answered. "I'll try." Then, in a quieter voice, she asked, "Mom, did you leave because of me? I wasn't very nice to you that morning you left. I know that. I guess I haven't been very nice to you for a while. I'm sorry if the way I acted made you want to leave. I promise I'll be better if you come home."

Maggie gasped as Kaia's words tumbled across the distance between them. Her eyes filled with tears. She'd never hurt her children intentionally, and the fact that Kaia thought it was her fault broke her heart. "Oh, sweetie, no. I didn't leave because of you. I love you. You didn't do anything wrong."

"Then why, Mom? Was it Dad? Was it Kyle? Why did you leave?"

"I just needed some time away," Maggie said honestly. "Honey, I know it's hard to understand, but so much has happened over the past couple of years that it all just crept up on me. I know running away isn't the right thing to do, but I really needed some time to myself. Can you understand that?"

"Because of Grandpa and Aunt Amy dying?" Kaia asked.

"Yes, that has a lot to do with it, honey."

"I know how sad you were when they both died," Kaia said. "I guess I can understand why you'd want to go away for a while. But it really scared us when we didn't know where you were. I was afraid something bad had happened to you and I'd never get to tell you how sorry I was for being such a brat."

"Oh, honey," Maggie said, wiping away tears. "I'm so sorry. It was thoughtless of me not to call right away. I never meant to scare any of you."

"Mom, you will be coming home, won't you?" Kaia asked, sounding like a little girl again.

"Yes, dear. I will be coming home. I could never leave you and Kyle," Maggie said with certainty. She knew how devastating it had felt when her mother walked away from her and Amy. She knew she would never do that to her own kids.

"Can I call you whenever I want?" Kaia asked, sounding relieved.

"Anytime you want," Maggie assured her.

"Okay."

"And Kaia? Will you help your dad out around the house? I think he's going to need your help more than ever while I'm gone."

"Sure," Kaia answered. "We're going grocery shopping after school, and then we're cooking dinner. Dinner hasn't been very good since you left."

Maggie laughed and that made Kaia giggle.

"Oh, Mom?"

"Yes, hon."

"About the piercing. Is it okay if I keep it?"

Maggie chuckled. A week ago, she would have said absolutely not, but a lot had changed since then. "Why don't you keep it for now, and we'll see how you feel about it when I get back, okay?"

"Thanks, Mom," Kaia squealed.

After they hung up, Maggie felt as if a weight had been lifted from her shoulders.

Since Maggie was already awake, she decided to get dressed and head off in search of breakfast. She hadn't ventured out the night before, opting instead to go to bed early. Her conversation with Andrew had dampened her spirits, and she knew she wouldn't enjoy herself if she'd gone out. But today was different. It was a beautiful day, and she wasn't going to waste it. She planned to drive outside of town to take photos of Reno, with the Sierra Nevada mountains as a backdrop. And then she would head for Lake Tahoe to take pictures of the lake and lush scenery.

Maggie took the elevator down to the casino and went in search of a restaurant that served breakfast. The casino was busy, even this early in the morning. Chandeliers twinkled overhead and slot machines jingled all around. Casinos were built for never-ending pleasure, with no clocks or windows. It was a make-believe world, and even though it was fun to visit, Maggie knew she wouldn't be staying long.

Maggie found a breakfast buffet and waited in a long line behind other hungry hotel guests. The hostess seated her at one of the many small tables that lined one side of the restaurant, each with a booth seat on one side and a chair on the other. As soon as the waitress took her order for a glass of milk, she pulled her purse and camera bag over her shoulder and headed over to serve herself from the buffet.

Maggie sat back down at her table with a full plate. There had been such a variety to choose from that she had taken a little of everything that looked delicious. She knew she was going to be out walking all day, so she didn't feel guilty about all the food she'd piled onto her plate.

Maggie was just biting into a crispy piece of bacon when she was startled by a shadow that fell over her. Looking up, she saw a woman with thick, curly brown hair and elaborate eye shadow staring down at her.

"Sorry to startle you," the woman said. "I've been walking all over this place, trying to find my table, but for the life of me, I can't find it. Honestly, I think someone else sat down at my table."

The woman had a large bag slung over her shoulder and was carrying a plate of food piled just as high as Maggie's. Looking around, Maggie couldn't see an empty table anywhere, either.

"Would you mind if I sit with you?" the woman asked. "It's just so crazy busy in here."

Maggie glanced at the woman before answering. She was of average height, just a little shorter than Maggie, and slightly on the plump side. Her dark hair was shoulder length, with lovely auburn highlights. Her makeup was applied thickly, and although her hot-pink T-shirt was a bit loud for Maggie's taste, her black trousers toned it down a bit. All in all, she seemed harmless, so Maggie waved at the empty chair. "Of course. Please, sit down."

The woman let out a sigh of relief as she plopped down into the seat, setting her plate on the table and letting her big, heavy bag drop off her shoulder and onto the floor. "Thanks so much. I wasn't sure what I was going to do, and that bag sure is heavy." Her face broke into a friendly smile. Her lipstick matched her hot-pink shirt. "I'm Roberta, but my friends call me Bobbi."

Maggie stopped chewing her bacon for a second as she stared at the woman across from her. Bobbi. Another Bob? Was this a joke? With a grin she said, "I'm Maggie. Nice to meet you, Bobbi."

Bobbi broke off a piece of the large blueberry muffin on her plate and popped it into her mouth. "So are you here for the hairstylist convention, too?" she asked.

"No, I'm just passing through. Is that why it's so busy in town? Because of the hairstylist convention?"

"Yep. I come to this one every year. The workshops help me keep up-to-date on the latest trends, and the casinos are just plain fun. Except this year, no one from the salon where I work came along, so I'm kind of on my own."

"Where do you live?" Maggie asked.

"San Diego. Ever been there?"

Maggie shook her head. "No, but we were stationed north of San Diego in San Pedro for a while when I was a kid, years ago before we moved back to Seattle, where my dad was from. I was a navy brat."

Bobbi grinned. "Navy brat, huh? Well, being from San Diego, I know a lot about navy brats, and you sure don't fit the part. Do you still live in Seattle?"

"No. I live in Minnesota now. A small town in the upper northwestern part of the state."

A waitress came by then and brought Maggie a refill on her milk. Bobbi ordered a diet soda.

"For breakfast?" Maggie asked.

"You sound like a mom. Is your family here with you?"

Maggie's eyebrows rose.

"I see your wedding ring. I'm just assuming you have a husband and family to go with it," Bobbi said.

"Oh, yeah, well, I do. But they're not with me. I'm doing some traveling on my way to see relatives in Seattle." Until she said this,

Maggie hadn't even considered going to Seattle, but now she realized that she'd been heading that way all along. Even though her sister and father were both gone, she had a cousin she was close to that she could stay with awhile. And the more she thought about it, the more she liked the idea of seeing Cassie and her husband, Matt, and their kids.

Maggie and Bobbi ate their food and watched as people came and went. The restaurant was very busy, and now that Bobbi had mentioned the hairstylist convention, Maggie noticed large groups of women eating breakfast together. Most had beautiful hair, or extreme hairstyles, and many were dressed professionally, as if they were going off to work. Maggie assumed that most of them were there for the convention. Seeing so many women in one place made her feel less out of place than she had when she arrived.

Some people were being seated at the next table, and Bobbi had to move her bag out of the way. She seemed to struggle under its weight, and Maggie was curious what was in it.

"Mind if I ask why such a big bag?"

Bobbi chuckled. "It's full of free samples and some of my hairstyling equipment I'll need for the next workshop. The workshops are very hands-on, and some have volunteers who let us try out new styles or techniques on them." Bobbi studied Maggie a minute with her big brown eyes. "Hey, would you like to volunteer at my coloring workshop? It's tomorrow morning, and I know they're still looking for more people for us to work on."

Maggie frowned as she reached up and touched her blond hair. "Is there something wrong with my hair the way it is?"

"Oh, no, don't take offense. It was just an idea. It'd be a great way to get a free color job. I was just thinking that you could use highlights, and I could help you get rid of that little bit of gray at the roots."

Maggie hadn't realized the gray in her hair was so obvious. "Thanks, but I'm not sure if I'll even still be here tomorrow."

"I'm sorry if I offended you," Bobbi said, looking contrite. "I just thought you might like to freshen up your color." When she'd finished everything on her plate, she asked Maggie if she'd mind watching her bag while she went to get more. Of course Maggie didn't mind.

Maggie felt full and satisfied by the time she'd emptied her plate. She and Bobbi had a pleasant conversation about Reno and Tahoe and the many things to do around there. They also talked a little about their lives. She found out that Bobbi was thirty-two years old and single, but still looking for Mr. Right. Maggie told Bobbi a little about her husband and kids, leaving out the details of why she was here without them. Bobbi seemed like a nice, normal person, and Maggie enjoyed her company. She was happy she hadn't eaten breakfast alone.

Bobbi looked at her watch and then said it was time to go to her workshop. "It was so nice visiting with you," she told Maggie. "This is my only workshop today. Any chance you might want to get together later and go casino hopping or see a show?"

"That sounds like fun, but I plan on spending the day driving around and taking pictures. I'm heading to Lake Tahoe in a couple of hours and hope to get a few good shots."

"Oooh . . . Could I go with you? I don't have my car here, and I'd love to see Tahoe. I mean, if I won't be in your way or anything. We could even eat dinner at one of the casinos there." Bobbi looked hopeful.

Maggie thought about it for only a moment. Bobbi had an easy, friendly way about her, and she seemed like good company. Maggie thought it might be fun to have someone go along. "I don't mind, but I have to warn you, we'll be walking a lot, especially in the woods."

Bobbi clapped her hands joyfully. "That sounds great. I'll be sure to put on my walking shoes and jeans. I can be ready by noon. Is that okay?"

Maggie smiled. She couldn't help it. Bobbi sounded so excited. "That's fine. I'll meet you at the door to the parking garage at noon."

Bobbi waved and left with her big bag slung over her shoulder. Maggie thought she might be in for an interesting day.

Maggie decided not to drive around in the busy traffic while she waited for Bobbi. Instead, she walked through downtown Reno and snapped a few pictures. She walked to the famous Reno welcome arch and shot a few pictures. She planned on taking pictures of the arch when it was colorfully lit up on her way back at the end of the day. She then walked across the street and took shots of the new CommRow building, where the historic Fitzgerald's Casino used to be. She stopped in front of the 164-foot climbing wall, the tallest in the country, located on the outside of the building, and marveled at the people who were brave enough to climb that high above the streets of Reno.

Downtown Reno was definitely not as colorful or exciting by day as it was at night, but Maggie managed to take a few great shots of the city and the interesting people strolling around. She was sure that tonight, from her hotel-room window, she could get a few great shots of the city lit up in all its glorious colors.

As promised, Bobbi was ready and waiting for Maggie at noon by the door leading out to the parking garage. She had changed from her hot-pink top to a yellow T-shirt and now wore jeans and sneakers. She'd also traded in her large bag for a smaller one, and she had a pair of sunglasses sitting on top of her head and a sweater slung over her arm.

"Ready to go?" Bobbi asked.

They were soon heading south on Highway 395 toward the curvy Highway 431 to Incline Village. From there, they would drive down Highway 50 along Lake Tahoe toward South Lake Tahoe.

They couldn't have asked for a more beautiful day to drive the curving, tree-studded road along Lake Tahoe's shore. The view was crystal clear, and the snowcapped mountains in the distance were spectacular. The traffic wasn't too heavy, so Maggie was able to periodically turn off at roadside stops to take pictures of the lush scenery that lay before them.

As the pair rode along, they talked about their lives, the best vacations they had ever taken, and the most beautiful scenery they'd ever seen. Both agreed that there weren't many places in the United States that could top the beauty they were enjoying today.

"Do you know what we really need?" Bobbi asked at one of the stops along the highway. "A convertible. Wouldn't it be amazing to drive along this highway, in this gorgeous weather, in a convertible sports car?"

Maggie agreed. With the warm sun on their backs and the sparkle of the lake below, riding along in a convertible sports car would've been perfect.

They turned into Lake Tahoe Nevada State Park at Sand Harbor, paid the fee, and parked in the tree-lined parking lot. From there, they walked down to the natural harbor, an inlet just off the larger body of water, where pine trees lined the shore and large boulders jutted out of pristine, crystal-clear water.

The air coming off the lake was fresh and crisp, and both women were happy they had brought heavy sweaters along. They walked over to some large boulders protruding out of the water along the shoreline. The rocks were bleached white from the sun, which made a sharp contrast against the blue-green water of the lake. The wind was just a whisper, and the huge body of water sat quiet. Maggie and Bobbi both stood a moment in awe of the beauty of the lake, the shoreline dotted with pines, and the snowcapped mountains in the distance. It was a spectacular view.

Excitedly, Maggie raised her camera and began snapping photos of the picturesque scenery. The beach was empty of tourists, enabling her to capture some breathtaking photos of unmarred shoreline.

Bobbi climbed up on one boulder and then made her way from boulder to boulder along the rocky shore. Once, when she almost fell into the icy-cold water, Maggie laughed out loud, which made Bobbi giggle. Bobbi finally sat down on a large boulder that sat far out in the water.

"Pose," Maggie called out to her, and turned her camera on Bobbi.

Bobbi smiled, then lifted her knees up, put one hand behind her head, and pursed her lips into a kissing pout, pinup girl–style. Maggie laughed again and took her picture, plus several more as Bobbi adopted different poses. With her bright lipstick, voluptuous figure, and mane of shiny hair—plus the blue-green water and the mountains as her backdrop—Bobbi actually did look like an old-time movie star glamming it up for the camera.

After a time, they walked along the shore to the strip of beach, then strode in the sand to the other end of the inlet. Tired at last, they sat on a boulder and enjoyed the view from the point.

"You're going to love those pictures I took of you," Maggie said. "The scenery is amazing."

Bobbi giggled. "I bet I looked silly, but I don't care. It's so beautiful here. This is nothing like a Southern California beach. It's so clean, and the water is clear."

Maggie agreed. Lake Tahoe wasn't an ocean, of course, but it was so large that it reminded her of one. "My husband and I came here when we were in college. It's exactly as it was then, beautiful."

"Why isn't your family here with you, Maggie?" Bobbi asked. "If you don't mind me asking."

Maggie sighed. She figured it seemed strange, her running around the country alone when she had a family at home. "I don't mind. I sort of ran away from home."

Bobbi's brown eyes grew wide. "Ran away? Really? Why?"

"It's kind of hard to explain. I hadn't planned on leaving. It just happened. Our marriage has had problems for a while, and I've had some family tragedies that added to the stress. I think I sort of lost it."

"Wow," Bobbi said. "You just seem like you have it all together. I guess even the best of us crack up now and again."

Maggie frowned at this, which only made Bobbi laugh.

"I don't mean you're crazy or anything. We all need to let off some steam once in a while, and it sounds like that's what happened to you. You just had to let go."

Maggie thought this over as she stared at the mountains in the distance. Maybe Bobbi was right. She had been holding in her feelings for so long, she finally just had to let them out.

"I know exactly what you need," Bobbi said, her eyes lighting up. "Tomorrow, we're going shopping, and tomorrow night, we're going to get you all dolled up. You're going to attend the banquet with me. We'll get some snazzy dresses, do up your hair and makeup, and you'll feel like a million bucks."

"Oh, I don't know," Maggie said. "I'm not really looking to go out and party like a teenager."

Bobbi chuckled. "Don't worry. You won't be. You'll be in a room of mainly women hairdressers and makeup artists. You can be my plus one. Come on. It'll be fun."

Maggie wasn't so sure about dressing up and going to a party. But then, she'd ridden on a motorcycle with Wild Bill and had a blast. It might be fun to dress up and look pretty for a change.

Maybe even dance a little. The more Maggie thought about the idea, the more she wanted to do it.

"Okay," Maggie told Bobbi. "It sounds like fun."

Bobbi grinned. "That's the spirit!"

# CHAPTER ELEVEN

Maggie and Bobbi walked back to the van and headed farther down the highway to South Lake Tahoe. They stopped several more times by the side of the road to take pictures of the lake. After crossing over the California state line, they entered South Lake Tahoe. As they drove through the town, trying to decide where they should stop to eat, Bobbi suddenly pointed and said excitedly, "Take a left. Pull in over there."

Startled, Maggie turned left into the parking lot that Bobbi had indicated. Once there, Maggie realized it wasn't a parking lot after all. It was a car dealership.

"Drive up ahead," Bobbi said, practically bouncing up and down in her seat. "Look. Right there."

Maggie pulled up and saw what Bobbi was pointing at. Two Mustang convertibles sat side by side. One was royal blue with a black top, and the other was cherry red, its black top down.

"Why in the world did you have us stop here?" Maggie asked, turning toward Bobbi. But Bobbi was already opening the passenger door and heading outside to stand beside the two convertibles.

"Aren't they beautiful?" Bobbi asked as Maggie stepped out of the van. "Can't you just imagine yourself driving the curvy Lake Tahoe road in one of these? I vote for the red one."

Maggie shook her head, and then smiled. Bobbi was as excited as a little kid with a new toy. "Yes, they're very pretty. But I don't need a new car today."

"Can I help you ladies?" A tall, slender middle-aged man wearing dress slacks and a sport coat walked up to Maggie, his hand extended. "I'm Jerry. What can I do for you today?"

Reluctantly, Maggie shook Jerry's hand. The last thing she wanted to do was talk to a salesman, especially since she wasn't serious about buying a car. "We're just looking," she said. No sooner had the words left her mouth than Bobbi piped up.

"She's interested in this red Mustang. Any chance we can take it for a test drive?"

Maggie looked at Bobbi, frowning and shaking her head. "No, I'm not really interested—"

"Sure. A test drive would be fine," Jerry interrupted. "You have good taste. I'll go get the keys." He smiled wide at Maggie, then hurried away to the office.

"What are you doing?" Maggie asked. "I don't want to buy a car."

Bobbi walked over to Maggie. "You don't have to buy it," she said. "We're just going for a little ride in it. It'll be fun."

"We're wasting this man's time."

Bobbi brushed her hand through the air. "Oh, he won't mind. Besides, I think he likes you. I saw him give you the once-over. If you decide to buy it, he may give you a great deal."

Maggie rolled her eyes. "He gave me the once-over to make sure I wasn't some insane person who'd drive off and not return. Come on. Let's get out of here before he comes back."

Bobbi grinned and pointed. "Too late."

Jerry headed toward them and handed a set of keys to Maggie. "All I need is to see your driver's license a minute. While I'm writing down the number, you can pull your van out of the way. Park it over by the office."

Maggie sighed. She didn't want to argue in front of the salesman, so she did as he said.

Jerry handed back her license. "Here you go." He walked over to the red Mustang and opened the driver's-side door for Maggie. "You picked a beauty. You know how to drive a stick shift, I hope."

Maggie walked over to the car and looked inside. The bucket seat did look inviting. And a stick shift? She thought back to her first car, when she was seventeen. It was a late-1970s-model sports car, beat-up but fast and fun to drive. She had loved that car.

"Oh yes, I know how to drive a stick," she told Jerry. As she climbed into the small car, Maggie felt twenty-five years younger.

Maggie and Bobbi were sailing up the Lake Tahoe road once again, with the sun on their faces and the wind in their hair. The Mustang hugged the curves in the road beautifully, and both Maggie and Bobbi laughed with delight at each turn. It felt delicious and decadent, driving along the scenic road in a gorgeous sports car.

"See, I told you this would be fun," Bobbi said, smiling over at Maggie. She turned the radio on and blasted it so they could hear the music above the rumble of the engine and the wind whipping around them.

Maggie gasped when she recognized the song, "Hollywood Nights," another song from her favorite Bob Seger album. He sang about driving miles and miles on those twisting, turning roads. Maggie laughed. It shouldn't have surprised her that Bob would be on the radio, singing that song, at this exact moment in time. First,

Bob the teacher in Deadwood, then Bobbi the hairdresser. Now, Bob as background music for their wild drive. It seemed to be a running theme for this entire crazy trip.

Eventually, Maggie turned the car around and headed back, even though she didn't want to any more than Bobbi did. As they pulled into the car lot, Bobbi looked over at her and winked.

"Think you might buy yourself a car?"

Maggie laughed. "You're crazy. I can't buy this. But you were right. It was fun."

Jerry was there to greet them as they stepped out of the Mustang. Maggie handed over the keys. "So did you have a great ride?" he asked.

Maggie nodded. "It's a fun car. Thanks for letting us give it a try."

"Is that your van, or is it a rental?"

Maggie looked over at her new van. She'd just bought it a few months ago when her old one was on its last legs. At the time, she'd thought of getting a car instead. Now that the kids were older, she didn't need as much room. But Andrew had told her to buy another van. He'd said they might want it for family vacations. So she bought another van, even though she hadn't really wanted one. As usual, Andrew got his way and she had just let him.

"It's my van," Maggie replied.

"It looks new. Is it this year's model?"

Maggie nodded. "I just bought it this past spring."

"Well, it's your lucky day," Jerry said, grinning. "I can give you a great deal on the Mustang if you want to trade in the van."

"Oh, I don't think so," Maggie said. She'd seen the price on the Mustang, and she knew the van was worth a little more. "Besides, I'm not from California. I live in Minnesota."

"That's not a problem, as long as you have the title and it's in your name. We can take care of everything online or over the phone, however you like. I'm assuming you have a loan on the van."

"Well, yes. It's through my bank."

"That's even better. You can switch your loan up and be off. If you're interested, I can hold the car for you over the weekend, and we can do the paperwork on Monday."

Maggie laughed. Even considering trading in her new van for a used Mustang was crazy. "I'll think about it," she told Jerry, though she didn't plan on giving it another thought.

It was late afternoon by the time Maggie and Bobbi parked in the Harrah's Lake Tahoe parking lot and were seated in the dining room of the Forest Buffet on the eighteenth floor. They were both famished from their long day. The view of the mountains out the floor-to-ceiling windows was breathtaking, and the food was delicious. They feasted on seafood, steak, and a variety of other entrees, and then loaded up on dessert as well.

"That sure was a beautiful car," Bobbi said as they both sat contemplating another dessert.

"Yes, it was," Maggie agreed, eyeing her cautiously.

"It was in really great shape for a 2010, too."

"Yes, it looked almost new."

"I think it was the GT model."

Maggie stared hard at Bobbi. "Are you getting a cut of Jerry's commission? You sound like you're trying to sell me that car."

Bobbi laughed. "No. I just think you'd have so much more fun driving around in that Mustang than in your mom van."

"Hey, I like my mom van. It's comfortable, it handles well, and it's practical."

Bobbi shrugged as she stood to get one more dessert. "Who wants to be practical? There's no fun in that." She threw Maggie a mischievous grin and headed to get another dessert.

Maggie sat there, gazing out the window at the snowcapped mountains. *"Practical."* She remembered a time when she hadn't always been practical. After spending years caring for her father and sister, going to college had opened a whole new world for her, giving her the freedom to be carefree and spontaneous. When she and Andrew started dating, he said it was her impractical side that he loved so much. Her ability to drop everything at a moment's notice and pack up a picnic, go for a drive or even a midnight stroll on the beach. Somewhere along the way, she'd lost that spontaneity. Had she simply grown up and become responsible, or had she just become too tired from responsibilities to try anymore? She'd stopped looking for the fun in life and had let herself become boring. Was that what caused Andrew to stop looking at her as a desirable woman, and instead only as his wife and the mother of his children? Is that what had made him search out another woman's affections?

*It's not your fault he had an affair. Stop blaming yourself.*

Maggie knew this was true, but taking responsibility for everything had become a way of life for her, and it was difficult for her to stop.

As Maggie sat there, contemplating this, her cell phone vibrated. It was a text from Kaia asking how to make lasagna. Maggie smiled. At least being boring had a few perks. Her daughter could count on her to know things like how to boil noodles and fry hamburger. She answered her, feeling happy to be needed as the practical mom that she was.

Andrew picked Kaia up from school and they drove to the store to buy groceries. He hated missing so much work, but he had no choice. He'd spread the story around his office about Maggie having to go to Seattle to help out a relative, so a least no one questioned his leaving early each day. In fact, a couple of the office women had told him how sweet it was of him to take care of his daughter. Even though he resented having to do Maggie's errands, he was pretty proud that he'd been able to make himself out to look like the good dad.

Kaia shook her head at him when they parked at the local grocery store. "What?" Andrew asked, perplexed.

"Mom always goes to Walmart first to buy most of the groceries, because it's cheaper. She only comes here to buy the meat, dairy products, and baked goods, because she says they're better here."

Andrew sighed. "Your mom has all the time in the world to go from store to store, but if we do that, we'll never get home in time to make lasagna. Besides, this store is one of our biggest sponsors for television advertising. We should support our local stores instead of the chain stores."

"Okay, but that's not how Mom does it," Kaia said as she stepped out of the car and followed Andrew into the store.

Andrew didn't care how Maggie bought groceries. He was in charge now, and they were doing it his way.

Kaia grabbed a cart and rolled it into the store, following her dad. She stopped at the apples and started carefully choosing ones to put in a plastic bag.

"Why are you scrutinizing every apple? Just grab a few and bag them."

"Geez, Dad. You have to look for bruises, holes, and broken stems. I don't want to eat a rotten apple."

Andrew frowned but didn't reply. He headed over to the lettuce and picked up a head. He didn't know the first thing about buying produce. In truth, he didn't know anything about grocery shopping. Maggie had always done the shopping and cooking, and he'd never paid any attention to it.

As he picked out a bunch of bananas, Kaia shook her head at him. "Now what?" he asked.

"Look at all the black spots on those. You're supposed to pick ones that are just a little green at the top, without all the spots. They'll be perfect in a day or two and last longer."

Andrew sighed but did as he was told. After placing the bananas into the cart, he asked, "How do you know so much about picking fruit?"

Kaia shot a condescending stare his way. "I go shopping with Mom all the time. I'm not stupid—I see what she does."

"Why do you always go? Do you like shopping?" Andrew asked. It never occurred to him that Kaia went everywhere with Maggie.

"Not really. At least, not this type of shopping. But it's an occupational hazard. I can't drive yet, so I have to go everywhere Mom goes."

Andrew laughed. "Occupational hazard? What in the world do you mean by that?"

"Well, duh, Dad. I have to do whatever the grown-ups are doing. It's an occupational hazard of being a teen without a driver's license."

Andrew shook his head and smiled. "You know, you're a funny kid."

Kaia just rolled her eyes and walked past her dad with the cart.

After filling the cart, they got in line to pay. Most of the checkout clerks and baggers knew Kaia, either from her shopping with Maggie or because a few were friends with Kyle. Andrew was surprised, and a little proud, that his daughter knew so many people. He'd always prided himself on being popular in town, and he liked that his daughter seemed to be, too. He had a smug look as he watched the computer screen total up their groceries.

"Hi, Kaia. Where's Maggie?" A young woman wearing a smock came up to the counter and opened a plastic bag for their groceries.

"Hi, Cindi. Mom's gone away for a while, but she'll be back soon," Kaia said, then asked how Cindi was doing.

As Andrew listened to the exchange between his daughter and Cindi, he watched the girl bagging his groceries. Her hands were small and wide, which made it awkward for her to pick up larger items. She had a friendly, round face and almond-shaped eyes. Her hair was cut short, and she had bangs framing her eyes. There was no mistaking she had Down syndrome, and Andrew wondered how Kaia knew her.

Kaia noticed her dad watching her, so she turned to him. "This is Cindi, Dad. Mom drives her here to work and sometimes takes Cindi shopping, too."

"Oh" was all Andrew managed to say. It dawned on him that Cindi was one of the residents of the group home where Maggie worked. Since he'd never really paid attention to what Maggie did or who she worked with, this surprised him.

"And bowling, too," Cindi interjected with a wide smile, making Kaia laugh.

"Yes, and we sometimes go bowling together, too," Kaia said.

"Bowling?" Andrew asked. But then the cashier told him the total of the bill, and his attention returned to the computer screen.

"How much did you say?" Andrew asked.

"Two hundred sixty-five dollars and ninety-eight cents," the boy said. He began helping Cindi bag the groceries.

Andrew frowned. Were groceries really this expensive? He looked over at Kaia.

"Told you," she said with a satisfied look.

Andrew shook his head and swiped his debit card to pay.

Cindi helped cart the groceries out to Andrew's black convertible and loaded them into the trunk and the backseat.

"This is a lot smaller than Maggie's van," Cindi commented as she tried to make everything fit.

Andrew bit his lip and didn't say anything.

"Bye, Kaia," Cindi said, waving. "Tell Maggie I miss her."

Kaia waved and slipped into the passenger seat as her dad got behind the wheel.

"Looks like Cindi and you know each other pretty well," he said as he started the car.

"Well, yeah. I hang out with Mom when she works in the summer, and I go along when she takes residents shopping or out for activities. Cindi is sweet. And you should see how great she bowls. She always beats me."

"Oh, I didn't know that you went to work with your mom," Andrew said.

"What did you think I did all these years? Sit at home alone while Mom worked? She never wanted me to be home alone, so she brought me along. Kyle used to come, too, but once he had a summer job, he stopped."

When Andrew thought about it, he did remember Maggie saying that the kids went to work with her sometimes in the summer. He hadn't really given it much thought. He'd always gone to work and didn't worry about where the kids or Maggie were. The kids were Maggie's job. Summers were always so busy when the kids were young, with Kyle in Little League and Kaia in tennis. He'd paid attention to their sports, because both baseball and tennis interested him, but the day-to-day stuff was lost on him. Now, he wondered why he hadn't paid more attention.

After Andrew and Kaia unloaded the groceries and carried them in, Kaia took charge and began putting everything away. "I doubt if you know where everything goes, anyway," she told her dad when he said he would help. Andrew frowned, but he had to admit she was right. "You can feed Bear and fill the cat-food bowls while I finish," she said.

"Fine." Andrew found the canned dog food and opened a can, then spilled the entire contents into Bear's bowl.

Kaia ran over and grabbed the bowl. "Only half a can. He gets half in the morning and half at night. And he gets dry food, too, in the other bowl." She started scraping food out of the bowl and back into the can, then found a plastic lid and capped it.

"What difference does it make?" Andrew asked, angry at being chastised by a teenager.

"Bear's getting too fat. Mom's limiting his canned food, and he eats diet dry food."

"Oh." Andrew walked over to the cat-food bowls with a container of dry food. "Can I feed the cats, or are they on a diet, too?"

Kaia only stared at her dad with raised eyebrows. She looked like Maggie when she looked at him that way. Andrew stopped being sarcastic and fed the cats.

"Maybe you should be in charge of feeding the animals so I don't mess it up," he suggested, and was rewarded with a sigh. *Cripes, do all women sigh so much? Or do I bring it out in them?*

"I'll start making the lasagna," Kaia said as she finished putting the groceries away. "Do you want to make the salad?"

"Do you think I can do it right?"

"*Daaaad!*"

"I'm just kidding. I'll do it," Andrew said, chuckling. And they both began working quietly, side by side, in the kitchen.

After Maggie and Bobbi had eaten their fill, they made the trek out to her van and got in for the drive back to Reno. But as they passed the car lot again, instead of driving right by it, Maggie found herself pulling in and stopping behind the red Mustang.

"Are you doing what I think you're doing?" Bobbi asked, her eyes wide with surprise.

"I'm just taking another look," Maggie said, but as the words left her mouth, she knew that wasn't true. She really wanted to drive the Mustang again. And again, and again. *Crap. I do want to buy it.*

The two women stepped out of the van and stood in silence, staring at the car as the sun sunk lower on the horizon.

"I really loved driving that car," Maggie said.

"It's a great car," Bobbi agreed.

"Is it crazy, wanting a sports car at my age?"

Bobbi looked over at Maggie. "At your age? I didn't know you were an old lady. Maybe we should be looking at a motorized scooter chair instead."

"Ha, ha."

Maggie continued staring at the car. *This is crazy. It's absolutely ridiculous. Moms don't drive convertibles. They drive vans.* But Maggie had loved how it felt driving that car. She could see herself in it— top down, the breeze caressing her face—driving to Seattle. *But what will Andrew say?* She frowned. *Who cares what Andrew says? He drives a convertible. Why shouldn't I?*

"Red or blue?" Maggie asked.

"Definitely red."

Maggie turned to Bobbi, her expression doubtful. "But doesn't red just shout out *midlife crisis?*"

Bobbi shrugged. "Well, isn't that kind of what this is?"

"Oh hell," Maggie said, and both women broke out in laughter. "Might as well just embrace it rather than fight it, huh?"

"Might as well," Bobbi agreed.

The door to the office opened, and Jerry came out, smiling wide. Maggie followed him back into the office to make arrangements to trade in her old life for her new one.

# CHAPTER TWELVE

Maggie sat cross-legged on the bed in her hotel room. She was looking at her computer screen to view the pictures she had taken that day when her phone buzzed. She glanced at her phone and saw the call was from home. She hesitated a moment. She'd had such a nice day, and she didn't want to end it by battling wits with Andrew again. But then she noticed the time and realized it was after eleven o'clock at home. Afraid there might be something wrong, she decided to answer.

"Hello?"

"Hi, Maggie. I didn't wake you, did I?" Andrew asked.

"No. You're up late. Is something wrong?"

"No, everything is fine here. I'm just calling to check on you."

Maggie's eyebrows rose. Andrew actually sounded like he was in a good mood for a change. "That's nice. How did the lasagna turn out? Was it edible?"

"How'd you know we ate lasagna?"

Maggie chuckled. "Kaia texted me a couple of times asking for directions."

"Oh, so that's how she knew how to make it. And here she had me thinking she was a super teenager, knowing how to cook so well." Andrew laughed, a happy sound, and it made Maggie smile. She hadn't heard him joke or laugh in a very long time.

"Well, she is pretty adept at doing things around the house and cooking a few dishes. So did it taste okay?"

"Yeah, it was just like your lasagna. She did a good job. She also made garlic toast, and she even allowed me to make the salad. We had a good dinner. It was actually fun."

*Wow*, Maggie thought. *Andrew actually helped with dinner.* She couldn't remember the last time he'd assisted her in making a meal, or even offered to help. "That's great. Kaia's a good kid. She can be a lot of fun when she isn't brooding. How did grocery shopping go?"

"Oh, it went fine. Kaia knew exactly what to buy. Groceries sure are expensive, though. I guess I never realized how much it cost for a week's worth of food."

Maggie frowned. "Didn't Kaia tell you where to buy groceries so you'd save money?"

"Oh, yeah, of course she did. Kaia knows everything. She's a big help. How was your day? What did you do?"

Maggie told him about her drive to Lake Tahoe and the photos she'd taken. She didn't mention the Mustang. She figured she'd spring that one on him later. She didn't want to ruin his good mood. "It was so much fun," Maggie said, her voice growing animated. "I'd forgotten how beautiful it is in Tahoe. Do you remember the beach we used to go to years ago?"

"Yes. I loved going there."

"I took some gorgeous pictures of the crystal-clear water and the snowcapped mountains there. It was so inspiring and gorgeous, I wished . . ." Maggie faltered.

"What did you wish?" Andrew asked, caught up in Maggie's excitement.

"I wished you and the kids were there with me to enjoy it."

"That would be fun. I wish we had been there, too," Andrew said softly.

Maggie paused at Andrew's words. He sounded sincere, and it warmed her heart to think he actually meant it.

"I was just looking at the pictures on my computer," she said. "I can't wait for you and the kids to see them."

"You always did take wonderful pictures," Andrew said. "You're very talented."

Maggie smiled. It had been a long time since Andrew had complimented her. "I forgot how much I loved taking pictures. I've really missed it."

"You should do more of it," Andrew said. "The kids are older now. I don't see why you couldn't spend more time taking photos."

"I've been thinking about that. Remember years ago, when we talked about me opening an art shop in town where I could sell my own photographs as well as other artists' work? I'd really love to do that."

"I don't know, Maggie. That would be expensive, and opening a new business is always a big risk."

Maggie sighed. Once again, Andrew's conservative side had come out when she talked about fulfilling a dream. "It was only an idea. It's something I've wanted to do for a long time."

"I didn't mean to sound so discouraging," Andrew said quickly. "Why don't we talk about it when you get back?"

Maggie's heart soared. She sat on the bed for a long time after they'd said good night, excited by their conversation. It had been a long time since they'd talked to each other without arguing, and it felt good. What had suddenly come over him? Had her leaving him made him wake up and realize how much he missed her? She hoped so. As she fell asleep that night, she had high hopes that their life together might turn out fine after all.

*Deanna Lynn Sletten*

After Andrew hung up the phone, he grimaced at the white lie he'd told Maggie about grocery shopping. Andrew didn't want to admit he hadn't listened to his fourteen-year-old daughter and therefore spent much more than he should have. After Kaia and he had eaten dinner, he'd compared what Maggie spent on groceries and found she actually saved about forty dollars a week by store hopping. He'd never given Maggie credit for being careful with the money, but now he understood that she was as careful as she could be—it was just that life was expensive. He should have told Maggie that, but his ego made him not want to admit it to her.

Staring at the family photos on the wall, he wondered why it was so hard for him to tell Maggie how he felt. And why had he been so quick to discourage Maggie about her idea for an art shop? They'd been having a good conversation, and Andrew had heard some of the old Maggie in her voice. The Maggie he'd known in college, who'd been full of ideas and dreams. He'd loved that about her. Why had he tried to quash her dream?

He was happy he'd stopped himself from being a total jerk, saying they could talk about her idea when she came home. The fact that she'd agreed made him think she was going to return soon. He knew they still had a long way to go to fix their marriage, but he was hopeful they were on the right track.

Saturday morning, the washing machine began clunking and banging in the laundry room. Sleepily, Kaia walked into the kitchen and glared at Andrew, who was standing by the washer, frowning.

"You woke me up," Kaia complained.

"It wasn't me—it's this damned washing machine," Andrew said. "Why does it keep doing that? No matter how I load the towels, it's unbalanced."

Kaia shrugged. "I don't know. It happens to Mom sometimes, too."

"What does she do?"

"Same thing you're doing. She moves the stuff around until it's balanced."

Andrew rolled his eyes. "Gee, thanks."

Kaia smirked. She eyed the dirty clothing in the basket on top of the dryer and nodded toward it. "Whatever you do, don't shrink my good shirts and sweaters," she warned him, then turned into the kitchen to get breakfast.

Andrew looked at the basket of clothes that Kaia had pointed out. Maggie had a system. The clothes were separated in four baskets: whites, towels, shirts, and jeans. There was also a pile of clothes on the floor that belonged to Kyle, all splattered with grease from his job at the motorcycle shop. Andrew had figured out how to wash the whites and the towels just fine, but he was at a loss with all the rest. He knew Maggie hung some of the clothes to dry so they didn't shrink, and he knew that some jeans were hung and others could go in the dryer. But for the life of him, he didn't know which went where.

"Kaia? Do you know how Mom washes and dries all these different clothes?" Andrew called out to his daughter, who was sitting at the kitchen table, eating cereal and watching the small television.

Kaia looked over at him. "Not really. You can't put my jeans or tops in the dryer for the full amount of time. They need to be hung after about fifteen minutes of drying. That's all I know." She returned her attention to the TV show.

"That's a lot of help," Andrew mumbled to himself. Why in the world was laundry so complicated? He reached for his phone in his jeans pocket, hesitated a moment, then went ahead and hit Maggie's number on autodial.

"Hi," Maggie said.

"Hi. I didn't wake you, did I?"

"No, I was just getting up. What's up?"

"I'm knee-deep in laundry here, and I'm afraid that I don't know what I'm doing. Can you help me with this so Kaia doesn't yell at me for ruining her clothes?"

Maggie chuckled. "I can help you with that. Do you have a pen and paper handy?"

"Really? Are you serious? Is doing laundry so difficult that I need to write it down?"

"Only if you want to remember everything," Maggie told him. She then started explaining what he needed to know: separating darks and lights, which clothes to put in the dryer for a full cycle, which ones to do for fifteen minutes and then hang dry. She told him which cycles to use, when to use fabric softener, and how long to dry certain items. Before long, Andrew had filled a page and a half of notebook paper with instructions.

"Geez, I never realized how much work goes into doing laundry. I thought you just put the stuff in the machines and took it out."

Maggie smiled. "Yeah, it's pretty crazy. So what's on the agenda for you and Kaia today? Besides laundry, of course."

Andrew frowned. He hadn't really thought of doing anything besides figuring out the laundry and maybe going out for dinner. Most Saturdays, he was involved with one of his community meetings or events and didn't do much with the family. He'd canceled going to most of his meetings for the next couple of weeks so he could be home with Kaia. He knew he wouldn't be able to do this for long, though. He had to get back to his community obligations.

"I'm not sure. What do you and she usually do?" Andrew asked.

"Well, sometimes, we go bowling with the residents from the group home. Other times, we go roller-skating at the rink, or we just go shopping and have lunch. She loves going to the bookstore and looking at the latest releases. Also, there's an arcade at the bowling alley that she likes to play games at. I guess it just depends on what you want to do."

"Bowling, huh? Kaia mentioned that yesterday in the grocery store. Since when do you like to bowl?" Andrew asked. He'd never gone bowling with Maggie or the kids.

Maggie laughed. "It started when I began taking the residents from the group home there to practice for Special Olympics. They needed volunteers to bowl with them, so I did, and when Kaia was older, she volunteered. Kyle did for a couple of years, too. Both kids are actually quite good."

Andrew racked his brain, but he couldn't remember Maggie or the kids ever talking about bowling. "Why didn't anyone ever tell me you three bowled so much? Where was I?"

"I'm sure the kids mentioned it to you. I remember them telling you scores every now and then. I guess you were just too busy with your own work and commitments to pay attention."

Andrew was quiet a moment. Maggie didn't sound resentful, but the amount of time he spent away from home volunteering was a bone of contention between them, and he was aware that this conversation could quickly turn from warm to cold. Instead of continuing on this topic, he changed the subject.

"Maybe I'll take Kaia bowling, if she wants to go. It might be fun," Andrew said, keeping his voice cheerful.

"That's a great idea. But watch out. Your daughter is as competitive as you are, and she has the upper hand. Don't let it get you too mad."

Andrew laughed. "I know all about her competitiveness. She's a killer on the tennis court."

After ending the call, Andrew thought about their conversation as he started a new load of laundry. There was so much he hadn't paid attention to around the house and his family, because he'd left everything for Maggie to do. Truthfully, he'd always thought she'd had it easy being home with the kids and only working part-time. But after the past few days, he'd come to realize how much she actually juggled. He felt like a heel for not appreciating all she did and taking her for granted. It was a hard thing for him to admit—he was a proud man—but he decided he had to tell Maggie he appreciated what she did for the family the next time they spoke.

# CHAPTER THIRTEEN

After talking to Andrew, Maggie showered and went downstairs to meet Bobbi for breakfast. After enjoying a variety of delicious foods again, the two of them planned to meet at noon and go shopping at an outlet mall that carried designer dresses for a fraction of the original cost.

"We're going to look *hot* tonight," Bobbi declared before heading off to another workshop. Maggie doubted she'd ever be considered *hot* but didn't argue the point with Bobbi, who seemed so excited about the banquet that night.

Twelve o'clock found Maggie and Bobbi back in the minivan, heading to the mall. Maggie wished she had the Mustang instead, but she couldn't pick it up until Monday, after all the paperwork was complete.

Bobbi gave directions, and soon they were parked at a large factory-outlet complex.

"I take it you've been here before," Maggie said.

Bobbi nodded. "Like I said, I come here every year for the convention, so I know this place well."

Bobbi led Maggie into one of the many designer dress shops. She started digging through the racks of dresses, pulling them out one by one and handing them to Maggie. "You're a size eight, right?" she asked as she continued pulling out short, sparkly dresses.

"More like a size ten," Maggie said, but Bobbi gave her the once-over and shook her head.

"Definitely an eight," she said.

"What makes you so sure?" Maggie asked.

"I worked in a fancy dress shop while I was going to beauty school. I can guess a woman's size by just looking at her."

After loading Maggie's arms with dozens of dresses, Bobbi led her to the dressing rooms. She stopped in front of a row of shoes, considered them a moment, and then picked out a pair of high-heeled sandals. She carried them to a dressing room and set them on a chair. "You can't try on dresses without the right shoes," Bobbi announced. She grabbed the dresses from Maggie and hung them on the hooks on the walls, then turned to her.

"You want me to try on all of these?" Maggie asked, staring dumbfounded at the dresses hanging in the room.

"Sure. We're here to have fun and to find a dress. You're sure to find one you like."

Maggie gave in. "Okay. But what about you? Aren't you going to try on dresses?"

"You bet I am. I just wanted to get you started first. I knew if I'd left you on your own, you'd have picked out one dowdy black dress to try on. This way, you're sure to find something *fun*."

"Hey, do I really seem that boring to you?" Maggie asked, insulted.

Bobbi chuckled. "Of course not. But from what I can tell, you've spent too many years taking care of your family and not thinking about yourself. I want you to have a good time tonight, and you will if you pick out a great dress."

Maggie realized that Bobbi was right. She hadn't done anything like this in a long time. So, in the spirit of fun, she began shimmying into the dresses Bobbi had picked out for her.

Soon, Bobbi was in the dressing room next to Maggie's with a pile of dresses of her own, and they were both moving in and out of their rooms, modeling their latest outfits. Maggie laughed at many of the dresses she tried on. Some were much too short, or too tight, or too bright. One even had purple feathers sewn onto it. They laughed, groaned, occasionally oohed and aahed, and enjoyed every minute of it.

Maggie finally settled on a deep-blue, strapless satin dress that hit slightly above the knee and wasn't so tight that she couldn't breathe. The black sandals Bobbi had chosen for her to try were perfect with it, so she kept them, too. And the dress and shoes were affordable—they cost less than a pair of jeans. She decided she should hit one of the casual shops at the mall to pick up some jeans and tops as well, since she had lost some weight and her clothes were getting loose.

"Well, it's not the most outrageous dress you tried on, but it does suit you," Bobbi said of Maggie's choice. "You'll definitely turn a few heads tonight."

"I'm not looking to turn any heads," Maggie assured her. "But it will be fun dressing up for a change."

Bobbi had chosen a more daring dress that was tight, short, low-necked, and turquoise blue with sequins on it. She'd also purchased a pair of silver platform sandals. Maggie had to admit, the dress suited Bobbi's outrageous style.

As Maggie went off to purchase jeans and tops, Bobbi headed out to shop on her own. An hour later, they met at the van. Maggie asked if Bobbi had found anything else to buy.

Bobbi looked at her sheepishly. "I hope you don't mind, but I bought some hair color and highlights for you. Please, please, please let me trim and color your hair for tonight. I promise you won't be sorry."

Maggie looked in the rearview mirror. Her hair used to be shiny blond, but now, it was dishwater blond with gray at the roots. She couldn't deny that it needed a little help.

"I guess I can't go driving around in that new Mustang next week with this hair," she told Bobbi with a grin.

"Yippee! You're going to be the belle of the ball tonight."

Maggie rolled her eyes. She might feel like a princess in her new dress, but she certainly wouldn't look like one.

Kaia stood on the approach, positioned her feet, held her ball at waist level, then walked four paces down the lane and released the ball. It dropped smoothly and rolled toward the pins, hitting another strike dead-on.

"That's strike number three. You'd better catch up, Dad, or I'll beat you again," Kaia said.

Andrew frowned. He'd lost by a large margin in game one, and she was already kicking his butt in game two in the first three frames. He knew he had a huge competitive streak, but he hadn't realized how big it was until Kaia started beating him today. Yet part of him was filled with pride at how well his daughter played the game.

"You're really good at this," he said, trying to be a good sport.

"It's a lot harder than it looks," Kaia replied. "People think that just anyone can bowl, but it takes practice."

"Hmm. I guess I'd better practice more," Andrew said. He stood on the approach, positioned himself in line with the pins, then took four steps and released the ball. The ball thumped loudly on the lane and rolled to the right, only knocking down the ten pin.

Kaia laughed.

Andrew took a deep breath, turned around, and walked over to Kaia. "Okay, smarty-pants. What did I do wrong?"

"First off, you don't aim the ball. You position it, using the dots and the arrows on the lanes. Where you position your feet on the approach will help determine where the ball will roll. Also, you want to keep your wrist straight when you release the ball. If you twist it, the ball will spin off in a different direction. Oh, and don't try to hit the one pin—that usually ends in a split. Try to direct the ball to hit between the one and the three pin for a strike."

Andrew stared at his daughter. "Who taught you all this?"

Kaia shrugged. "Mostly Carl and Cindi. Carl has been bowling for years and has won several tournaments for Special Olympics."

Andrew turned back to the approach, lifted his ball, and positioned his feet in the middle of the approach.

"No, Dad. Start over on the right side, but run your ball over that arrow," Kaia instructed. She pointed to where Andrew should throw the ball. "You still want to hit it like a strike so you can pick up the spare."

Andrew sighed but did as he was told. He moved over closer to the right side of the lane, took four steps up to the line, and rolled the ball over the arrow Kaia had pointed out. His ball hit perfectly between the first and third pins, and all nine pins clattered down for a spare.

"I did it," he said with a big smile as he turned toward Kaia, then realized how loudly he'd said it. He cringed as several people in the bowling alley looked up and stared at him.

Kaia smiled smugly. "Told you."

Andrew didn't care who stared at them or how smug Kaia was. He was having fun with his daughter for the first time in years, and that was all that mattered. Overtime at work or committee meetings didn't compare to seeing the smile on his daughter's face.

After they had bowled a few games, Andrew offered to take Kaia out for pizza—and she was all for it. He called Kyle to see if he'd like to eat with them.

"Thanks, Dad," Kyle said. "But I already have plans."

"I've barely seen you this week. Can't you eat with us this one time?" Andrew asked.

"I've already told Ashley we'd go out to eat and to a movie tonight," Kyle said.

Ashley? Andrew's brow furrowed. He remembered meeting a girl once. Kyle had brought her home to watch a movie on television, but Andrew couldn't remember her name. "Why don't you and Ashley come to dinner with us? Then you can go to your movie."

Kyle hesitated, and then finally agreed.

"So fill me in on Ashley," Andrew said as he and Kaia headed out to the car.

"Geez, Dad. Where have you been? Kyle has been going out with Ashley for the past six months."

Andrew ignored Kaia's tone—it was getting easier to ignore the more time he spent with her—and asked, "What's she like?"

Kaia shrugged. "She's nice. She doesn't come out to the house very often, but Mom and I have had dinner with Ashley and Kyle a few times. They graduated together, and she goes to college with Kyle."

When Andrew and Kaia met the young couple in the pizza place, Andrew suddenly recognized Ashley as the girl who'd come to the house. Kyle was quiet at first, but Ashley happily answered Andrew's questions, and she and Kaia joked around. Andrew liked her. She was outgoing and friendly and had a cute smile. And when Kyle looked at her, Andrew saw a sparkle in his eye. He imagined it was the same way he used to look at Maggie when they'd first started dating. He was happy Kyle had a special girl in his life.

Andrew enjoyed spending time with the kids. It had been a long time since they'd sat around like this and just had fun, talking. Ashley told a funny story about a customer's antics at her part-time job at the movie theater, and Kyle talked about a Harley-Davidson motorcycle he'd worked on at the shop. Andrew rarely heard stories from the kids anymore, and he really enjoyed them. It surprised him how grown-up they'd become.

When Maggie had been gone before, to handle her father's and then her sister's affairs, Kaia had stayed with a friend, and Kyle was already driving and working after school. Andrew hadn't had to deal with taking care of the kids then. Now, he realized that he'd missed out on spending time with them. He should have taken vacation time to be home with the kids. *How is it that I never realized what I was missing?* Maggie's leaving had actually given him time to reconnect with the kids, and even though he'd resented having to do so at first, he was really enjoying it now. He hoped to do more of this in the future.

Maggie sat still in front of the bathroom mirror as Bobbi ran goo through thick strands of her hair and folded strips of foil over them. She looked like an alien. But Bobbi assured her that the highlighting was going to brighten her hair and make her look years younger. They had already dyed her hair a soft blond color to cover the gray, and now she was highlighting it. Maggie liked having the gray gone but was afraid that highlighting might overprocess her fine hair.

"Don't worry," Bobbi kept assuring her. "I've done this a million times."

Maggie watched Bobbi work and admired how skillfully she managed her hair. She was happy she'd run into her that first morning. Bobbi was like a breath of fresh air, with her bubbly personality and positive attitude. She was a pretty woman, especially when she didn't pile on the makeup, and she seemed to love her life and her job. Maggie wondered why Bobbi hadn't yet found the right person to share her life with.

"Why hasn't anyone scooped you up yet?" Maggie asked.

Bobbi shrugged and smiled. "Guess I'm too picky."

"Has there ever been anyone serious?"

Bobbi stopped working a moment and sighed. "Yeah. I was involved with someone a few years ago. We lived together for several years, and I thought we were happy, but he never brought up marriage. When I finally asked him if he'd ever consider marriage, he said he didn't want to. After that, we started to drift apart, and he moved on. I wanted the whole package—marriage, kids, a house, and a dog. But he didn't."

Maggie frowned. "Sorry. I shouldn't have pried."

"No, that's okay. The worst part is he ended up married to someone else a year later, and they have a kid on the way now. I guess I just wasn't the right one for him."

Maggie smiled reassuringly. "I'm sure you'll meet the right man soon. You have so much going for you. You deserve a great guy."

Bobbi looked up and stared at Maggie in the mirror, her expression serious. "What about you, Maggie? You have it all, yet you're here and your family is in Minnesota. Is marriage not everything it's cracked up to be?"

Maggie sighed. "Marriage is wonderful. Except sometimes, people get lost in their roles of husband, wife, mother, and father, and forget to be their real selves. I was lost in my marriage, and that's what I'm doing here—trying to find the real me again. But that doesn't happen to everyone. You have a great sense of who you are. You won't let marriage change you like it did me."

"I hope everything works out for you, Maggie. You're a good person, and after I'm done with you, you'll be the hottest mom on the planet. Your husband won't be able to keep his hands off you."

Maggie laughed. Being with Bobbi was just what she needed. It was therapeutic.

Two hours later, Maggie and Bobbi were heading down to the private banquet room, wearing their new dresses and shoes. Maggie's hair had turned out beautifully, and Bobbi had trimmed it to softly frame her face. She'd then curled it lightly to give it some bounce, and Maggie looked years younger, as promised. Bobbi had talked her into adding more makeup and outlining her blue eyes. She also gave her some sample lipsticks to enhance her smile. Maggie was shocked when she finally looked in the mirror. She had to admit— she didn't look bad at all.

Like two giggly teenagers on the way to the prom, Maggie and Bobbi entered the banquet room and began to mingle. Chandeliers sparkled overhead, and the tables were set beautifully with gold tablecloths, silverware, and crystal goblets. Waiters walked among the crowd, offering champagne and wine to the guests, and a bar was set up for those wanting mixed drinks.

Bobbi picked up two glasses of champagne from a tray and handed one to Maggie, who looked at it and frowned. "I don't usually drink," Maggie told her.

Bobbi just laughed. "Enjoy it. It's free."

Maggie accepted it and took a sip. The bubbles tickled as they made their way down her throat. She couldn't remember the last time she'd had champagne, but with each sip, she enjoyed it even more.

Bobbi introduced Maggie to a few people she knew from past conferences, and soon, they were all sitting down, enjoying the delicious food and the entertainment the conference officials had hired. A band started tuning up after dinner, and the tables were cleared away to make room for a dance floor. By the time the band started belting out popular tunes from the seventies and eighties, Maggie had drunk a bit more champagne than she'd intended, and she didn't resist when a young man—he couldn't have been older than his late twenties—asked her to dance. Maggie just let herself go and enjoyed the moment.

Bobbi and Maggie each took several turns around the dance floor with different men. At one point, the two women stopped to catch their breath.

"I really shouldn't be dancing with strange men," Maggie said loudly over the band to Bobbi.

Bobbi laughed. "Don't worry too much about it. Most of the guys here are gay."

Maggie practically spit out her champagne as she tried to hold back a laugh. She hadn't realized the young men asking her to dance were gay. Knowing that, she felt better about being out and having a good time. For the first time in years, Maggie felt young, attractive, and feminine, and she wanted to hold on to that feeling for as long as possible..

Andrew lay in bed that night feeling good about the way the day had played out. He felt he'd made a strong connection with Kaia over the past several days. Even though Kyle seemed distant with him, he thought that if he asked him to be home more often, maybe they could become closer, too. He decided to talk to Kyle tomorrow about coming home for dinner at least a couple of nights a week so the three of them could spend time together as a family.

The only missing piece was Maggie. He thought about how he could talk Maggie into coming home. Maybe if he told her he'd give up some of his committee work and spend more time with the family, she'd consider forgiving him for his affair. It had been more than a year since Maggie had found out about it and he'd ended it, though a bit reluctantly. But now, he was actually relieved that she'd found out and made him end it. The woman he'd been having the affair with wasn't someone he'd have wanted to lose his marriage over, or someone he'd want to spend the rest of his life with. She had just been there, convenient and willing, and despite knowing it was wrong, Andrew had given in to temptation.

He'd been seeing the other woman for almost a year when Maggie had told him she knew about the affair and that he either had to end it or lose his family. Though he'd been embarrassed at being caught, he'd resented her ultimatum. But he also hadn't wanted her to leave him. So he'd ended it. They had never discussed it again, but they also had never reconciled their marriage completely, either. Maggie stayed distant, no longer asking him to join her and the kids for family activities or even something as simple as a meal out together. He'd gone his way, and she'd gone hers. He'd immersed himself even more in his volunteer activities, and he'd paid little attention to how Maggie and the kids spent their time.

His resentment grew and he figured hers did, too, but they didn't know how to get past it. It was easier to ignore than to rehash the past. Their marriage had been teetering on the edge for so long, he'd been afraid that if they actually talked about their problems, they'd fall over the cliff. He knew that Maggie hadn't forgiven him and he really couldn't blame her. And now she was gone. After being home with Kaia and seeing all that Maggie did for the family, Andrew realized that he missed her—not only for everything she did but also because she made their family complete. And the sooner he told her that, the better.

# CHAPTER FOURTEEN

Maggie awoke slowly, her head throbbing, and her body feeling as if she'd run a marathon. Squinting, she looked at the clock. One thirty p.m. She turned her head slightly and saw a thin ray of sunshine through a crack in the drapes. She couldn't believe she'd slept so late. But then again, she and Bobbi had stayed out until three in the morning, going from one casino to another with a small group of people from the banquet. At each spot, Maggie had only one drink, but along with the champagne earlier in the evening, it was much more alcohol than she was used to. By the time she'd returned to her room, she was feeling queasy, and she'd collapsed into bed, only taking enough time to remove her shoes and dress.

Maggie tried raising her head from the pillow, made it only a few inches, and then dropped back down as she moaned in pain. Her stomach churned. Now, she remembered quite clearly why she rarely drank alcohol. It just wasn't worth feeling this miserable the next day.

The room's phone rang at an earsplitting volume, startling Maggie. She put the pillow over her head, trying to block out the noise. Then, her good sense returned, and she realized it might be important, so she forced herself to roll over and pick up the receiver.

"Hello."

"Hey, are you still alive in there?" a cheerful voice rang out over the phone. "I knocked on your door around eleven to see if you were up and ready for breakfast, but there was no answer."

Maggie moaned again. How in the world could Bobbi be so wide-awake and cheerful after the night they'd had?

"I tried calling your cell phone, but it went right to voice mail," Bobbi continued. "Did I wake you?"

Maggie squeezed her eyes shut, trying hard to fight off the headache. "My head feels like the band is still playing inside it. I'd kill for some Tylenol."

Bobbi laughed heartily. "I'll come over now and we'll fix you right up. It's your last day in Reno. You don't want to spend it in bed."

Maggie couldn't think of anywhere else she'd rather spend today than in bed.

Spying her cell phone on the nightstand, Maggie pulled it to her and tried switching it on. Dead. The only charger she had was in the van, so she'd have to recharge it in there. The last call she'd had was from Kaia, who'd phoned during the banquet when the band had been playing an old rock song. They'd talked for a few minutes, but since they couldn't hear each other very well, Maggie said she'd call her the next day. Kaia had been excited about beating Andrew in bowling, and Maggie definitely wanted to hear more about it.

An hour later, feeling more awake after a long shower, and her headache almost gone after two Tylenol, Maggie headed off with Bobbi in search of a late lunch. After plugging her phone into the jack in the van, they found a decent café nearby. Being out in the sunlight and away from the constant clanging of slot machines also helped relieve Maggie's headache. Once she'd eaten, Maggie felt a little better, and the two women walked through the casinos and played the slots here and there, not winning any money but having fun. When Maggie's headache returned a couple of hours later, she told Bobbi that she had to go back to her room and sleep it off.

"I'm still driving you to the airport tomorrow in my new Mustang," Maggie said as they parted at the elevators back at Circus Circus.

"I can take the shuttle if it's too much trouble," Bobbi said.

Maggie shook her head. "You have to ride in the new car one more time. After all, I never would have bought it if it wasn't for you."

They settled on a time to meet the next day, and Maggie went up to her room. As soon as she slipped into bed, she realized she'd left her phone in the van. She had no desire to walk all the way back to the parking garage to retrieve it. She fell asleep as soon as her head hit the pillow.

Andrew awoke in a cheerful mood. He showered and dressed and headed downstairs to the kitchen with plans of what he and the kids could do together that day. Kyle and Kaia were already sitting at the kitchen table, eating bowls of Cheerios and watching cartoons on the small kitchen television.

"Wow. Some things never change," Andrew said with a chuckle. All he got in return was a grunt from Kaia. Pulling out a carton of eggs from the refrigerator, he asked, "How about some scrambled eggs for breakfast? Or maybe fried?"

Kaia and Kyle both shook their heads, keeping their eyes on the television screen.

Andrew pulled out a frying pan and started making himself two eggs over easy. He certainly wasn't a chef, but he was adept at making eggs of all styles, and cooking on the grill. "Why don't we all do something together today? Then we can grill steaks for dinner."

Kyle looked up at his dad. "I can't. I'm going over to Ashley's for the day. I already told her I'd be eating there with her family."

Andrew frowned but tried not to sound discouraged. "Well, why don't you and Ashley hang out here today? She's more than welcome to have dinner with us."

"Naw, that's okay. I'll just go over there. Maybe we can hang out here some other time." Kyle got up from his seat, rinsed out his bowl in the sink, then headed upstairs to his room.

As Andrew flipped the eggs, he wondered why Kyle seemed so distant. He and his son once had been close, watching football on weekends together, working on model cars, and playing video games. Of course, that was years ago, and Kyle was nineteen now. He decided not to take it personally. Kyle was just growing up and building his own life.

Andrew slid his eggs onto a plate and buttered his toast. He sat down in the chair Kyle had vacated. "Well, it looks like it's just you and me today," he told Kaia. "What do you want to do?"

Kaia shrugged. "I have a lot of homework, so I should just stay home." She passed the TV remote over to her dad and took her bowl to the sink. "I'm going to spend the night over at Megan's house Monday. Her mom will pick us up after school. We have a history report we're doing together and need to work on it."

Andrew's eyebrows rose. "Don't you mean 'May I spend the night at Megan's house'?"

Kaia grinned. "Don't be silly, Dad. You weren't invited."

"Ha, ha. I guess it's okay, but I'll need Megan's mom's phone number first, so I can confirm she's picking you up."

"You've figured out this dad thing pretty fast," Kaia said, still grinning, and then walked out of the room.

Andrew sighed. Keeping up with these kids was a lot more work than he'd thought.

Later, after doing a couple of loads of laundry and going for a walk around the neighborhood with Kaia and Bear, Andrew grilled two small steaks along with some corn on the cob wrapped in tin-foil. This was one task he knew how to do, and it made him feel competent at something around the house.

Earlier, he'd tried calling Maggie to check on her, but his call had gone directly to voice mail. After a couple of tries, he began to worry. He didn't know which hotel she was staying at in Reno, or if she'd already left there. He hoped she was okay. Maybe the battery had died. Did she even have a charger with her? He hoped so. He figured he'd try again later. He was beginning to enjoy their conversations, now that they weren't arguing.

After dinner, as Kaia started rinsing the dishes and putting them into the dishwasher, Andrew stared at her in disbelief. A few days ago, she hadn't offered to help him with anything. Now, she was doing it on her own. He'd always thought Maggie spoiled the kids by not making them do chores, but now he knew differently.

"What?" Kaia asked, sounding annoyed.

"Nothing," Andrew said, smiling, and headed to the laundry room to finish folding the last pile of towels.

He tried calling Maggie that evening, but again, his call went to voice mail. Andrew's worry grew.

"Have you talked to your mom today?" he asked Kaia as she worked on her homework at the kitchen table.

"I talked to her last night," Kaia said. "But her battery was low, and there was too much noise, so she couldn't hear me. She said she'd call me back today."

Andrew cocked his head. "Noise? What type of noise?"

"There was a band playing some old rock music. You know, like the stuff you and Mom listen to. She said she was at dinner with someone named Bobby, and there was a band."

Andrew stared at Kaia, but she just went back to writing in her notebook. *Bobby? Maggie was out with some guy named Bobby, having dinner and listening to a band in Reno?*

Kaia looked up and saw her dad staring at her. "Now what?"

Andrew regained his composure. "Did your mother call you back today?"

"No. I figured she was busy doing something, or maybe she left Reno and was driving somewhere else and forgot. I'm sure I'll hear from her soon."

As Kaia went back to her schoolwork, Andrew thought about what she'd said. Out to dinner with someone named Bobby. Listening to a loud band. She was probably in some bar in Reno, in one of the casinos, with some strange guy. *Oh, my God.* He was getting angrier by the second. Here he was, playing house dad and actually starting to feel good about their relationship, and she was out with some guy she'd met in a casino.

Andrew stormed out of the kitchen and headed upstairs to his bedroom. He tried calling Maggie again, but there was still no answer. This time, he left a message to call him immediately. If she thought she was going to make him jealous, then she was wrong. He might be angry, but he wasn't jealous. If she wanted to pick up strange men, then that was her problem. All he knew for sure was that when he talked to her, he was going to give her an ultimatum, and she'd better make the right choice—or else.

Maggie awoke once again to sunshine peeking through the drapes. When she saw it was eight in the morning, she was dumbfounded. Had she actually slept from late afternoon until the next morning? Tentatively, she rose to a sitting position and was relieved her headache was gone. She stepped out of bed and opened the drapes.

It was another beautiful, sunny day. Then she remembered that she was picking up her new car today. With renewed energy, she hurried to shower and dress, and then headed out the door of her room for the last time.

At one o'clock, Maggie pulled up to the front entrance of Circus Circus in her new Mustang. The top was down, and the car sparkled in the sun. People stared as they walked past, and Maggie felt like a movie star.

When Bobbi came out, a big smile spread across her face and she ran over to the car. "It's so beautiful!" she exclaimed. Maggie helped her put her luggage in the backseat, and the two of them hopped in and drove to the airport.

The ride was too short as the two women enjoyed the warm desert air whipping across their faces and their hair blowing in the wind. Maggie stopped at the terminal entrance for Bobbi's flight, and then stepped out to help unload her luggage.

"I'm going to miss you, Maggie," Bobbi said as she gave her a hug good-bye. "We sure had some fun. Don't forget to keep in touch."

"How can I forget my new friend?" Maggie asked, laughing. "After all, you're the first person in years to bring out *hot* Maggie again." Both women laughed. "Seriously, though, Reno and Tahoe wouldn't have been the same without you. Thanks for making my stay such fun."

"Anytime, girl. Anytime." Bobbi lifted her carry-on onto her shoulder and pulled her suitcase behind her to the automatic sliding-glass doors. She turned, waved to Maggie, and then was gone.

Maggie ran around her new Mustang and slid back into the driver's seat, thinking how she'd never have had the courage to buy this gorgeous car without Bobbi's encouragement. She popped open the compartment between the front seats, pulled out her Bob Seger CD, and slipped it into the player. As Maggie drove out of the airport, Bob began to sing her favorite song. The song that had started her on this journey and then kept her driving west. "Roll me away, Bob," she said, smiling as she exited onto Interstate 80 west toward San Francisco.

# CHAPTER FIFTEEN

Monday night found Andrew sitting in Two Rivers Pub on a stool at the bar. It was after seven in the evening. He'd just finished eating a hamburger and fries and was now nursing his second mug of beer. He was alone. Kaia was at her friend's house for the night, and Kyle was God knows where. Andrew had tried to persuade Kyle to join him for a burger, just the guys, but he'd declined. Andrew was irritated with him. Why couldn't his only son spend just an hour with him? They'd been close when Kyle was younger. Andrew had coached his Little League teams, and they'd played catch and one-on-one basketball in the driveway many nights after school and work. Sure, Andrew had been busy the past few years with work and committee meetings, but Kyle was older and had been busy, too. He just couldn't understand why Kyle was giving him the cold shoulder.

Andrew glanced up and spotted the owner, Russ Peterson, behind the bar, pouring two mugs of beer. He and Russ had graduated together from high school, and he had a son the same age as Kyle.

"Hey, Russ. What's your son up to these days?"

"He's going to the college here, same as your kid. Business major," Russ answered as he placed the mugs of beer on a tray and started mixing a drink.

"Do you and he ever spend time together anymore?"

Russ chuckled. "If you count him working here on the weekends, then sure. Otherwise, not much time. He's busy with school and working here, and he has a girlfriend. Not much time for the old man."

"Hmm," Andrew muttered into his beer as he watched Russ finish mixing the drink, then take the tray out to some customers on the far side of the room. Maybe it was normal for grown kids not to spend time with their parents. Maybe he shouldn't read too much into it. But it still irked him.

"Trouble at home?"

Andrew turned to see who'd asked him that question and had to stop himself from grimacing when he saw Clyde at the end of the bar. Everyone in town knew Clyde. He was an old drunk who hung out in all the local bars and mooched off his friends to buy him drinks. He'd been a logger years ago but had long since retired. Clyde's wife had passed years ago, and his kids had left town. But Clyde had been a presence in the bars around town long before his wife died. He nosed around in other people's business, and that was why Andrew didn't like him much.

"No. No trouble at home. Why do you ask?" Andrew said, barely managing to hold back his contempt.

Clyde shrugged. "No reason. Just that you're here alone and not with that pretty wife of yours. That's all."

Andrew ignored Clyde and turned away, looking into the wall-length mirror behind the bar. He and Maggie hadn't come here together to eat in a long time. Not that there was anything wrong with the pub. It was a family-friendly place that served good food. The atmosphere was cozy, with warm oak-paneled walls, high-backed booths lining the outer walls, and big, heavy wooden tables and chairs in the center. A jukebox sat against one wall near the popcorn machine filled with fresh popcorn. He, Maggie, and the kids used to come here often for burgers and fries, usually on a Friday or Saturday night. That was before things became tense between Maggie and him.

At the thought of Maggie, he grew angry all over again. He still hadn't heard from her, and he'd be damned if he was going to try calling her again. The more he thought of her being out with another man, the angrier he became. Yes, he had cheated on her a year ago, and yes, he knew he'd been wrong. But did that make it okay for her to do the same thing? Was she trying to get even with him?

"Hey, Andrew, how's it going?" Derrick Weis walked up to the bar and stood beside him.

"Fine. Just having dinner," Andrew answered.

Russ came over and asked Derrick what he'd like.

"Two beers on tap," Derrick answered. Russ began to draw beer into frosted mugs.

Andrew turned, noticing that Derrick wasn't wearing his uniform. "Off duty tonight?"

Derrick nodded. "Wouldn't be drinking if I was on duty." He looked Andrew directly in the eye. "How's Maggie? Has she come home yet?"

Andrew stiffened. He didn't like Derrick's tone. "She's still out in Seattle, visiting family," he lied. He wasn't sharing his family problems with Derrick.

"Well, that's good to hear. I'm surprised she didn't take Kaia along with her, though. I see those two together all over town. They're inseparable."

*That's because it's an occupational hazard of being a young teen.* A grin settled on Andrew's face as he thought of what Kaia had told him. He didn't share this with Derrick, though. "She has school."

Russ came over and placed the two beers in front of Derrick, then stood there, joining in on the conversation. "Maggie's been gone? I didn't know that. What happened, Andrew? You two have a fight?" He chuckled, and Andrew glared at him.. Derrick's eyebrows rose as he waited for Andrew to answer.

"No, we didn't have a fight, as if it's any of your business," Andrew snapped back.

"Cripes, man. Don't bite my head off. It was just a joke. I'm just surprised Maggie left now that school is in session. She's always so active in the schools, volunteering in the classrooms and with the PTA," Russ said.

Andrew frowned. He knew Maggie used to be in the PTA but didn't know she still was an active member. He didn't want to admit this to these two goons, though.

"She's usually in charge of the middle-school dances, too. The fall dance is coming up, so I'm surprised she left this time of year," Derrick said, eyeing Andrew.

Andrew turned his frown on Derrick. "She had her reasons, okay?"

"Oh, I'm sure she had her reasons," Derrick said in a tone that irritated Andrew. Russ snickered from behind the bar.

Andrew's eyes narrowed. "What's that supposed to mean?"

Derrick stared hard at Andrew. "I think you know what it means. This is a small town, Andrew. You know that as well as I do. People talk. Did you really think you could keep your affair a secret? Everyone in this town likes Maggie. She's a nice person, a good mother, and she gives her time to help benefit this community. She didn't deserve what you did to her."

Andrew stood and faced Derrick. They were practically the same height, but Derrick was built thicker than Andrew. He didn't care—if Derrick wanted a fight, he'd give him one. "None of this is your business, Derrick. Why don't you worry about your own wife and family, and butt out of mine."

"Oh, just calm down, Andrew. I'm in no mood to fight with you," Derrick said as Clyde chuckled at the end of the bar.

"I do a lot of volunteer work in this community, too, you know," Andrew said, trying to save face. "I spend my free time helping this community grow, bringing jobs into this town, and making it a nice place for our families. Maggie's not the only one who gives her time."

"Yes, I know all about your volunteer work in this town," Derrick said. "But there's a big difference between what you do and what Maggie does. She does it from the heart. You do it for the recognition."

Andrew glared at Derrick, unable to come up with a retort.

Derrick lowered his voice. "I've known you a long time, Andrew. We went to school together, and we coached Little League together. I know, deep down, you're a good guy. But what you did to Maggie . . . that was low. You know, when you first came home from college and brought Maggie back with you, there wasn't a guy in this town who wasn't jealous of you. She was beautiful, sweet, and kind. We all envied you. And as the years went on, she just proved over and over again what a valued member of this community she is."

Andrew stared at Derrick, dumbfounded. Russ nodded in agreement. "So you all had a crush on my wife. How would your wife like to hear you say all these things about Maggie, huh?"

Derrick frowned at him, his face turning red with anger. He looked to the back of the room where his wife sat, wearing her scrubs and waiting for him, in a booth. "I love my wife. She's a good person, and I'm proud of everything she does, too. So don't turn this around on me. The point I'm making is that you have a pretty wife who cares about other people and who is a good mother, and how did you repay her? You cheated on her with a woman who wasn't even half the woman Maggie is. It was Maggie who had to go through each day, trying to hold her head up high and ignore the whispers behind her back and pretend that everything was okay. You didn't even have the decency to hide your affair. You paraded around town with that woman at your side. So you're right. Maggie had her reasons for leaving. And her number one reason for leaving was you."

Maggie found a comfortable hotel in San Francisco near Fisherman's Wharf to settle into for the night. Even though it was only a four-hour drive from Reno to San Francisco, she'd hit the city in the middle of rush hour so it had taken her an extra hour to find a hotel. Now, she just wanted to clean up and walk to the wharf to take pictures and eat a delicious seafood dinner.

Kaia had called Maggie earlier to tell her about her weekend with Andrew and that she was spending the night at Megan's house to work on a school project.

"So what's your father up to without you at home tonight?" Maggie had asked her. Kaia said he'd planned on going out for a bite with Kyle, but that was about all.

"Is everything going fine at home?" Maggie asked, curious about how Kaia and Andrew were getting along. This morning she'd listened to the message from Andrew, and he'd sounded irritated. Hearing his tone, Maggie had decided that she didn't want to talk to him just yet. She'd let him settle down first from whatever had set him off. They'd been getting along so well the past few days that she didn't want to ruin it by talking to him when he was miffed.

"Yeah, it going good," Kaia answered. "Dad's calmed down a lot. I think he's actually having fun being home more, and he isn't acting as stressed out as he usually does."

After saying good-bye to Kaia, Maggie had pondered her words as she drove along the highway toward San Francisco. Maybe her going away had been good for both of them. It was not only giving her a chance to sort out her life but also allowing Andrew more time to spend with the family. She was happy that Kaia and he were getting along so well. But if everything was fine, why had he sounded so angry in his last message? She'd decided that if she didn't hear from Andrew by tonight, she'd call him first thing in the morning.

Grabbing a sweater and her camera, Maggie headed out to get as many pictures as she could before sunset, and then eat dinner.

Andrew fumed all the way home and slammed the door in the back porch, scaring Bear and making the cats scatter. *"Maggie had her reasons for leaving. And her number one reason for leaving was you."* Andrew grew angrier the more he thought about Derrick's words.

"How dare he butt his nose into my life?" he yelled into the empty room. "Who the hell does he think he is?" Seeing Bear stare at him with big, droopy eyes brought Andrew back to reality, and he walked over and gently rubbed the dog's ears. Once Bear started wagging his tail, Andrew took him outside and hooked him to his leash so he could do his business. Andrew put down food for Bear, then fed the cats and refilled their water bowls, and by the time he was done, he'd calmed down a little.

Maggie hadn't called him back. This upset him more than he wanted to admit. He had no idea where she was, or who she was with. Could she really have found another man that easily? Was he that easy to replace? He winced at the thought that Maggie had probably wondered the same things when she'd found out about his affair.

Upstairs in the bedroom, Andrew changed out of his suit and into sweats. The house was cool, proving that fall was upon them and winter was close behind. As he glanced at the phone on the nightstand, he saw the message light blinking. Had Maggie called the house phone instead of his cell? When he checked caller ID, he saw that the last caller had been his mother. Ignoring her message, he reluctantly called her back.

"Hello," his mother's brisk voice said after the second ring.

"Hi, Mom. It's Andrew. I see that you called earlier."

"Yes, I did. I thought you'd be home, but apparently, you weren't."

Andrew sighed. "I went out for a bite to eat. Was there something you needed?"

"No. What I want to know is what is going on with your family?"

Andrew's brow wrinkled. "What do you mean by that?"

Marcia spoke in a clipped manner. "There are rumors going around town that Maggie has left you. What's that all about? Has your wife left you for another man?"

Andrew stood there, dumbfounded. Who in the world was spreading these rumors? "No. Of course she hasn't. I told you, Maggie went to Seattle to see her cousin. Where did you hear such a thing?"

"It's all over town. People are saying that Maggie left you and the kids, and you've been left to take care of everything. It doesn't surprise me one bit, you know. Maggie was never one of us. I'm surprised she didn't leave years ago."

Andrew's heart pounded as he ran his hand through his hair. *"Maggie was never one of us"*? He knew his mother never approved of Maggie, but how dare she say that? But he also knew arguing with his mother was useless. He weighed his words carefully. "These rumors aren't true. They're all lies. Besides, who cares what goes on between Maggie and me? That's our business, and no one else's."

"Who cares?" Marcia asked indignantly. "Well, for one, I do. And you should, too. You've worked very hard carving out your position in this town. Just because Maggie doesn't care about it doesn't mean that you shouldn't. A rumor like this can ruin your chances when you run for mayor next year."

Andrew let out a long breath. His mother didn't care that there were problems between him and his wife. She didn't care how it affected his children. All she cared about were his chances of becoming mayor. "Maggie cares about this town, Mother. She volunteers in the schools, and people around here like her very much. There's no basis for these rumors, so don't pay any attention to them."

"Well, you'd better get your house in order and tell your wife to come home," his mother said curtly. "It doesn't look good, her gallivanting around the country, abandoning her family. She should feel very lucky to have you for a husband. You're highly respected in this town."

Andrew snorted, laughter rolling from deep inside his throat. "Really, Mom? Respected? If only you knew the truth. I'm not as highly respected in this town as you think. In fact, Maggie has a much higher standing with everyone right now than I do."

"Don't be ridiculous. If you're referring to that little indiscretion of yours last year . . . well, no one really cares about that. Men cheat all the time. It's in their DNA. No one will hold that against you."

Andrew stopped laughing, shocked by what his mother had said. "You know about that?"

"I heard the rumors. I don't condone it, but I'm not surprised by it, either. It happens. If that's why Maggie has run off, then she just needs to get over it. All that matters is that you're a good provider for your family and you have a nice future in this community. People won't hold you responsible for a little indiscretion."

"*A little indiscretion*"? Is that what his mother called cheating on your spouse? Andrew thought about his childhood and how cold his parents were to each other. Back then, he had heard rumors about his father cheating, but no one ever told him to his face. And his parents had always stayed together, so he figured the rumors couldn't possibly have been true. But now, he wondered. Did his dad have a few *little indiscretions*?

Andrew assured his mother that Maggie would be home soon, and hung up the phone. He mulled over what she'd said. Her tone bothered him as much as her words. She sounded cold, unfeeling, and uncaring. Was that how he sounded to Maggie? All his mother worried about was her standing in the community and her own activities. Family wasn't important to her. It came as an unwelcome shock to realize that he could be accused of acting exactly the same way. He'd placed his job, the community, and his own aspirations ahead of Maggie and the kids. And he'd strayed. He'd told himself that Maggie was the one who didn't make time for him. He'd allowed himself to believe that he'd been justified in having the affair. But at this very moment, standing in this silent house, he came to a crushing realization that there were no excuses. He was the only one to blame.

Downstairs, the back door opened and closed, and footsteps pounded on the staircase. Andrew looked out his bedroom door as Kyle appeared at the top of the stairs.

"Hey, buddy, you're finally home," Andrew said, keeping his voice light. He glanced at his watch and saw that it was a little after nine o'clock. "Did you do anything fun tonight?"

Kyle frowned. "Not really. Just hung out with Ashley and a couple of the guys."

"So how is school going?" Andrew asked.

Kyle shrugged. "Okay, I guess."

Andrew sighed. Getting Kyle to talk to him was like pulling teeth. "So what are you majoring in at school? I talked to Russ down at the pub tonight, and he said his son was majoring in business."

"I haven't declared a major. I'm just doing my general education right now. I haven't found anything that interests me yet."

Andrew grinned. "Well, maybe you should try a business or communications major like your dad."

Kyle shook his head. "I don't think so, Dad. I'm not really into that stuff." He started backing away toward his bedroom. "I need to get some homework done before tomorrow. I'll see you in the morning."

Andrew took a step toward Kyle. "It's after nine and you don't have your homework done yet? You really should come home earlier at night so you can work on it. You spend too much time at the motorcycle shop and hanging out with friends. You need to concentrate on your schoolwork."

"Dad," Kyle said, making it clear by his tone that he didn't want to talk about it.

Andrew realized this probably wasn't the best time, but he hardly ever saw his son and he wasn't going to be put off. "Listen, Kyle. You need to think about your future more and do better in school. Sure, cycles are a lot of fun, but there's no future there." When Kyle only stared at him, Andrew grew irritated. "I don't understand why you don't like college. I loved going to college, and your mom did, too. I'm sure she'd agree with me that you need to have a good education."

"Like you know what Mom thinks," Kyle said softly.

Andrew's brow furrowed. "What did you say?"

"Forget it, Dad. I'm tired, and I have homework to do. Good night." Kyle turned and headed into his bedroom.

"Fine," Andrew said curtly. "But I want you to come home earlier at night and spend more time on your homework and less time messing around town."

Kyle didn't answer him. He just quietly closed his door against Andrew's words.

# CHAPTER SIXTEEN

Andrew's mood hadn't improved much the next morning. He tried talking to Kyle again, but all he got were grunts in return, so he gave up. *Spoiled kid.* He headed out to his car. *He doesn't appreciate anything.*

The day was sunny, and the trees that lined the neighborhood streets were beginning to turn vibrant yellows and reds, but Andrew didn't notice any of it. He was too angry. *Like you know what Mom thinks*, Kyle had said last night. What had he meant by that? Did Kyle know what happened between him and Maggie? Did Maggie tell him? That thought really infuriated him. What happened between him and Maggie was their business, and there was no reason to bring the kids into it.

Since he didn't have to drive Kaia to school, he headed directly to the office and started work early. It felt good, working before the office became busy and noisy. He had his own office, since he was the lead advertising associate and needed the privacy to talk to clients. But that didn't stop the noise from filtering in as the rest of the staff talked to customers on the phone or people grouped, gossiping in the hallways. Today, he was able to complete a load of work by coming in that extra hour early.

A little after noon, the bookkeeper came in and dropped off the daily deposit for the bank. Andrew had been taking the deposit to the bank every day for years. Since he usually left the office to talk to clients, it saved a trip for the bookkeeper, so he didn't mind doing it.

He'd had a productive morning, and it felt good. As he slipped on his suit jacket and headed out to his car, his thoughts turned once more to Maggie. He decided it was time to stop being so defensive and to just talk things out with her. He didn't want to fight anymore. He wanted to get past everything that had happened between them and move forward. Tonight, when he got home, he'd call her to talk about their future. He hoped the conversation would end with her deciding to come home.

Andrew headed into the bank and dropped off the deposit with one of the tellers. He had been banking here his entire life, since he was ten years old and had saved money by mowing lawns and shoveling snow for neighbors, so he knew almost everyone who worked here. He'd either gone to school with them, or he knew them through his parents. He even knew some of the young tellers because Kyle had gone to school with them. He waved and smiled at employees as he walked past them toward the door to leave.

From the corner of his eye, Andrew saw Charlie Larson, one of the bank's loan officers, hurrying toward him with a folder in his hand. Andrew sighed and slowed down, wondering what Charlie wanted.

"Hey, Andrew. I'm glad I caught up with you. Figured you were here to sign the loan papers," Charlie said, looking up at Andrew with a smile.

Andrew frowned. "What loan papers?"

"For Maggie's new car. She said she'd come in and sign the papers when she came home, but I figured you might as well since you're here. Can't say I wasn't surprised when Maggie called from Tahoe saying she was changing over the loan, but I can't blame her.

This car's a beaut." Charlie opened the folder and handed Andrew a picture of the red Mustang convertible that Maggie had purchased. "The car dealer sent me this photo and the car stats for the paperwork. Of course I'm sure you've already seen it, but you can't look at a car that fabulous too much, eh, Andrew?"

As Andrew stared at the photo of the cherry-red Mustang convertible, it was all he could do not to let his mouth drop open in shock. He looked up to see Charlie still smiling at him, his eyes crinkled behind his big glasses. Andrew collected himself as best he could, not wanting Charlie to realize that he knew nothing about his wife's purchase.

"You're right, Charlie. It's a beautiful car. I was so busy at work today, I almost forgot about it. You know, I have to get back to the office. Do you mind if we sign those papers later this week?"

"No problem at all," Charlie said, closing up the folder. "I'm not worried. I know you and Maggie are good for it. Besides, she's just replacing the loan on the van for the Mustang, so the money has already been approved." Charlie looked at Andrew curiously. "You know, I didn't expect to see you here today. Figured you were in Tahoe with Maggie."

Andrew looked up from the car picture and saw Charlie's eyes sparkle with anticipation. He could tell that, like everyone else in this small town, Charlie wanted a juicy bit of gossip to spread around. "Maggie's on her way to see her cousin in Seattle," Andrew lied as casually as he could. "She's been wanting a car like this for a long time, so when she saw it, we both agreed it would be fun to buy." *Oh, God. When is all this craziness going to end?*

"Well, it was a smart purchase. That car suits Maggie better than that mom van. Hope she enjoys it."

Andrew just nodded, wondering what Charlie meant by that. *Geez, does he have a crush on Maggie, too?* What was wrong with the men in this town? He started to walk away when he realized he still had the picture of the Mustang in his hand.

"Mind if I keep this photo?" he asked Charlie. "You know, to show the kids."

"Sure, no problem. Catch you later."

Andrew stepped outside into the sunny day and just stood there, dazed. A Mustang convertible? A *red* Mustang convertible? What the hell was Maggie thinking?

Maggie woke up early the next morning and headed out to take a few more pictures around San Francisco before driving across the Golden Gate Bridge and connecting with Highway 1 along the coast. Eventually, she'd have to head inland to Interstate 5 for a quicker route to Seattle. But for now, she wanted to enjoy the calming view of the ocean, the small seaside towns, and the feel of the salty air on her cheeks as she rode the winding curves with the top down.

Oh, how she missed the ocean. Living far north in the middle of the country, she always forgot how soothing ocean views were until she was back here on the West Coast. Before she married Andrew, he had made it clear he wanted to go home, back to Woodroe, to live, work, and raise a family. At the time, Maggie hadn't minded. Being a child of a navy serviceman, she'd moved often and had lived all over the United States. She didn't mind moving to Minnesota, as long as she and Andrew were together. But even after all these years, when she was here by the ocean, feeling the breeze and taking in the beauty of the cliffs, beaches, and frothy water, she felt more at home than she ever did in Minnesota.

Maggie stopped several times to take photos along the way. She took one of an elderly woman who was selling fresh fruit and vegetables at a roadside stand, with the cliffs and ocean as a backdrop. She stopped again to take a picture of a run-down gas station, with old rusted pumps and an antique 7UP clock in the dusty window. Maggie loved capturing these slice-of-life photos that showed America as it was and as it still is.

Once Maggie crossed the Oregon border, she found a quaint bed-and-breakfast to stop at for the night. She decided that tomorrow morning, she'd cross over to Interstate 5 so she could be in Seattle, at Cassie's house, before nightfall. As she sat on the bed in her cozy room, loading the latest photos into her computer, her phone buzzed. It was Andrew. Tentatively, she answered with a soft "Hello."

"You bought a Mustang? A *red* Mustang?" Andrew bellowed.

"Hello, Andrew. How are you? I'm fine," Maggie said, knowing it would piss him off but not caring. How dare he just start yelling at her?

"Don't act smart. Did you really think I wouldn't find out? Charlie Larson at the bank couldn't wait to corner me and tell me about it. What in the world were you thinking? You traded in our brand-new van for a useless convertible? Do you realize how senseless that is?"

Maggie took a deep breath to hold back the anger that was building inside her. "First of all, stop yelling at me or I'll hang up. Second, you drive a convertible sports car. Remember? And it's much more expensive than the one I bought."

There was a pause before Andrew answered in a calmer voice. "That's different. I need a car that looks good to my clients. Perception is important in my job. A nice car makes me appear successful, and people spend more on ads if I look like I know what I'm doing. But you don't need a flashy car. You're a mom. You need a car to drive kids and groceries around in, not a car to pick up men with."

Maggie laughed. "Are you kidding me? I don't drive kids around anymore. The only person I drive around is Kaia, and I'm sure she'll fit inside this car. And pick up men? What men, exactly, am I picking up?"

"What about that Bobby guy you picked up in Reno? Yeah, Kaia told me you were out at a bar with him the other night. What were you thinking, picking up some random guy, going to a bar, and then telling our *fourteen-year-old daughter* about him?"

"Bobby? You think I was out with some guy named Bobby?" Maggie laughed. This conversation was so ridiculous that she couldn't help herself. "It's *Bobbi* with an *i*—short for Roberta. I was at a hairstylist convention's banquet with a woman I met in Reno named Roberta. Honestly, Andrew. Do you really believe I'd go out and pick up some random guy?"

"How the hell was I supposed to know Bobbi was a woman?" Andrew sputtered. "And what am I supposed to believe anymore? You run away, then you go and trade in our minivan for a Mustang. I have no idea what you're capable of these days."

"Don't be ridiculous. So I traded in the van for a cute car. I agree, that isn't something I'd normally do, but what's so wrong with it? After all, the loan for the Mustang is less than what we owed on the van, so I even made a little money on the trade-in. The guy at the dealership said he could sell that van in a heartbeat, so he gave me a good deal. I've been doing everything for everyone else for so long. What's wrong with me having a fun car of my own for a change?"

There was a long pause, and then Andrew asked, "How are you able to afford all this? Where is the money coming from? You can't possibly have saved enough money from your small paychecks to go running around the country."

"Don't worry, Andrew. I know how much you love your money. I wouldn't dream of using the family money frivolously," Maggie said. "I have actually saved some of the money from my paychecks over the years. Believe it or not, I don't throw away money the way you think I do. And have you forgotten that I inherited money from my father, from the sale of his house?"

"That couldn't have been very much money, considering you had to share half with your sister," Andrew said.

"If you'd pay attention to what I tell you once in a while, you'd know exactly how much it was. The house sold for over four hundred thousand dollars, and the mortgage had been paid off years ago. By then, Amy knew she had cancer, so she told me to keep the money in my name. I spent almost one hundred thousand of it on her living and medical expenses that weren't covered by insurance before she died. Other than that, I've only used the money for Kyle's college expenses. So, basically, I have enough money to travel for as long as I'd like."

"Why didn't I know all this?" Andrew asked, sounding stunned.

"Because when I tried to tell you, you told me you didn't care what I did with my *little* inheritance. As usual, you didn't pay attention to what was going on."

"And you've been paying for Kyle's college tuition? I thought we were paying that out of our savings."

"I haven't touched our savings. I knew my father would have wanted me to use the money for the children, so that's what I'm doing. I'm hoping to have enough for Kyle and Kaia. But that depends on what happens to us." Maggie was surprised as the words left her mouth. Even though their marriage problems had been brewing for a long time, it was the first time either of them had acknowledged it out loud.

"What are you saying, Maggie?"

Maggie sighed. "This isn't a conversation I'm ready to have yet, especially over the phone. Let's just give it a rest for a while. I'm tired of arguing."

"Then come home, Maggie, so we can talk face-to-face," Andrew said. "You've had your fun, and you've bought your toy. It's time for you to turn around and come home. I just want things to get back to normal again."

Maggie sighed. He still didn't get it. She didn't want to go home and "get back to normal." She wanted things between them to change. "I can't come home yet," she said. "I'm not ready. *We're* not ready."

"What's *that* supposed to mean?" Andrew asked, exasperated.

"If I come home now, our life will just go back to the way it was before I left. But I don't want to go back to that life. I want it to change. We need to change, Andrew. Don't you understand that?"

Andrew ran his hand through his hair as he paced the floor of their bedroom. "But we can't even try to change anything if you're not here. I know now that I should spend more time with the family and I plan to do that. I do realize how hard you work around here, and I'm willing to try to help. Just come home so we can work on our relationship and be a family again."

Maggie's heart dropped. While it was nice to hear Andrew say those things, there was still the fact that their marriage was broken. "Oh, Andrew, all that is nice, but it's not enough. We have so much more to fix."

"What more do you want?" Andrew asked, sounding exasperated.

"The fact that you have to ask means you still don't understand. Too much has happened and too much has been left unsaid for things to change between us. I'm tired of just sweeping everything under the rug and ignoring it. But that's what you do, Andrew, instead of facing it. I can't tell you—you have to be the one to figure out what *you* need to do to fix this."

"You know, Maggie? I'm beginning to think you just don't want to come home," Andrew said contemptuously. "You want to flit around and play and forget about your family and your responsibilities. You ended up being just like your mother after all. You walked away and left your family behind, just like she did."

Maggie gasped. Andrew couldn't have hurt her any more if he had stabbed her in the heart. "How dare you compare me to my mother?" she said, her voice low and menacing. "You left us long before I ever drove away. I was the one who raised the kids while you made excuses to be at work late or volunteer all over town. I was the one to drive them to school, care for them when they were sick, take them to activities, and attend all their sporting events, school conferences, field trips, and plays. I was with our children every second of every day, taking care of their needs and yours. I didn't abandon them, you did. Just like you abandoned me." Maggie paused a moment, giving Andrew a chance to digest her words. "I'm driving up to Cassie's place. Don't bother calling me until you're ready to apologize." Without another word, Maggie clicked off her phone.

Andrew knew he'd gone too far the moment the words came out of his mouth: *"You ended up being just like your mother after all."* He couldn't believe he'd said such a thing, let alone with such vehemence. He knew Maggie was a good mother. She was nothing like the woman who had left her family without so much as a good-bye. Yet there it was. He'd said it.

Andrew groaned. Why did he keep saying things to hurt Maggie? Why couldn't they just talk this through? He was such an articulate, organized person. He liked his life running smoothly, the way it used to. He just wanted to get everything back to the way it had been.

*"You have to be the one to figure out what* you *need to do to fix this,"* Maggie had told him. He didn't understand what she meant.

He'd apologized for the affair. He'd stayed in the marriage. What more could he possibly do?

"And now she's going to her cousin's house," he said aloud, shaking his head. Cassie didn't like him, and he knew it. They'd never gotten along, and he knew she really hated him now, ever since the affair. Cassie and Maggie were as close as sisters, so he was certain Maggie had told her about it. Now, her being in Cassie's home wouldn't bode well for him, especially since he wasn't there to defend himself.

Andrew heard Kyle come in downstairs, his heavy work boots pounding on the wooden floor, then on the staircase. Andrew looked at the clock. It was after ten.

"Hey, Dad," Kyle said as he stopped in front of Andrew's door. He smelled of oil and gas. There were stains on his jacket, and his backpack was slung over his shoulder. He lifted the picture of the red Mustang. "What's this? I saw it on the table. Are you thinking of getting a different car?"

Andrew stared at the photo. He'd left it on the table by accident. "That's your mother's new car," he said. "Apparently, the minivan wasn't good enough for her anymore."

"Cool," Kyle said, studying the picture. "I can't wait till she comes home so I can test-drive it."

Kyle's total acceptance of anything his mother did irritated Andrew. Kaia had also said how cool she thought the car was when she'd seen the picture this evening. Why did the kids always judge him harshly but let Maggie have a free pass all the time? With his nerves already frayed from his conversation with Maggie, he lashed out at Kyle. "Why are you home so late? I thought I told you to come home early enough to do your homework."

Kyle glared at his dad. "I did it at Ashley's. Ate dinner there, too. I'm going to bed. Good night."

Before Andrew could reply, Kyle was in his room, his door shut. Andrew backed up and dropped onto the bed, defeated. "When will this mess end?" he asked aloud in the empty bedroom.

# CHAPTER SEVENTEEN

Maggie's phone vibrated only minutes after she'd hung up on Andrew. *He'd better not be calling to yell at me some more.* She picked up the phone. To her surprise, it was Kyle.

"Hi, Kyle," she said, smiling. She knew that Kaia had kept him updated on what was going on, and that's why she hadn't called him. They had a good relationship, but getting Kyle to say more than a few words, let alone a whole phone conversation, was like pulling teeth. Maggie had learned not to prod him. Sooner or later, he'd talk if he felt he had something to say.

"Hi, Mom," Kyle said, his voice deep and sounding so much like his father's. "Where are you tonight?"

"I'm staying at a cute oceanside bed-and-breakfast on the Oregon Coast."

"That sounds fun. Hey, I hear you bought a Mustang. Way cool. How is it to drive?"

Maggie grinned, hearing the enthusiasm in her son's voice. He'd always loved anything with a motor. She remembered when he was just a toddler, making *vroom, vroom* noises with his toy cars long before he could even talk. "It drives like a dream. It has five on the floor and hugs every curve in the road. I'm sure you'd love to drive it."

"Sounds like I get my love of cars from you," Kyle teased.

"That's probably true," Maggie said, laughing. "So how's everything going with you? How's school?"

Kyle's tone grew serious. "Everything's okay, I guess. But school isn't going so well. I just can't get into it this semester."

"Well, maybe it's time we talk about you trying something different after this semester ends. I know you aren't happy at college. Have you thought about going to the tech school?"

Kyle snorted. "Yeah, like Dad would agree to that. He thinks working on bikes and cars is a waste of time."

"Don't worry about your dad. You need to do what makes you happy. Speaking of your dad, how is everything going there?"

"I don't know. Dad's being kind of weird. One minute, he's trying to act like our friend, and the next minute, he's bossing Kaia and me around. It's weird, you not being here."

"Your dad's trying to do his best, I'm sure. He's just not used to being in charge of you kids." Maggie was trying her best to sound positive about Andrew, even though she was mad as hell with him.

"Yeah, I suppose." Kyle grew quiet. After a moment, he continued. "Will you be coming home soon?"

Maggie's heart swelled. She really missed the kids, and it felt good knowing that they missed her, but she just couldn't go home yet. Her last conversation with Andrew proved that he still didn't get it. She didn't want to go back and fall into the same old rut—things had to change. "Probably not for a little while yet, honey. I still need some time to sort things out. I'm going up to your aunt Cassie's for a few days, and then we'll see what happens." Even though Cassie and Maggie were cousins, they had always been as close as sisters and each one's children referred to the other woman as their aunt.

"I'm sorry about everything, Mom. Sometimes I wish . . ."

Maggie interrupted him. "This is not your fault, Kyle. Don't ever think it is. This is between your dad and me. You kids didn't do anything wrong, okay?"

After a pause, Kyle said, "Okay, Mom. I hope everything works out."

"Try getting along with your dad, and I'll be home soon. Okay? I love you, Kyle," Maggie added softly.

"Me, too, Mom. Talk to you later."

Maggie hung up the phone, her heart heavy for her oldest child. He was a kind, warmhearted person, and the complete opposite of Andrew. She hoped the two of them wouldn't clash too much while she was away.

Maggie thought back to last year and sighed. She wished Kyle had never learned what his father had done. She knew it weighed heavily on him. She'd told him she'd take care of it and not to worry, but maybe that had been asking too much. The reason she'd never just packed up and left after finding out about Andrew's affair was because she wanted to protect the children. But maybe that had been the wrong thing to do. Maybe she should have fought harder with Andrew back then to work things out—or end their marriage. She'd been too drained from everything that had happened to deal with it at the time. But now, it was all coming out anyway.

Maggie lay back on the bed, exhausted. She was glad she'd decided to go to Cassie's after all. She would finally have someone she could talk openly with. Maybe there, with family around, she could make a decision on what her next move should be.

After a long day of highway driving and hitting three hours of "rush hour" traffic, Maggie pulled into the driveway of her cousin's Puget Sound home and sighed, relieved to finally be there. Maggie parked in front of the four-stall garage on the brick-paved driveway and sat quietly for a moment, admiring her cousin's beachfront mansion. Cassandra Wiles and she were the same age, and they had both been raised in modest, not-quite-middle-class families, with few luxuries. Now, Cassie, her husband, Matt, and their two children lived in a home of over six thousand square feet with amazing views of the sound because Matt had been in the right business at the right time. Ten years ago, Matt, a computer program designer, and his business partner struck it rich when they designed software that Microsoft wanted. They sold their company to Microsoft for millions. Despite their ridiculous wealth, Cassie and Matt were still the same down-to-earth couple they had been when they were surviving on soup and grilled-cheese sandwiches in the lean years before success. And although Cassie bluntly spoke her mind whether she'd been asked for advice or not, Maggie still loved her as much now as she did when they were children.

Maggie stepped out of her car and walked up to the set of large double doors at the front of the house. She hadn't called Cassie to tell her she was coming, because she wanted to surprise her. She rang the bell and waited, hoping they were home.

When Cassie answered the door, she broke into a broad smile and pulled Maggie into a hug.

"Oh, my God! Maggie! This is such a great surprise. Why didn't you tell me you were coming?" Cassie said everything as if in one sentence, and Maggie laughed as she hugged her cousin tight.

Cassie pulled away and focused intently on Maggie. "Wow, you look amazing. Have you lost weight? I love your hair. You look so . . . happy." Before Maggie could respond, Cassie started looking around as if something was missing. "Where are the kids? I can't wait to give them a big hug. It seems like forever since I've seen them. Are they still in the van?" She ran past Maggie out to the driveway before Maggie could tell her they weren't with her. Cassie stopped short when she saw the red Mustang and no one else in sight. She turned and stared at Maggie, looking confused.

"You have a Mustang? A red Mustang? Where's the van? Where are the kids?"

Maggie walked over to her cousin. "I'm here alone," she said softly.

Cassie's brown eyes searched Maggie's blue ones. Suddenly, it was as if a lightbulb had turned on in her head. "You left Andrew?" Cassie asked. Then she smiled wide and blurted out, "You finally left Andrew. Well, thank the good Lord you've come to your senses. But where are the kids? Why are you alone?"

Maggie shook her head. It was just like Cassie to jump to conclusions and not give her a chance to explain. She stepped up to her cousin and put her arm around her waist, walking her toward the front door. "No, I haven't left Andrew, and the kids are with him. Let's go inside and I'll explain everything."

As Cassie and Maggie entered the home, Maggie once again marveled at its grandeur. The entryway was two stories high, with sunlight pouring in through the tall windows. A shiny tan-and-cream marble floor stretched out beneath their feet and adjoined with the gleaming natural oak floor in the expansive living room, complete with a two-story river-rock fireplace flanked by floor-to-ceiling windows. To the left of the living room was the massive kitchen with an attached family room and another, smaller fireplace. The entire house was surrounded by an outside deck that offered views of the sound, the Olympic Mountains, and Maury and Vashon Islands, depending on which side of the house you were on.

Entering the kitchen, Cassie poured some freshly brewed coffee into heavy mugs. Once they were seated on the stools at the island, Cassie finally looked Maggie in the eye and said, "Dish it, girl."

Maggie stared at her cousin and smiled. They were from the same family and yet were as different as could be. But they still melded perfectly. Cassie was tall and athletic, a natural runner, and always participating in the latest fitness craze, from spin classes to suspension training. She wore her mahogany-brown hair short and stylish, generally used very little makeup, and was a no-nonsense sort of woman when it came to clothes. Yoga pants and running shorts dominated her closet, with a dress or two for special occasions. Maggie, on the other hand, rarely exercised, wore jeans, khakis, and T-shirts, and couldn't imagine cutting her hair short. But she and Cassie had always gotten along well. When Maggie was ten, she and her sister had lived with Cassie's family for almost a year while their father was assigned overseas. Maggie really liked Cassie's mother, Karen, who was her father's sister. Cassie's family had become Maggie's second family during that year. They were as close as sisters, and since losing her father and sister during the past two years, Maggie was even more grateful for having Cassie in her life.

Maggie began explaining to Cassie about her trip, and how she'd just driven away one day after dropping Kaia off at school and hadn't returned. She told her about meeting Wild Bill in Deadwood and their ride up to Mount Rushmore, about her days in Reno with the vivacious Bobbi, and about the conversations she'd had with Andrew throughout her journey. She left out her last conversation with him, when he had accused her of being just like her mother, because it hurt too much to repeat. Cassie already didn't like Andrew, and his remark would make her dislike him even more.

Cassie sat, stunned by all Maggie was telling her. Maggie was the good girl, the one who never made waves. And here she was, running away from home and standing up against Andrew's demands that she return.

"You just drove away and kept on going?" Cassie asked, still trying to comprehend it all. She grinned. "That's so unlike you. I'm so proud of you. You finally stood up to that tyrant of a husband. It's about time."

"Cassie, Andrew isn't a tyrant. He's a good man and a good father. He's just made a few mistakes lately."

Cassie frowned at Maggie. "A few mistakes? Maggie, he cheated on you. And after you caught him, he just wanted you to forget it ever happened and go back to the way things were. That's terrible. He didn't even care how his cheating affected you. If Matt ever cheated on me, I'd throw his ass out the door and never let him in again."

Maggie sighed. "It isn't as easy as that when it actually happens to you," she said sadly. "I thought I'd never stay with a man who cheated, but when you have a family, everything changes. Kyle was in his last year of high school, and I didn't want anything to disrupt it. And Kaia would have been devastated if I'd left Andrew. I just didn't have the energy then to face it. At the time, staying seemed easier."

Cassie sat quietly a moment, taking a sip of her coffee and staring out the window at the calm water. Finally, she said, "You're right. Leaving isn't always easy, especially with a family. But here you are. You did finally walk away. Now what?"

Maggie shrugged. "That's what I'm trying to figure out."

Cassie reached over and hugged her tight, then pulled away and smiled. "Well, let's get you settled in the guest room, and we'll figure it out together, okay? Let's go get your luggage."

The two women went out to the car and pulled out Maggie's suitcase, camera, and laptop.

"Is this all you have?" Cassie asked, surprised.

"I didn't know I was leaving until I was gone. I didn't pack anything. This is what I've picked up along the way."

As they headed back inside and up the stairs to the bedrooms, Maggie asked, "Where are Matt and the kids? It seems too quiet around here."

"They're down on the beach. It's almost dinnertime, though, so I'm sure they'll be back soon."

As Maggie turned toward the bedroom she'd stayed in before, Cassie stopped her. "Sorry, that one's taken. You'll have to stay in the one down the hall this time."

"Taken? What, are you renting out rooms to pay for this monster house?" Maggie joked.

Cassie reached out and pinched Maggie's arm. "No. Matt's old business partner is staying for a few days. You remember Robert. He came up from his place in California to visit and see what Matt's up to."

Maggie stopped and stared at Cassie, her eyes wide. "Robert?"

"Yeah, Robert Barnes. Well, we call him Rob. I'm sure you two have met before."

Maggie shook her head and chuckled. *Rob? Well, at least it isn't another Bob.*

The two women entered Maggie's room. It was as beautiful as the other guest room. There was a queen-size bed nestled in an oak sleigh frame, covered in the fluffiest blue comforter Maggie had ever seen, on one side, with a gas fireplace opposite it. An antique oak dresser stood against another wall. Windows lined the room, one of which was a bay with a window seat. Maggie walked over to it and looked out at the sound and the beach below. The two kids were running around, tossing a ball, and Matt and Rob sat on a large log in front of an unlit fire pit.

"You know, I've never met Rob before," Maggie said. "What's he like?"

Cassie looked up, surprised. "Really? I thought for sure you had. Although you and Andrew didn't come visit much during the years Matt was in business." She set Maggie's suitcase on the bed and started unzipping it. "You'll love him. He's a sweetheart. Very down-to-earth. He rode up here along the coast road on his Harley-Davidson. He's really into his boy toys."

"A Harley, huh?" Maggie said quietly as she continued staring out the window at the beach. She turned when she heard Cassie let out a shriek.

"What the heck are these?" Cassie pulled out a pair of black leather chaps.

Maggie laughed at the shocked look on Cassie's face. "Those are my leathers, of course. It's been an interesting trip."

Cassie dropped the chaps onto the bed and pulled out the matching leather jacket. Looking seriously at Maggie, she said, "You really have to catch me up on what you've been up to."

Still laughing, Maggie walked over to Cassie and took the jacket out of her hands, laying it back in the suitcase. "Let's unpack later. I want to see those kids of yours, and that crazy husband, too."

Linked arm in arm, they headed down the hallway toward the stairs. "I'll order pizza for dinner and call everyone up to the house," Cassie said.

Maggie grinned. "Pizza delivery? What do you think the pizza-delivery guy thinks when he pulls up to a house like this?"

Cassie winked at her. "He probably thinks he's going to get one heck of a tip."

Andrew didn't sleep well after fighting with both Maggie and Kyle. The next morning, he barely said a word to Kaia before dropping her off at school, which only resulted in her becoming moody toward him. At work, he felt like he was behind all day. Then, he had to leave early to pick up Kaia, which left him with a pile of unfinished work on his desk. By the time he returned home that afternoon, he was agitated and short-tempered.

"What are we having for dinner tonight?" Kaia asked as they walked through the door and Bear slid past them to go outside.

"Geez, Kaia. We just got home. How would I know what we're having for dinner yet?" Andrew snapped.

Kaia glared at him. "Didn't you take anything out to cook? You're supposed to take out meat or something before we leave in the morning so it can thaw. That's what Mom does."

"I don't give a shit what your mom does. I'm in charge now," Andrew said. As soon as the words left his mouth, he was sorry, but Kaia didn't give him a chance to apologize.

"You don't give a shit about anything!" she yelled at him, tears filling her eyes. "You don't care that Mom's gone, you don't want to drive me to school, and all you do is argue with Kyle. And look . . ." Kaia pointed out the window at Bear. He had crossed the street and was doing his business in the neighbor's yard. "You let Bear out again without putting him on his leash. A car could have hit him. You just don't care about anything."

"I can't do everything!" Andrew yelled.

"Mom can. And you won't even apologize to her so she'll come home. All you do is fight with her. I heard you last night. You're wrong. Mom isn't like her mother. She didn't leave us forever. She just needed to get away for a while."

Andrew's tone grew quiet. "But she's not here, is she? She did leave us."

Kaia's face turned red. "I hate you. I thought you were changing, but you're not. You're mean to everyone. If anyone is like their mother, it's you." She turned and stormed up the stairs, slamming her bedroom door shut behind her.

Andrew started to follow her up the stairs, and then thought better of it. He looked out the window and saw the neighbor yelling at Bear. With a defeated sigh, Andrew went outside to apologize—yet again—and collect the dog.

Later, after feeding Bear and the cats and giving himself a chance to calm down, Andrew knocked on Kaia's door. "Hey, can I come in?"

"No. Go away," Kaia said in a small voice.

Andrew sighed. He could hear Kaia crying. He felt helpless. "I'm sorry I yelled at you, Kaia. I didn't mean anything I said. I'm just frustrated. Why don't I order a pizza, and we can talk while we eat."

"No. I don't want pizza *again*. I'll get something myself later. Just go away and leave me alone."

Andrew remained in the hallway, with the door between them, trying to decide what to do. What he really wanted was to open the door, walk in, and make Kaia talk to him. But he knew that would only make matters worse. He sighed and went across the hallway to his bedroom. He changed out of his work clothes into jeans and a sweatshirt, then headed downstairs and called to order a pizza. He hoped that the smell would entice Kaia to come downstairs so they could talk.

The pizza came, but Kaia didn't come down. Andrew put it away in the fridge and did a load of laundry.

*"If anyone is like their mother, it's you."* Kaia's words stuck in Andrew's head all evening. His mother had never been close with the kids, and he couldn't blame Kaia for thinking she was mean, but did Kaia really think he was as cold and heartless as his mother? He thought he'd been making progress with Kaia, but now, everything was unraveling.

As Andrew sat in the living room, trying to forget all his problems and concentrate on a television show, his cell phone vibrated in his pocket. He pulled it out, hoping it was Maggie. He knew he should apologize. He hadn't meant what he'd said about her mother.

But it wasn't Maggie, it was Craig Henderson, one of the men he volunteered with on the new airport-planning committee.

"Hi, Craig. What's up?" Andrew asked.

"You tell me, Andrew. Where are you? The meeting started ten minutes ago, and you're still not here."

"Oh, crap." Andrew thumped the palm of his hand on the side of his head. "I'm sorry, Craig. I forgot all about it. I won't be able to come tonight."

"It's not like you to forget about a meeting," Craig said. "Is everything okay at home?"

Craig worked at the bank with Charlie Larson and was also friends with Derrick Weis. Andrew was pretty sure he'd already heard there were problems at home. He wasn't about to discuss them with Craig, though. "Everything's fine," he said tersely. "I've just been really busy. I promise I'll make it to the next meeting."

"You know, Andrew, what we're doing is very important. If I remember right, you asked to be on this committee. If you can't fulfill your obligations, just say so, and we'll ask someone else to join instead."

Andrew took a deep breath. He had to, or else he'd tell snooty Craig Henderson where he could put his committee. He spoke in a controlled voice. "I understand how serious this committee's agenda is, Craig. I do want to be a part of redeveloping our town's airport. But I just can't make it tonight. I promise I'll be at the next meeting."

"Fine. I'll e-mail you the notes and the date of the next meeting. Just make sure you come, okay?"

Andrew hung up after promising again not to miss the next meeting. He wanted to throw his phone across the room but refrained from doing so. His life was a mess. He was missing meetings, fighting with Maggie and the kids, and barely hanging on at work. He didn't know who to be mad at—Maggie or himself. As he sat there, pondering how his life was going to hell, he heard Kyle come in the back door. Andrew stood and walked into the kitchen just as Kyle did.

"Hey. I see you're home a little earlier," Andrew said, noting it was only eight o'clock. "There's fresh pizza in the fridge, if you're hungry."

Kyle stared warily at Andrew. "I already ate with Ashley. I'm going up to my room to finish my homework."

Andrew frowned. Why was he having so much trouble connecting with Kyle? When he reached out and touched Kyle's sleeve to stop him from leaving the room, Kyle pulled away so quickly he dropped his backpack, and books spilled out on the floor.

"Geez, Kyle, what's going on? You won't even give me a minute of your time. Why are you so angry with me?" Andrew asked, exasperated.

Kyle knelt down and shoved his books back into his backpack. He stood and looked his dad straight in the eye. "You wanted me home earlier, so here I am. I did what you asked. Why can't you just leave it at that?"

"What's going on with you?" Andrew asked. "Since your mother left, you've done everything you can to ignore me. What the hell did I do to make you so mad at me?"

"I don't want to talk about this anymore," Kyle said, taking a step back toward the hallway.

"Well, I do," Andrew said. "I'm tired of everything that's going on around here. If you have a beef with me, I want to know what it is. You want to be treated like a grown-up, so act like one. What the hell is going on?"

Kyle dropped his backpack on the floor with a thump and took a step toward his dad. "You're the problem. You ignore everything that's going on here for years, and then all of a sudden, you think you're in charge."

"I didn't have a choice!" Andrew yelled. "Your mom ran off, leaving everything in my lap. I had to take charge."

"Mom didn't just run off. You made her leave. It's your fault she's gone, but you're trying to blame everyone else for it."

Andrew leveled his gaze on Kyle. "You don't know anything about what happened between your mom and me. You have no right to blame me."

Kyle took another step toward his dad and pointed a finger at him. "You don't even know what's going on right in front of you. All you care about is your stupid job and all those committees you're on to help improve this town. Yet you don't even care what goes on in your own family." Kyle stooped, picked up his backpack, and turned toward the stairs.

Andrew grabbed Kyle's arm and turned him back to face him. "That *stupid* job of mine is what pays for everything for this family. I support all of you. Don't forget that. If you knew what it was really like to be responsible for other people, you wouldn't be so quick to condemn me. Maybe you'd even appreciate what you have for a change."

"Like you appreciate what you have? Like you appreciate everything Mom does for you? Or how you appreciate your kids? You're the one who doesn't appreciate anything."

Kyle glared at his dad. For an instant, it looked like he was going to hit Andrew.

Andrew didn't budge, but the anger in Kyle's eyes was so blatant, it sent chills up his spine.

Finally, Kyle turned toward the back porch.

"I'm out of here. I won't bum off of you any longer," Kyle said.

Andrew snorted. "And where the hell do you think you're going to stay? At Ashley's? Are you going to mooch off her parents now?"

"No, I'm going to Nick's. I'll come pack up my stuff when you're not here."

"Fine. Go. Maybe if you have to pay rent and bills, you'll finally see how hard it is to live without handouts from your parents!" Andrew yelled at Kyle's retreating figure. The back door slammed shut, and Andrew heard Kyle's truck roar to a start and squeal out of the neighborhood.

Andrew turned and was surprised to see Kaia standing on the bottom step.

"What have you done?" Kaia asked, her voice just above a whisper.

As Andrew looked at Kaia's distraught face, he wondered the same thing.

# CHAPTER EIGHTEEN

Maggie, Cassie, Matt, and Rob all sat on logs by the burning fire pit as nighttime settled over Puget Sound. Despite the fire, Maggie and Cassie were each wrapped in wool blankets to ward off the autumn-evening chill. The two kids, Jessie and Brandon, were just saying good night to the adults and heading up to their rooms for the night. The kids wanted to stay up longer, but they both had school the next day.

Maggie stood and hugged each kid tightly before they left. "I'm so happy to see you both. I wish Kaia and Kyle were here. They'd love to see you, too."

Jessie hugged her aunt longer than her brother had. "You'll still be here tomorrow after school, won't you, Aunt Maggie?" Jessie was twelve years old and was already the spitting image of her mother, except her brown hair was long and straight. She reminded Maggie of Cassie as a child.

"Of course. I may be here so long, you'll get sick of me," Maggie said, giving the girl a kiss on the cheek.

"Don't forget, you promised me a ride in your new car," Brandon said. He tossed his head for the umpteenth time, flicking his longish brown hair out of his eyes. At fourteen years old, he was tall and gangly, but he was a good-looking boy.

Maggie laughed. "I won't forget."

Once the kids had left, Maggie settled back onto the log and pulled her blanket tightly around her. "I forgot how cold it gets by the water at night. Especially this time of year."

"This is nothing compared to that icebox you live in six months out of the year," Cassie said.

Rob sat on the other side of Maggie, holding his mug of coffee in his hands. Matt had loaned him a heavy coat, since all he had was his leather riding jacket. He smiled at Maggie. "What part of Minnesota do you live in?"

"The northwestern section, about a hundred and fifty miles south of the Canadian border."

"What's the coldest you've seen there?" Rob asked.

Maggie glanced at Rob. She hadn't had much of a chance to talk to him since they'd met earlier over pizza in the kitchen. He seemed like a nice man, though. At first, she was taken aback by how handsome he was. He had wavy, dark hair that was a little long but styled nicely, and a well-groomed beard and mustache. His deep-blue eyes twinkled when he smiled. He was tall, about as tall as Andrew, but huskier, yet definitely not fat. All he needed was a bandana and his riding leathers, and he'd look like he belonged on a Harley. He sort of reminded her of a younger Bob Seger. He had a quick smile and a good sense of humor.

"Thirty below zero isn't unheard of in December or January," she told Rob.

"Ah, but it isn't the cold that gets to you. It's the wind, right?" he said with a grin, and they both laughed.

"Yeah, but thirty below is thirty below, wind or no wind. It's a crazy place to live in the winter, but the summer and fall are beautiful," Maggie said.

"Give me good old Seattle anytime," Cassie said. "I need to live by the ocean."

Maggie nodded. "I miss the ocean, that's for sure. When I drove up the coast road yesterday, I just couldn't get enough of it."

Matt had been sitting across the pit from them but now came over and sat close to Cassie. He refilled his coffee mug from the thermos they had brought down and offered some more to the others. Maggie had always liked Matt. He was easygoing and cute for a computer nerd. He also had longish brown hair like Rob, but Matt's was shaggier. He was clean-shaven, and his brown eyes lit up when he smiled. Cassie and Matt were the perfect pair, with Cassie's intense personality complementing Matt's laid-back one.

"Rob lives near the ocean. He owns an enormous house in the middle of a vineyard in Northern California," Matt said. He placed his arm around Cassie, who snuggled in closer to him.

Maggie turned to Rob. "You own a vineyard?"

Rob laughed. "Yes, I own the land and house, but someone else grows the grapes and makes the wine. We share in the profits."

"You think our house is amazing, but you should see his," Cassie said. "It looks like a Tuscan villa, sitting on top of a hill, overlooking the vineyard. It's beautiful."

"Sounds lovely," Maggie said.

They sat there on the beach until the fire began to fade. Maggie enjoyed Rob's company. He was intelligent but didn't flaunt it, and he'd traveled extensively. She was surprised he was single. Women usually snapped up the good-looking rich men quickly.

They all parted ways at the top of the stairs to go to their own rooms. Cassie gave Maggie a hug good night before following Matt into their bedroom at the end of the hall. Maggie went into her room and couldn't wait to snuggle under the thick comforter. It had been a long day and she was beat. As soon as her head hit the pillows, she fell asleep.

The next day, Maggie rose late in the morning after a restful night's sleep. The long drive yesterday, along with the late night and fresh air, had worn her out. She felt good as she headed downstairs to the kitchen in search of breakfast. Rob was sitting at the island counter, drinking coffee and reading the paper, when Maggie entered.

"Good morning. Did you sleep well?" he asked, his face crinkling into a smile.

"Good morning," Maggie replied. She pulled a mug out of the cupboard and poured herself some coffee. "I slept great. Where are Cassie and Matt?"

"Cassie went for a run and Matt's working in his den on a new video game."

"Oh." Maggie dug in the refrigerator and pulled out a large bowl of cut-up fruit and a hard-boiled egg. "Have you eaten breakfast yet?"

"Yep. You go ahead. I may steal some of that fruit, though," Rob said.

They sat quietly for a few minutes while Maggie ate and sipped her coffee, and Rob continued reading the paper. After he was done reading, he offered it to Maggie, who shook her head.

"I have enough going on in my life right now. I don't need to read bad news, too," she said.

Rob nodded. "Cassie said you and your husband were going through a rough patch. She didn't elaborate, though."

Maggie nodded. She really didn't want to talk about Andrew today. "Looks like a beautiful day outside. I should be out there instead of inside, I guess."

"I was thinking about driving into Seattle and going to Pike Place Market. I haven't been there in a while," Rob said.

"Oh, that sounds like fun."

"Would you like to come? I'm going to pick up some fresh salmon for Matt to grill tonight."

Maggie considered Rob's offer. It would be fun to go, and she could bring her camera along. "Sure. We can take my car, if you'd like."

"Sounds like a plan." Rob stood and rinsed out his coffee mug. "I'll go tell Matt we're leaving, and we can get going."

Maggie ran upstairs and grabbed her camera, car keys, and a sweater, then met Rob in the entryway. She handed him the keys.

"Are you sure you want me to drive?" he asked, surprised.

"If you don't mind. I'm kind of tired of driving."

"I don't know," he said as they walked out to her shiny red car. "It might be a hardship driving this car, but I guess I'll manage." He winked at Maggie and opened her door for her, then ran around to the other side and slipped in behind the wheel.

Maggie smiled at the look of joy on Rob's face. "How does it feel?"

"Fits like a glove," he said. He started it up, and they were off.

With the top down, and the wind whistling between them, they didn't need to fill the quiet with conversation as they sped along the highway into Seattle. Once there, they parked in a crowded lot near the market and made their way to the shops and vendors lining the street.

The day was clear and sunny, perfect for taking pictures. Maggie snapped several photos of colorful buckets of flowers in front of a florist shop, and a few of a young child and his mother buying ice cream from a sidewalk vendor. She managed to snap the photo just as the child stood up on tiptoe, reaching for his freshly scooped cone. It was adorable.

"Do you work as a professional photographer at home?" Rob asked after Maggie had taken dozens of photos.

"No. I've always loved taking pictures, though. I majored in art in college, or at least for the two years I was there. Photography was my first love. After I married Andrew and moved to his hometown, my dreams of becoming a professional photographer slowly slipped away. I've always wanted to own an artists' shop, where I could sell my photos and art by other local artists, too. That's something I'd like to look into when I go home."

Rob nodded. "You certainly seem to have a knack for finding the perfect shots. Maybe you'll get some good ones here at the fish market."

Maggie soon learned that was an understatement. As they entered Pike Place Fish Market, they both had to duck as a huge salmon flew across the aisle. People clapped and cheered as a guy caught it easily. Maggie readied her camera and snapped a picture of the next flying fish in midair, just as it was about to enter the arms of the man catching it. While Rob went up to the counter to buy fresh salmon for dinner, Maggie walked around and took photos of the bustling market. She snapped photos of a child staring into the unseeing eyes of a fish, his own eyes wide, and of the men who worked the counters as they nimbly wrapped up fish for customers. It was a carnival atmosphere, and a wonderful place to immortalize an iconic piece of Americana in photos.

Afterward, Rob offered to buy Maggie an ice-cream cone, and they sat on a bench in the sun, enjoying the cold treat.

"That was amazing," Maggie said as she captured a drip of chocolate ice cream with her tongue. "I took so many great pictures. I can't wait to see them on my computer."

Rob smiled at her. "It is fun, isn't it? You know, before we sold the company, all I did was work. I never enjoyed a nice sunny day. I rarely took my bike out for a coastal ride, and I certainly didn't go to a place like this to buy fish. I ran to the local store, got what I needed, went home, and ate it. I feel very lucky that now I can take my time, enjoy more in life, and work less."

"You and Matt worked very hard to get where you are. It's not like they just handed you free money. But it must be nice, not having to worry anymore about money, and just enjoy life," Maggie said.

"Yeah, but money isn't everything. I had always hoped to find someone to share my life with and have children, like Cassie and Matt. Their life is so full. I just wasn't lucky enough to find the right one."

Maggie studied Rob thoughtfully. He was smart, good-looking, and had a kind disposition. She couldn't imagine why he'd never been able to find someone to settle down with.

"Do I have ice cream on my face?" Rob asked, wiping his mouth and beard with his napkin.

Maggie felt her face heat up. She hadn't realized she'd been staring at him for so long. "No, no. I didn't mean to stare. Has anyone ever told you that you look a lot like the singer Bob Seger?"

Rob broke out in laughter. "Actually, I have had a couple of people say that. Especially since I grew this beard. I take it as a compliment, though. I like his songs."

"Me, too. I was listening to Bob's music when this whole crazy journey began. And ever since I left, I keep running into people with variations of his name. Bob, Bobbi, and now Rob. There's definitely a theme going on here," Maggie said. She told Rob about her encounters with Wild Bill and Bobbi.

"You have had an interesting trip," he agreed.

Cassie was happy to see them when they returned to the house, and especially pleased to see the fresh fish for dinner. While she and Maggie got to work in the kitchen, Rob, Matt, and the kids went into the den to play Matt's latest video game, trying to find errors in it.

Once Maggie finished helping Cassie, she brought her computer down to the kitchen and uploaded the day's photos. The picture of the child reaching for his ice-cream cone was adorable, and the ones in the fish market had turned out beautifully. The colors were vibrant and alive as the slick salmon flew through the air. Maggie was pleased and started adding the best ones to a folder of her favorites from the trip.

"Wow. That's a beautiful shot. Did you take it?" Cassie asked as she came up behind Maggie, wiping her hands on a kitchen towel. They were looking at one of the photos of Lake Tahoe.

"Yes, I did. Isn't it wonderful? The water is so crystal clear by the shore, and then deepens in color as the water becomes deeper." Maggie began clicking through the different pictures for Cassie.

"Who's that?" Cassie asked when a photo of Wild Bill came up on screen. He was standing with his back to Maggie, looking up at Mount Rushmore. Maggie had changed the photo into sepia tone for an old-fashioned look.

"That's Wild Bill. What's more American than a photo of an everyday citizen admiring a national landmark? I think the sepia tone adds impact, don't you?"

Cassie stared in awe at the photos. "I forget just how talented you are," she said. "You really need to start doing this for a living. This is what you love, and you're brilliant at it."

Maggie smiled up at Cassie. "Thanks, sweetie. I've been thinking about that more and more. I spoke to Andrew about opening that artists' shop I've always talked about. He's not too thrilled with the idea, but he said we could talk about it."

Cassie grunted and turned back to the dirty pans in the sink. "You don't need his permission to do what you want. Don't you still have some money left from your dad's house? You could use that to start your business. Forget what Andrew thinks. He only cares about his own ambitions."

Maggie looked over at Cassie. "What is it about Andrew that you dislike so much?"

Cassie stopped washing dishes and turned toward Maggie. "You mean besides the fact that he cheated on you?"

"You've never liked him, even before that happened. Why?"

"He's always been so damn arrogant. Even when you first met him, he just had a way about him that irked me. And his attitude has become worse over the years. I figured that he'd mellow with time, but he's become more self-involved. Plus, he takes you for granted."

Maggie stood and walked over to Cassie. She wasn't angry with her cousin for speaking her mind, but it did make her sad that two people close to her didn't like each other.

"He's not as bad as all that, you know. Andrew comes from a very proud family, and it comes off as arrogance sometimes, but he doesn't mean it to. Most of the time, I think he's torn between being the man he wants to be and living up to his mother's expectations."

"And did his mother's expectations include him cheating on you with some bimbo from his office?" Cassie asked.

Maggie sighed. "No. I don't know what he was thinking when he did that. We never really discussed it. That's the biggest problem between us. We haven't sorted all that out the way we should have right away. We both just ignored our problems. It seemed easier at the time, but now, I realize that was wrong. It's why I left. All those buried emotions finally came to the surface, and I ran away from them."

Cassie stared hard at her. "This isn't your fault, so don't blame yourself. You always make excuses for him. It's time he accepted the blame for his behavior."

"We've been together for a long time, Cassie. We have two children together. What am I supposed to do?"

Cassie reached out and squeezed Maggie's arm. "I just want you to be happy. I want you to have what Matt and I have. Someone who cares about you and wants to make you happy."

"Andrew was that guy, once. We've just gotten off track." Maggie wasn't sure if she believed her words, but she hoped she was right. She'd spent too many years with Andrew to just throw their relationship away. Even after all they'd been through, she had to believe they could find a way to fix their marriage. They had loved each other once, and she wanted to believe that their love was still there, somewhere, buried under all the pain.

Cassie turned back to her dishes. "If you weren't married, I'd try setting you up with Rob. He's a sweetie. You two would be perfect for each other."

Maggie walked over to her computer and sat down again. She couldn't believe what Cassie had just said. She hadn't even thought of Rob that way. As she continued working on her photos, Cassie's words kept tugging at her thoughts.

A while later, Maggie's phone vibrated on the island's counter. She was happy to see it was Kaia.

"Hi, honey. How are you?"

"Mom, you won't believe what Dad has done," Kaia blurted out.

Maggie frowned. She walked into the living room so she could talk to Kaia privately. "What's going on?"

"He had a big argument with Kyle last night, and now Kyle has moved out. He was just here, packing up his clothes and stuff. He told me not to worry about it, that he'd be okay at his friend's apartment. But I'm worried. You should have heard them arguing, Mom. It was so awful. At one point, I thought Kyle was going to punch Dad." Kaia started crying.

Kaia's tears tore at Maggie's heart. She took a deep breath. She was so furious with Andrew right now, but she didn't want to say anything that would upset Kaia further. "I'm so sorry, honey.

Everything will be fine. I'll talk to your dad, and we'll settle this. Did Kyle say which friend's place he was staying at?"

"Nick's apartment," Kaia said, sniffling. "Mom, you have to come home. Dad is just going crazy. He's nice one minute and angry the next. Please come home."

Maggie felt terrible. She wanted more than anything to reach through the phone, hug Kaia, and tell her everything was going to be fine. But she was fifteen hundred miles away, and even if she left this very minute, she wouldn't be home for at least two days. Besides, Andrew was the one who had made this mess, and he was the one who had to fix it—and fix it fast.

"Kaia, I promise you everything will be fine. Let me talk to your dad, and we can sort this out."

"He's not here. He's still at work," Kaia said.

"What? He didn't pick you up from school this afternoon?" Maggie asked, growing angrier by the minute.

"He wasn't in a very good mood this morning, and he asked me to take the bus home. He said he had a lot of work to do and had to stay all day. After last night, I just did what he said."

Maggie bit her lip as she paced the living room. She wanted to scream. Instead, she calmed Kaia down as best she could, then hung up and immediately hit Andrew's name on her phone. When he didn't answer, she clicked her phone off and swore under her breath. She decided to wait until he was home from work before confronting him, because if she knew him at all, they were in for a hell of a fight.

Andrew's day was a nightmare. He couldn't concentrate on work, because he couldn't get the fight he'd had with Kyle off his mind. And then there was Kaia's reaction. When he'd seen the distraught look on her face, he'd realized exactly what he'd done. He'd allowed his emotions to get the best of him and let his son walk out of the house. He should have stopped him, but he didn't.

Why had Kyle been so angry with him when all he wanted to do was spend some time with him? Kyle had insinuated he knew why he and Maggie were having problems, and that infuriated Andrew. If she told the kids what he'd done, that was unforgivable.

Andrew knew that Kaia was also angry with him for telling her to take the bus home so he could get some work done, but he didn't have much choice. His work had suffered ever since Maggie left, and it was driving him crazy. He liked being organized. He liked following a schedule and keeping to it. But his schedule had gone all to hell, and he found himself constantly apologizing to coworkers and clients for not getting projects done on time. As if all that weren't enough, he was upset about missing the airport-planning committee meeting last night, too. He hated to admit that without Maggie, his life was falling apart. He had never realized just how much she did to make things easy for him, and it irritated him to have to acknowledge that.

He saw a call come in from Maggie in the late afternoon, but he didn't answer it. He figured she'd probably found out about Kyle leaving home, and he didn't want to have that argument with her at work. Even though he didn't like the way things happened last night, he didn't think it would kill Kyle to live with one of his buddies for a while and learn what it was like to be responsible for his own bills. Maybe then he'd appreciate getting an education instead of complaining about it. Andrew decided that he'd call Maggie when he got home that night and they could sort things out. Until then, he had work to do.

# CHAPTER NINETEEN

Maggie kept her family problems to herself as they all sat down to dinner and ate the delicious salmon Matt had grilled and the asparagus tips, roasted potatoes, and salad she and Cassie had made. After dinner, the kids headed to their rooms to do their homework. The adults sat in the living room and chatted easily, and at one point, Rob said that he'd be leaving the next day for home.

"I didn't know you were leaving so soon," Maggie said, sorry to hear he was going. She was just getting to know him, and had hoped to spend a little more time with him while she was here.

"I don't want to wear out my welcome," Rob said. "Besides, the weather is supposed to be clear the next couple of days, so I know it will be good for biking along the coast."

"You know we'd never throw you out, Rob," Cassie said, sipping the last of her white wine. "Even if we were sick of you, we'd still let you stay."

Rob chuckled. "That's why I'm leaving. That way, you'll want me to come back soon."

"I'll bet that's a beautiful ride on a motorcycle," Maggie said. "A lot of amazing pictures just waiting to be taken."

"Gee, Maggie, you should ride along with Rob. After all, you already have the leathers," Cassie teased.

Maggie glared at her.

"Leathers?" Matt asked. "What type of leathers do you have, exactly?" He waggled his eyebrows at her suggestively.

"Riding leathers, you idiot," Maggie said, reaching out to hit Matt on the arm. "Keep your mind out of the gutter."

Rob smiled at Maggie. "They must be from your wild ride with Wild Bill," he said, winking.

Maggie rolled her eyes.

"Actually, it's not a bad idea," Rob said. "We could stop along the way so you could take pictures, and you could get some beautiful photos of my vineyard. It might be fun."

Maggie glanced around the table. Cassie was nodding and Matt said it was a good idea, too. "That's nice of you to invite me, but I couldn't impose on you that way. The last thing you want is someone making you pull over every few miles."

"I think it would be fun having you along. You might enjoy yourself," Rob said.

"Yeah, Maggie, you should go. You can always hop a plane when you're ready to come back. You'd have a great time," Cassie said.

Maggie wavered a moment. Riding down the coast road on a motorcycle without a care in the world did sound like fun, but she couldn't brush away her problems that easily. She had to get Andrew to fix what he had done, and she might even have to go home. But for a split second, she wished she could go with Rob.

"It's a nice idea," Maggie finally said. "But I really shouldn't. Thanks for asking, though."

"You can change your mind anytime. I'm serious when I say I'd be happy to have you along."

Maggie nodded, but she knew she couldn't accept. Her life was complicated enough without her traveling down the road with another man, no matter how innocent it was. Isn't that what Andrew had accused her of? Picking up random guys? *At least I'm not sleeping with them*, she thought spitefully.

She thought about how nice it would be to be free of responsibility and travel wherever the wind took her. Ever since she'd left home, she'd felt so much lighter and happier, not having to worry about everyone else's needs. She knew it was selfish to feel that way, but she couldn't help it. She loved her children and had unselfishly given of herself to them all these years. She couldn't even think of a life without them. But every once in a while, it would be nice to have time for herself. She wished she could collect the carefree feelings of the trip in a bottle and open it from time to time after she returned home, to remember how it felt. Maybe her life wouldn't feel as heavy anymore.

Later, after Maggie had gone off to her room to work on her photos, her phone buzzed. She answered it instantly when she saw it was Andrew calling.

"I tried calling you today," Maggie said, dispensing with any pleasantries.

"I know. I'm calling you back," Andrew said. "What's up?"

"What's up? Really? You tell me. What the hell happened between you and Kyle last night?"

"Oh, you've heard about that," Andrew said calmly. "It's no big deal, really. We had a disagreement. He went to stay with some friends. It'll blow over in a few days, and I'm sure Kyle will move home then."

Andrew's flippant tone infuriated Maggie. "Andrew, you listen to me. I don't know what you and Kyle were fighting about, but you need to go get him and bring him home. I don't want him staying at Nick's apartment."

"Oh, get off it, Maggie. You're right. You don't know what happened. And it won't kill Kyle to be away from home for a little while. Weren't you the one who said he's old enough to make his own decisions? Well, he decided he couldn't live under the same roof as me, so he moved out. Thanks to you," Andrew added nastily.

Maggie's blood boiled. She got off the bed and started pacing, trying not to scream and scare everyone in the house. "*Thanks to me?* What on earth do you mean by that?"

"You know damn well what I mean. Kyle insinuated that he knows what happened between you and me last year. How dare you tell the children? That's pretty low. Our problems are between us. Telling them so they'd hate me is . . . unforgivable."

Maggie stopped pacing. "How dare you blame me? I didn't tell Kyle anything. And I never said a word to Kaia, either. I can't believe you'd think I was even capable of doing such a thing. I have never tried to play the kids against you. No matter what you did."

"Then how does he know? And why is he so hateful toward me while he acts like you can do no wrong? I've never given Kyle any reason to hate me. You're the only one who could have done that."

Maggie shook her head. He was so clueless. Did he really think he could run around town with another woman and no one would know? "You really don't get it, do you?" Maggie asked, her voice quiet now. "The night that I confronted you about your affair with that woman, you never even asked me how I knew. Didn't you ever wonder how I found out about her?"

"No," Andrew replied sharply. "I just figured some nosy person like Derrick told you."

"No, Andrew, Derrick didn't tell me. No one in town told me, even though I'm sure everyone knew about it. Everyone, that is, except your wife."

"Then how did you find out?"

"Kyle told me. Our eighteen-year-old son, who was driving around with his friends and saw you and that woman in front of a downtown bar, kissing."

"Oh, my God," Andrew said.

"Imagine how he felt," Maggie continued. "His friends seeing what he saw. His father betraying his mother. He was devastated. He was so upset when he came home that I asked him what was wrong. I could see he didn't want to tell me, to hurt me, but he also knew I needed to know. So he told me what he'd seen. I had to hear about my husband's affair from my son. Can you even begin to imagine how that made me feel?"

"I'm so sorry, Maggie. I had no idea. You never told me," Andrew said, his voice barely a whisper.

"I never told you because I didn't want Kyle to be in the middle of this mess. He felt bad enough. He was afraid that by telling me, our marriage would be over. I told him not to say anything to you, and that I'd take care of it. Why do you think I didn't just pack up and leave you? Why do you think I didn't push the issue? I didn't want Kyle to feel like it was his fault that our marriage was over. *Because it wasn't his fault.* He didn't create this mess, you did. And now you've created yet another mess." Maggie sat back down on the bed, exhausted. She really didn't know how much more she could take.

"I'll fix this, Maggie. I'll go see Kyle and talk to him. I'll try to get him to come home," Andrew said.

"You can't just try, Andrew. You have to bring him home. I don't want him living at Nick's place," Maggie said urgently.

"All I can do is try," Andrew said.

"No, Andrew. You have to do more than try. Kyle can't stay there. Nick throws parties all the time and keeps illegal drugs at his place. Kyle only hangs out with him at work, or to go out to eat, but he never goes over there. He's afraid of getting into trouble for the drugs if he's there. Andrew, you have to bring him home. Now."

"Oh, shit. I didn't know that, either," Andrew said.

"There's a lot you don't know, Andrew, because you haven't been paying attention. You need to smooth things over with Kaia, too. She was really upset about the fight you had with Kyle."

"I'll go talk to her now, and then I'll go get Kyle," Andrew said. "I'll fix this, Maggie. I promise I will."

"You have to, Andrew. Because I can't cover for your mistakes any longer. It's up to you to bring your family back together again. I'm tired of trying to do it all on my own."

After Maggie hung up, she lay down and closed her eyes. She didn't know how she felt about Andrew anymore. Was there any love left between them? Too much anger and too many angry words had passed between them. They had loved each other once—truly loved each other. They'd built a life, and had a family. When the kids were young, everything had been fine. But slowly, their life had unraveled. She'd held on because she'd thought that, eventually, they'd be able to find the love lost between them. And then he'd hit her with the final blow. His affair had made her feel inadequate as a woman and a wife. It hadn't mattered that he'd chosen her over the other woman in the end. He'd broken her trust, and he hadn't yet proved to her that he was truly sorry for it. She was tired of making excuses for him. There were no excuses left.

Maggie no longer knew if their problems could be resolved. She just wanted to be happy. She wanted to feel whole again. And she wasn't sure she could ever feel that way with Andrew again.

Feeling defeated, Maggie went downstairs for a glass of water and was surprised to see Rob sitting in front of the fireplace in the semidark living room.

"Still up?" he asked. He was lounging in the corner of the sofa, his long legs spread out in front of him, looking relaxed and comfortable. Maggie wished she could feel as relaxed as he looked.

"Yeah. Just came down to get some water." She went to the kitchen and poured a glass of water, then headed back into the living room. "Did Cassie and Matt go up to bed?"

"Yep. I'm the only one up, except you."

"I figured you'd be asleep already since you have a long drive tomorrow," Maggie said as she perched on the arm of the sofa.

"Yeah, I probably should get some sleep. It's nice sitting down here, though, in front of the fire in the silent house."

They sat quietly a moment as Maggie stared into the crackling fire. When she looked up, she saw Rob gazing at her. He smiled warmly. She felt her face heat up. She wasn't used to men looking at her that way.

"My offer is still open if you'd like to join me. We'd have a good time. You could wear your leathers," he added, his eyes twinkling.

Maggie laughed. Maybe that's exactly what she needed—to ride along the coast and forget all about Andrew, their problems, and the trouble he'd caused. At least for a few days. *Why not?* Maggie threw caution to the wind.

"I think you've talked me into it. It might be fun. Just two friends on a ride, right?" she asked, hoping she was making the "friends" point clear.

Rob nodded. "Just two friends on a ride."

# CHAPTER TWENTY

Andrew sat on his bed, stunned at what Maggie had just revealed to him. The fact that Kyle had seen him with the other woman horrified him. No wonder his son couldn't stand to be around him. How could he have been so stupid? Had he really believed in a town this size he could carry on with another woman and not be found out? Was he really that arrogant?

Andrew ran his hand through his hair and paced the room. The last few years passed before his eyes. He thought of how he'd traded time with his family to pursue his ambitions. Maggie was right. He'd left them long before she ever drove away. What an idiot he'd been.

Andrew had a lot of work to do to fix his broken family.

He went to Kaia's room and apologized to her for the fight he'd had with Kyle. He assured her he was going to fix everything and bring her brother home. Kaia just stared at him with big, sad eyes. Andrew realized for the first time how much she had been through since Maggie left. The eyebrow piercing winked at him in the light, reminding him of those first few tense days. But things had been gradually getting better, until now. He didn't want to lose the relationship he'd rebuilt with his daughter just because he was a stubborn idiot.

Andrew walked across the room and drew Kaia into a hug. Tears filled his eyes when she hugged him back. He loved his children. How could he have let himself become so distant from them? When he finally left to go get Kyle, he hoped he had mended the gap in the bridge he and Kaia had started building.

Nick lived in an apartment above a coffee shop downtown. Andrew knew this only because he'd seen Nick coming out of the door between the buildings in the morning, when Andrew occasionally stopped there to pick up coffee and muffins for the office staff. He didn't know Nick very well, other than he was a little older than Kyle and worked in the parts department at the motorcycle shop.

The streetlights spilled shadows on the empty street as Andrew pulled up in front of the coffee shop. This was the old section of downtown, where two-story brick buildings, built in the late 1800s and early 1900s, housed family-owned businesses downstairs and musty old apartments upstairs. All the businesses downtown closed by six o'clock in the evening, leaving the streets deserted.

Andrew stood on the dark street a moment, looking up at the light in the upstairs window. He took a deep breath. He wasn't used to apologizing. He always believed he was right. But it was one thing to be proud, another to be stupid. Steeling himself, he rang the buzzer beside the door.

Andrew waited a while before Kyle appeared at the door. He opened it hesitantly and looked at his dad.

"Hi, Kyle. Can we talk?" Andrew asked.

Kyle frowned but turned and headed up the narrow staircase, leading the way. Andrew followed him up to the apartment.

Andrew surveyed his surroundings. There was a ratty brown couch in the center with a scarred wooden coffee table in front of it.

An old, green Naugahyde recliner next to the couch had silver duct tape holding the arms together and cigarette holes burned into the seat. A new flat-screen television was perched on a battered stand across from the couch. On the other side of the room was an old wooden dining table with four rickety chairs. The table and coffee table were littered with old pizza boxes and empty beer and soda cans. The place reeked of moldy food, beer, cigarette smoke, and God knew what else.

Kyle had sat down on the couch and was now staring at his dad. "It's not a palace, I know. But it's somewhere to stay."

Andrew walked over to the couch and tentatively sat down next to Kyle. "Is anyone else here?" he asked, not wanting Kyle's friends to overhear their conversation.

Kyle shook his head.

Andrew took a deep breath in anticipation of what he was about to say, then regretted it when he got a lungful of the horrible stench. "Kyle, I'm sorry I blew up at you. I'd like for you to come home."

Kyle rolled his eyes. "So that's it? All you have to do is apologize, and everything is better?"

Andrew looked down at his hands, not quite sure what to say. When Kyle was younger, he had looked up to him like he was his hero. Andrew remembered when Kyle was ten and gazed at him in awe when he'd taught him how to throw a curveball. But now, Kyle knew differently. He knew his dad was only human and made mistakes. He wished things were still as easy as they'd been back then, but those days were long gone.

"No, son, that isn't it," Andrew said, and looked Kyle directly in the eye. "I'm sorry that you saw me that night with that woman. I had no idea you had seen me. I'm so sorry that you had to be the one to tell your mom."

Kyle glared at Andrew. "Why? Because you got caught?"

Andrew shook his head. "No. I was wrong. I never should have done that to your mother. I embarrassed you in front of your friends. You were caught in the middle and forced to take sides. Worst of all, you shouldn't have had to be the one to tell your mom. I can't even imagine how heartbreaking that was for you to have to do. I was selfish and self-absorbed when I should have been thinking about what I was doing to my family. I'm so, so sorry, Kyle."

Kyle's pinched face softened. "I appreciate that, Dad. But aren't you apologizing to the wrong person? You hurt Mom more than you hurt me."

Andrew ran his hand through his hair in frustration. "I have apologized to her. We're still trying to work things out."

"Did you mean it, though? When you apologized? Or did you just say the words, like you do about so many things?"

Andrew stared at his son, shocked by his question. "Of course I meant it. Why do you say that?"

"Sometimes, you just say what you think the other person wants to hear, but you don't follow through. You don't really mean what you say. I think you've been a salesman for so long, you just say the right thing to manipulate people and get what you want. It's the same with all your committee work. You twist the truth into knots to get your way."

Andrew started to protest, then stopped himself. He thought about his life over the past few years. The way he'd slowly alienated his family with the excuse that he was doing good for the community, convincing himself that it made him a better person. But he barely knew his kids anymore. And he and Maggie had grown so far out of touch that he'd gone looking for comfort elsewhere. Without realizing it, he'd become a combination of his father and his mother, a coldhearted, unfeeling jerk. His kids knew it, and his wife knew it. Heck, the whole town seemed to know it.

"My God, how could I have not seen what I was doing? I'm so sorry, Kyle. I didn't mean to become that way." Andrew dropped his head in his hands, distraught at what he'd finally realized.

Kyle placed his hand on his dad's shoulder. "Dad, you are a good guy. But I want to go back to when you spent time with us and really listened to me and Kaia. We've both missed that."

Andrew raised his head and looked at his son. He was so grown-up. Andrew was suddenly so proud of the man he was becoming. Thanks to Maggie, Kyle was becoming a better man than he was.

"I want that, too," Andrew said softly. "And I'll start by listening to what you really want to do instead of going to college."

Kyle's brown eyes grew serious. "I just don't like college, Dad. I know that you think I need to go, but it just isn't for me. Mom and I talked about me going to the tech college this spring. I really enjoy working with engines, and I'm good at it, too. I think I'd rather pursue that instead."

Andrew took a deep breath. If he'd meant what he'd said about changing, then he had to start now. "Maybe that would be a good idea. You're good with your hands, and you're smart. Working on cars and small engines is getting more complicated these days, with all the computerized parts. I think the tech school might be a better fit for you."

Kyle smiled. "Thanks, Dad. I know you'd rather I go into business or something, but I don't think I'm cut out for that kind of work."

Andrew nodded. He actually felt relieved. He couldn't force Kyle to become someone he wasn't. He didn't know why he'd tried to push him in the wrong direction for the past two years. If working on engines made Kyle happy, so be it.

"So will you come home now? I promise, no more fighting," Andrew said.

Kyle looked around the apartment and grinned. "You mean you want me to leave all of this behind?"

Andrew chuckled. "I know it will be hard, but I'm sure you'll survive. Let's pack up your stuff and get you out of here, okay?"

Kyle stood and looked at his dad seriously. "What about Mom? How are you going to convince her to come home?"

"I don't know yet," Andrew said honestly. "But I'll keep trying. I promise."

Maggie and Rob headed out early Friday morning, just as the sun was burning off the morning fog. Cassie had been surprised, but pleased, to hear that Maggie was going after all, and she helped Maggie pack the few items she'd need for the trip. She couldn't take much, since everything had to fit in one of Rob's saddlebags. She left her leather chaps behind but wore her leather jacket for warmth and protection. She also chose to wear the pair of low-heeled ankle boots she'd bought in Deadwood and a new pair of jeans that fit perfectly. Maggie only packed a few personal items, another pair of jeans, a couple of T-shirts, and a pair of lightweight sneakers. She also squeezed in her camera, an essential for her.

She was in good spirits that morning, no longer worried about Kyle and Kaia. Last night, Andrew had texted her that he'd talked to Kyle and brought him home, and that he'd also smoothed things over with Kaia. She didn't call him back, because she was still upset with him. She just wanted to go on this trip with Rob, enjoy the view, and not think about her problems for a few days.

They headed down I-5 south, and then turned onto Highway 101. After only a couple of hours, they stopped at a small gas station to stretch and walk around. Maggie took photos of the ocean view from the rocky cliffs above. Down below, there was a sandy beach hidden in a cove, and a few people in wet suits were braving the water with surfboards. Maggie took pictures of the surfers on their colorful boards, cruising over the waves.

Soon, they were back on the bike and riding south again. Maggie sat behind Rob, holding him lightly around the waist for balance. The seat was generous in size and comfortable. She wasn't used to the helmet yet, but understood its necessity. She was happy she hadn't tried to style her hair this morning, because it would've just been a flat mess by this evening anyway.

Maggie loved riding on the bike. The freedom of the open road felt exhilarating with the wind brushing over her and the powerful bike beneath her. Her body became one with the bike, almost by instinct. Each curve in the road required her to lean, and soon, she was doing so without giving it any thought. It felt nice holding on to Rob, too. He was firm and strong, giving her a real sense of trust in his ability to keep them safe on the road.

After crossing the border into Oregon, they stopped in the town of Seaside at a roadside café for lunch. Once they were seated in a booth and handed menus, Rob asked, "How are you doing so far? Sometimes it can get uncomfortable, riding a cycle when you're not used to it."

"So far, I'm okay," Maggie said. "I can't promise that will be true tomorrow, though."

Rob chuckled. "We'll stop tonight about halfway to my place so we don't overdo it. I don't know about you, but my back gets sore on the bike after a few hours. It's the price of getting old."

Maggie smiled and nodded as the waitress came back for their order. Once she was gone again, Rob asked, "Does your husband own a cycle?"

Maggie shook her head. "No, you couldn't get Andrew anywhere near a motorcycle. He likes nice cars, but he's not much for toys like motorcycles, boats, or snowmobiles. My son, Kyle, loves anything with an engine. He has a smaller cycle he rides in the summer. It scares the crap out of me, but he seems to be careful."

"Yeah, that's how it starts. One toy, then another, then you have to have bigger and bigger," Rob said, and grinned. "How old is your son?"

"He's nineteen. He goes to college and works part-time at the local cycle shop. He doesn't like college, though. I think he's going to try the tech college next."

Rob nodded. "Sounds like it would be perfect for him. Did I also hear you have a daughter?"

"Yes, I do. She's fourteen, and her name is Kaia. She's very smart, too, like her brother, and athletic, something I never was. She plays tennis on the middle-school tennis team. She used to play volleyball, too, but it got to be too much."

"And I bet she's as pretty as her mother," Rob said softly.

Maggie blushed. She wasn't used to getting compliments. "Oh, she's much prettier. She has gorgeous, thick auburn hair and blue eyes. She takes more after her father's side of the family."

As they ate, they talked about the places they'd lived, books they'd read, and their favorite music. Maggie loved romance novels and mysteries, and old rock 'n' roll from the '70s and '80s. Rob enjoyed horror and mystery novels, especially Stephen King, and the same music as Maggie.

"Nothing better than an old Eagles tune," he said. "And, of course, Bob Seger," he added with a wink.

"Do you know where we'll be stopping tonight?" Maggie asked as they finished eating their lunch.

"Yep. There's a great place a few hours from here, right on the Oregon Coast. I stop there every time I travel up to Seattle. Wait until you see it. You'll be amazed."

Maggie was indeed amazed when they pulled up to the Victorian Bed & Breakfast, which sat on a cliff, overlooking the ocean. The home was beautiful, but in the haze of the evening fog, it looked like a house right out of a creepy movie.

"My goodness, this place looks like something out of a 1940s movie, where the heroine is pushed off the cliff and comes back to haunt the house," Maggie said as she stared up at the old home in the mist.

"That's exactly what it looks like. Or from the cover of one of those old historical romance novels, where a woman in a long, sweeping dress is running away from the house," Rob said, laughing. "In fact, this house was used in several old movies because of its location. Don't worry, though, it's cozy inside, and the owner is a sweetheart."

Rob was right. The interior was warm and cheery, with a crackling fire in the hearth and charming Victorian period furniture. The owner, Mrs. Nebish, was a sweet older lady. She wore a calico skirt and cream-colored cardigan sweater over a frilly blouse. Her silver hair was rolled up in a bun on her head, and she wore small half-moon reading glasses on the end of her nose. She set Maggie and Rob up in two very comfortable rooms, and placed a plate of sandwiches, homemade cookies, and two glasses of milk out for them in the kitchen.

Maggie loved the place. It was like going to your grandmother's house, and she said as much to Rob, who nodded his agreement.

"That's why I love this place. Mrs. Nebish makes it so inviting that I feel like I'm right at home," Rob said.

It was late by the time they finished their food, so they said good night at Maggie's door. "This has been so much fun," Maggie told him. "Thank you for inviting me along. It was just what I needed."

Rob bent over and brushed a friendly kiss on Maggie's cheek. "I'm happy you came, too," he said quietly. "Good night."

Once Maggie was tucked away in her room, sitting on the cushy double bed with the gas fireplace turned on to ward off the evening chill, she thought about Rob's kiss. Had it meant anything, or was he just being friendly? She had to admit it had felt nice. Rob was such a sweet guy, and handsome, too. What would she do if he seriously flirted with her? Would she kiss him? *Stop it. You have enough problems. You don't need another one.*

Her phone buzzed, pulling her out of her thoughts. She looked at it, thinking it would be Andrew. He'd been texting her all day, asking her to call him, but she'd ignored him. The last thing she wanted to do tonight was fight. To her surprise, it was Cassie calling.

"Hi. What's up?"

"Hi. I hope you've stopped for the night," Cassie said.

"Yes. We stopped a couple of hours ago, right before dark."

"Did he take you to that creepy old house where the owner looks like a sweet grandma but is probably Norman Bates's mother?" Cassie asked, chuckling.

"Cassie! That's terrible. Mrs. Nebish is a sweet lady. But you're right. The outside gave me the creeps when we pulled up. I can't wait until tomorrow morning, so I can take pictures of it before we leave."

"So how was your first day on the road with Rob?" Cassie asked. Her tone sounded like that of one of Kaia's teenage friends teasing her about a new boyfriend.

Maggie rolled her eyes. "Fine. We pulled over a few times so I could take pictures, had lunch, and then stopped for the night. And yes, nosy, we each have a room to ourselves. So get your mind out of the gutter."

"He's a sweetie, though. Don't you think? And he's cute, too," Cassie said.

"Cassie, stop it. We're just friends, and you know that," Maggie warned.

"Hey, I can always hope."

Maggie smiled and shook her head. "Did you call for a reason, or just to act like a twelve-year-old?"

Cassie sighed. "I called because I wanted to see how your day went and to tell you that Andrew called here today."

"He did? Why?"

"He said you weren't answering your phone, and he asked if he could talk to you. I hope you don't mind, but I told him you were riding down to a California vineyard with a friend, and you probably couldn't be reached."

"You told him that? Why?"

"Because it's the truth. I didn't tell him who you're with, though. So I wanted to warn you about him knowing where you are in case you talk to him."

"Gee, thanks. You're a big help," Maggie told her.

"You're welcome. Have fun with Rob."

Maggie clicked off her phone before Cassie could tease her anymore.

Maggie thought about calling Andrew, but it was already late and she didn't want to wake him. It would only make him crabbier. She knew she wouldn't have time in the morning to call. Besides, if they argued, he'd ruin her day. So she decided it would be best to call him tomorrow night when they arrived at Rob's house.

As Maggie drifted off to sleep, she thought about her life with Andrew over the past twenty-three years and how much they both had changed. How had they grown so far apart? You marry and look forward to all the possibilities together, then slowly pull away from each other as those dreams become reality. She also thought about the kids, and how soon they'd be gone and starting their own lives. Where would that leave her and Andrew? And then, she thought about the innocent kiss Rob had placed on her cheek. Andrew hadn't made a sweet gesture like that in a long time. She finally fell asleep, no longer thinking of her problems but instead marveling at how such a simple kiss could make her feel so alive.

# CHAPTER TWENTY-ONE

When Andrew awoke on Friday, he felt content for the first time in years. He was especially happy he'd reconciled with Kyle. He knew he had a long road ahead of him, but he was intent on working to rebuild their relationship and, hopefully, make up for his terrible transgression. He and Kaia were once again on good terms, and he was going to work hard to keep it that way. Even though the most difficult part still lay ahead of him—finding a way to win Maggie's forgiveness—he felt he was on the right path.

Throughout the day, Andrew tried, without luck, calling Maggie on her cell phone. He'd left messages and texts, but she still hadn't replied. By midafternoon, he was getting desperate to talk to her, so he swallowed his pride and called Cassie. She and he had never gotten along well, and to be honest, he never really understood why. But he wanted to talk to Maggie, and if he had to go through Cassie, then so be it.

"Maggie's not here," Cassie told Andrew after a cool hello.

"Can you ask her to call me when she returns?" Andrew asked. He figured she was out shopping or maybe on the beach with the kids. He knew how much Maggie loved the ocean and that she'd make sure to enjoy the beach as much as possible while staying there.

"I don't know when she'll be back," Cassie said bluntly. "She left to go down to California wine country with a friend today, and she's staying at his home for a few days. She didn't say when she'd be back."

Andrew was stunned. *His home*, Cassie had said. Who was *he*? Not wanting to get into a sparring match with Cassie, he ignored what she'd told him and asked whether she'd tell Maggie to call him if she heard from her.

When he hung up, Andrew wondered if Maggie had really taken off with another man, or if Cassie was just trying to make him jealous. Cassie could be a pain, but she had never purposely tried to start an argument between him and Maggie. Nevertheless, he spent the rest of the day at work worrying about who Maggie was with.

Andrew didn't have time to think about Cassie's words after picking up Kaia and heading off with her to buy groceries. This time, he heeded Kaia's advice, and they stopped at Walmart to buy most of what they needed, and then went to the local grocery store for a few items. The teenage boy who bagged their groceries talked to Kaia like he knew her, and Andrew noticed her smiling and blushing in response to his attention. After the bags had been stowed and they were in the car, Andrew asked, "Do you know that kid?"

Kaia's smile faded and she slid her gaze toward her dad. "His sister is in my class. He's a junior in high school. Why?"

Andrew saw her defenses going up immediately. "I was just asking," he said nonchalantly, then he started the car and they drove home. During the drive, however, he wondered about the way Kaia acted around the boy. She was fourteen, just a child as far as he was concerned. But it seemed like she had a crush on that older boy. For the first time, he noticed that his little girl was actually growing into a young woman, and that terrified him.

"Can I ask you a question without you getting mad at me?" Andrew asked.

Kaia continued staring out the window. "Okay."

"Do you have a boyfriend?"

Kaia's eyes grew wide, and she turned to stare at her dad. "Daaaad!"

"Don't get mad at me. I was just asking. I thought maybe you liked that boy."

Kaia crossed her arms dramatically and sighed, looking straight ahead of her. "We're just friends."

"Do you like him, though?" Andrew asked.

"Dad, stop asking me that."

"Why?" Andrew asked. "I mean, if you like him, why wouldn't you tell me?"

Kaia stared at her dad. "Because you're my dad. And because you still think I'm a little kid."

"Do you talk to your mom about stuff like this?" Andrew asked, feeling offended that Kaia didn't trust him enough to talk about boys with him.

Kaia shrugged. "Sometimes. But that's different. Mom doesn't treat me like I'm eight. She knows I'm growing up, and she's okay with it. You're different. You haven't noticed I'm growing up."

Kaia's words surprised Andrew. "I know you're growing up. I just didn't expect it to happen so fast." He paused before saying, "Can I ask you another question?"

"Not about boys, I hope."

Andrew chuckled. "No. Not about boys. Kyle said it bothered him that I was never around and didn't know what went on with the family. Do you feel the same way? Do you feel like I'm not around enough?"

Kaia looked down at her hands. "Yeah, sort of," she said. She turned and peered at her dad. "You used to be around and do stuff with us, but these past few years, you're never home. We just got used to doing everything with Mom instead."

Andrew pulled into the driveway and stopped the car. He reached over and placed his hand on Kaia's shoulder. "I'm sorry," he told her, looking into her eyes. "I never meant for that to happen. I guess I told myself that you and Kyle were getting older and didn't need me around as much, and you always had your mother. But that was wrong. I promise I'll try to be around more, okay?"

Kaia smiled shyly. "Okay. I'd like that."

Andrew smiled warmly. It felt good to have everything out in the open. "And you know, you can come to me if you ever want to talk about boys," he said seriously.

Kaia rolled her eyes, making Andrew laugh.

Andrew and Kaia quickly unloaded the groceries and put them away. They planned to meet Kyle and Ashley for burgers. Just as they were finishing up, the front doorbell rang.

Andrew went to the door, wondering who it could be. Everyone they knew used the back door. When he opened it, he was surprised to see a girl standing there, wearing a bike helmet and smiling up at him. "Can I help you?" he asked, recognizing her round face but not remembering from where.

"Is Maggie home?" the girl asked.

"No, I'm sorry. She's not home," Andrew said. He suddenly realized who she was. He had met her last week at the grocery store when she bagged and loaded their groceries. He looked past her and saw a three-wheeled bike with a basket attached sitting on the main sidewalk.

"Cindi?" Kaia had come up behind her dad. "What are you doing all the way out here?" Their home was eight miles from downtown, which meant Cindi had ridden a long way.

"I was hoping Maggie had come home. I miss her. When is she coming home?" Cindi asked.

Kaia invited Cindi to come in. Cindi walked calmly past a stunned Andrew, who stood beside the open door, staring out at her bike.

"Did you ride your bike all the way from town?" he asked, as Cindi and Kaia walked into the kitchen and sat down at the table.

"Sure," Cindi answered. She took off her helmet. "I ride my bike everywhere."

Andrew closed the door and followed the girls into the kitchen. Kaia was already placing a few chocolate-chip cookies she'd made earlier in the week onto a plate and pouring a glass of milk for their guest. Cindi's face lit up when Kaia placed the cookies and milk in front of her.

"Is Maggie coming home soon?" Cindi asked between bites.

Andrew sat at the table with the girls. Cindi stared at him with that sweet smile, waiting for an answer. "We're not really sure when she'll be home," he said. "Hopefully, soon."

Cindi's smile turned into a frown. "I really miss Maggie. I like it when she takes me places. The new lady who's been driving me around is okay, but Maggie's more fun."

Andrew felt bad that he couldn't give Cindi a definite answer. "I'm sorry. I'm sure Maggie misses you, too," he said.

"Dad. We should drive Cindi home. It's getting late, and they'll be wondering where she is."

"Should I call someone?" he asked Kaia. He knew nothing about the rules for the group home's residents and didn't know if Cindi was even allowed to ride her bike this far from town.

"No. We should just take her home," Kaia said.

After Cindi had eaten her fill of cookies and drunk all her milk, the trio went out to Andrew's car. Andrew rolled Cindi's bike to the car but realized there was no way it would fit in the trunk.

"We'll have Kyle bring your bike home tonight," he told Cindi. "It's too big for my car."

Cindi nodded and didn't seem too worried about it. She obviously trusted Maggie's family to take care of her prized possession. Andrew rolled it into the garage and closed the door.

Cindi and Kaia sat in the backseat and talked all the way back to the group home. Andrew could tell that Cindi was much older than Kaia, probably in her late twenties, but she liked many of the same things as Kaia did—movies, television shows, and music. As he listened to the two of them chatting easily, he was once again proud of how kind and patient Kaia was with Cindi. Kaia had a good heart, and he knew she'd gotten it from Maggie.

Andrew wasn't exactly sure where Cindi's home was, so Kaia gave him directions, and soon they pulled up to the older two-story home. There was a nicely kept lawn and garden in front, and the house had been freshly painted. The trees in the yard boasted leaves of gold, orange, and red, and the house looked cheerful and welcoming.

Andrew and Kaia followed Cindi to the screened-in front porch, through the door, and into the house. As soon as they entered, a tall woman with short brown hair, wearing jeans and a blue T-shirt, appeared in the living room where they stood.

"Hi, Cindi. Where have you been?" the woman asked, smiling over at Andrew and Kaia.

"I rode my bike over to Maggie's house, but she wasn't there," Cindi answered.

The woman walked over to Kaia and gave her a hug. "Hi, Kaia," she said. "I haven't seen you for a while. Is this your dad?" She turned to Andrew as Kaia nodded.

"I'm Andrew," he said.

"I'm Jan." She shook hands with Andrew. "It's nice to finally meet you. I live here with the residents full-time."

"Oh, so you're Maggie's boss," Andrew said, finally understanding who the woman was. "You have a nice home here."

Jan laughed. "Actually, the state owns the home. I just run it for them. But thank you. We like it."

Cindi grabbed Kaia's hand and led her to the staircase. "Come with me to my room," she said. "I'll show you my CD collection." Kaia followed Cindi upstairs, leaving Andrew in the living room.

"I hope Cindi wasn't any trouble," Jan said. "She really misses Maggie. I didn't think she'd ride out to your house, though."

"No, she wasn't any trouble. Her bike is still at our house. I'll have Kyle bring it back here in his truck tonight," Andrew said.

"Kyle is such a nice young man. And Kaia is a sweetheart. You're so lucky to have two wonderful children like them," Jan said.

Andrew nodded but didn't know how to reply. Obviously, this woman knew his kids well, yet he'd never met her. Just then, an older woman came into the room and stood beside Jan. She was short and round and had short gray hair.

"This is Marie," Jan said. "Marie, this is Maggie's husband, Andrew."

Marie peered through her square, thick eyeglasses at Andrew, and then smiled. "We like Maggie a lot," she said. "When is she coming back?"

Before Andrew could answer, another resident walked into the room. "Are you talking about Maggie? Is she here?" he asked. His arms and legs were twisted, but he was still able to walk with the use of forearm crutches. He cocked his head and stared at Andrew. "Who are you?" he asked.

"Joseph, this is Maggie's husband, Andrew," Jan said. Joseph made his way to the sofa near where Andrew was standing and lowered himself down onto it.

"Oh, I was hoping Maggie was back," Joseph said sadly.

Andrew looked around at the people Maggie worked with. Even though he'd known she worked with people with disabilities, he'd never put a face or name to any of them. His admiration for Maggie grew as he stood there. Not only because she worked here but also because everyone seemed to like her so much.

"Maggie is really missed around here, I see," Andrew said to Jan as she led him into the cheery kitchen and offered him a mug of coffee.

"Yes, she is. Maggie's really good with the residents, and they respond well to her. She takes an active interest in every one of them. And she's been working here for almost five years, so they've all become quite attached."

"How many residents live here?" Andrew asked as he looked around the kitchen. There was a small table by a sunny window, colorful mugs hanging from hooks under the cabinets, and a glass jar filled with cookies on the shiny white counter. The place looked like any family might live there, and from what Andrew could tell, the group of people who did were a family in their own right.

"We have six total," Jan said. "Two of the residents are at their jobs, and one is visiting her mother for the day."

Andrew looked surprised. "Her mother lives around here?"

Jan nodded. "Yes. Her mother is older and could no longer care for her on her own. Plus, living in a place like this helps the residents gain independence. Most earn their own money and enjoy full lives, just like you and I do. The only difference is they may need a little supervision, so that's why they live here. We also help them keep track of any medications they take and doctor visits. Otherwise, they're all very self-sufficient."

Andrew was impressed. There was so much more to Maggie's job than he'd given her credit for.

After saying good-bye to Jan, Cindi, and the other residents, Andrew and Kaia drove to the burger place and met up with Kyle and Ashley. As they ate, the kids talked about school, new movies that had just come out, and their plans for the weekend. The mood was light and easy, and Andrew was happy to see Kyle smiling and at ease. Best of all, he enjoyed feeling like he was a part of his kids' lives again. After all they'd been through the past couple of weeks, he was finally back on the right track, and it felt good.

That night, before going to bed, Andrew tried one more time to call Maggie, but she didn't answer. He left a message, asking her to call him on Saturday, and then turned out the light. As he lay there in the darkened room, he wondered where Maggie was, and who she was with. He realized that Maggie may have done that very same thing, months ago, in this very bed, wondering about him. He hoped he'd get a chance to make it up to her.

# CHAPTER TWENTY-TWO

Maggie and Rob took off on his bike the next morning, after Maggie had taken a few photos of the Victorian home and the rolling surf below the cliff on which the house sat. The home looked regal and inviting in the daylight, which made Maggie feel silly for thinking how spooky it had looked the night before. Soon, they were huddled on the bike, riding the curvy scenic highway and enjoying the beautiful ocean views.

Today, they didn't make as many stops so they could get to their destination before nightfall. They stopped for lunch around one o'clock at a cute little roadside café and ate greasy burgers and fries. Rob promised the food at his home would be healthier than what they'd been eating.

"I have a lovely housekeeper who preps dinner for me every night before leaving for the day. I usually grill something and eat a salad or pasta. If I ate like this all the time, I'd weigh a ton," Rob said as they sat in the red-vinyl booth and let their lunch settle.

"Wow, a housekeeper, huh? Must be nice," Maggie teased.

Rob shrugged. "I'm not very good at that stuff. Emma, she's a gem. She makes sure everything runs smoothly so I can just have fun."

Maggie shook her head and grinned. "Spoiled."

At Mendocino, they turned off the coast road onto Highway 128 toward Navarro. Rob's home was tucked away in the Anderson Valley, part of Mendocino Wine Country. As they rode through hills and valleys, Maggie admired the miles of perfect rows of vineyards. Giant pine trees lined properties, and homes sat high on hills, overlooking the acres of luscious grapes. Maggie marveled at the fall colors of the plants. Rows and rows of red, yellow, and orange leaves created a breathtaking scene for the eye to behold.

Rob eventually turned into a driveway that led them slowly up a steady incline toward a Tuscan home. When Rob pulled up in front of it and stopped, Maggie felt like she was staring at a palace.

Maggie slid off the bike and removed her helmet, shaking out her hair. She stared at the beautiful stucco home that boasted a large veranda, arched doorways, and a tiled roof. It was painted a soft mustard color and trimmed in reddish-brown. If Maggie hadn't known better, she'd have thought they were in Italy.

"This is your home?" she asked Rob, her eyes wide.

Rob grinned. "Yes. This is it. Do you like it?"

"It's beautiful," she said. She turned and looked all around. In the driveway was a lovely stone fountain. Well-tended rose bushes, red and pink geraniums, and an array of other colorful flowers grew around the base of the home as ivy trailed up the walls. The arched front entry was framed in red brick, matching other brick accents around the exterior. Across the driveway from the home was a five-car garage, built to match the house. Maggie wondered just how many cars Rob owned that he needed such a large garage.

"Let's go inside," Rob offered. He'd taken the saddlebags off the motorcycle, and Maggie followed him around the side of the house and under the upstairs veranda to a large pair of glass doors. Above them, the upstairs veranda spread out over the entire side of the home, with a black wrought-iron railing flanking the edge. He unlocked the doors, and they entered the combination kitchen–family room area.

Maggie marveled at the beauty of the interior. The tile floor gleamed, and large, thick rugs lay beneath the leather sofas and the long oak dining-room table. The kitchen was a mixture of brick, oak, and copper, with creamy marble countertops softening the masculine look of the room. A tall, open red-brick fireplace separated the family room from the large living room, so the fire could be enjoyed from both sides. The place was magnificent, yet very cozy, and suited its owner to perfection.

Maggie followed Rob through the living room into the foyer and up the stairs, which were made of gleaming mahogany and covered with a cream-colored runner. Black wrought-iron railing flanked the stairs and curled up to the second floor. They turned right at the top and followed a hallway that overlooked the main living room below. At last, Rob turned right again and opened a door for Maggie.

"Here we go. I hope you'll be comfortable in here," Rob said as he entered the room and set one of the saddlebags on the bed.

Maggie laughed with pure joy. She'd never seen such an elegant yet welcoming bedroom in her entire life.

"What's so funny?" Rob asked, frowning. "Don't you like it?"

Maggie smiled wide as she spun and took in the beauty of the room. The brick fireplace, oversize four-poster bed, thick coverlet in gold and brown tones, cushy rugs, and gorgeous dark-red tile floors were incredible. A large arched window stretched across one entire wall, dressed up in creamy-white sheers, muting but not blocking the setting sun.

"Of course I like it," she said, smiling up at Rob. "A person would be crazy not to like this room. I'm laughing because I can't believe how incredible your house is."

Rob grinned. "It is pretty amazing, isn't it? I never set out to own a Tuscan mansion on a hill, but here I am. I've been blessed."

Maggie walked to the window and pulled aside the sheer curtain for a better view. Looking out over the valley from this hilltop home made her feel like she was standing on the top of the world. She looked to her left and saw, far below, down by the highway, an adorable smaller version of Rob's home. "Who lives down there?"

Rob walked up behind Maggie and looked in the direction she was pointing. "That's not a house. That's where my neighbors have wine-tasting events for tourists. As a matter of fact, they're having a group here tomorrow night, and we're invited. It's kind of an end-of-season harvest festival. There will be music, food, and, of course, wine."

Maggie was suddenly conscious of how close Rob was behind her. She felt the warmth of his breath on her neck and smelled the scent of the outdoors on him from their long ride. She turned and smiled up at him, trying to act casual about his closeness. "That sounds fun" was all she could manage to say.

Rob stood there, gazing down at Maggie. His brown eyes were a rich mahogany. Maggie took a breath as she stared up at him. Goose bumps tickled her skin. Finally, he smiled warmly and turned toward the bedroom door.

"I'll check to see what Emma left us for dinner tonight," Rob said, his voice husky. "I called her earlier and told her I had a guest, so I'm sure she made us something delicious."

Maggie watched as Rob walked across the hallway and dropped the other saddlebag in front of a closed door, then turned and headed back down the hallway. She stared at the door across the hallway for a long time, trying to calm her pounding heart. *We're just friends*, she told herself. She didn't understand exactly why his standing so close to her had unnerved her, but it had. *It's been a long day. That's all it is.* She would feel better once she cleaned off the dust from the ride and changed clothes. Then everything would feel normal again.

Later, after a delicious grilled steak and freshly tossed salad, Maggie and Rob sat in front of the fireplace in soft leather chairs as the logs snapped and crackled. Outside, the night air had chilled and fog rolled in from the coast, nestling into the crooks and crannies of the valley. Inside, the fire fought against the cold and won, filling the room with a warm glow.

Maggie was relaxed and happy, sitting in her cushy chair, enjoying Rob's company and the coziness of the family room. She hadn't felt this content in a long time. Rob had served a delightful red wine with dinner, and although Maggie had been careful not to overindulge, it had lifted her spirits and softened any tension she'd felt earlier.

"Tomorrow, I can take you on a tour of the vineyards and introduce you to my neighbors, the DeLucas," Rob offered. "Gino and Adrianna are third-generation vintners. Their family came over from Italy in the early 1900s and have owned the winery and vineyards here ever since."

"That sounds nice, to be a part of something like that for generations. You don't hear of family businesses being passed down much anymore. It's heartwarming to think they've been here for so long," Maggie said as she gazed into the fire. "Is that their wine-tasting building that I pointed out earlier?"

Rob nodded. "They're the people who invited us there tomorrow night. Would you like to go?"

"It sounds lovely," Maggie said, smiling over at Rob. "All I brought were jeans, though. Will I have to dress up?"

Rob waved a hand through the air to brush away Maggie's concern. "Don't worry. I'll take care of it."

Maggie wasn't sure what he meant by that, but didn't care. She was enjoying the moment, and that was all that mattered.

Later, they headed upstairs to their rooms. Rob stopped at the door to Maggie's room to say good night.

"I'm happy you came," Rob said, standing close to Maggie. "This is the most fun I've had in a very long time."

Maggie smiled up at Rob. It was hard not to be affected by his nearness. He was so easy to be around that Maggie felt as if she'd known him for years instead of days. "I'm glad I came, too," she said.

Rob leaned down. He was so close she could feel his breath on her cheek. "Good night, Maggie."

Maggie stared up into Rob's eyes and held her breath. She thought, for one moment, he was going to kiss her. And, as bad as it sounded, a little part of her wished he would. But then she thought of Andrew and the kids, and she backed up toward the door. "Good night, Rob," she said, then made a swift retreat into her bedroom.

Maggie changed for bed, then pulled back the cozy comforter and crawled between the soft sheets. The light on the nightstand gave the room a warm, golden glow. She lay back against the plump pillows and thought about her day with Rob. It had been like a dream, riding along the coast road, then through the golden valley as the sun sunk slowly in the west. Coming to this beautiful hilltop home, and then relaxing by the fire, so comfortable and content. Maggie had felt carefree and unencumbered, as if she had no responsibilities or ties to hold her back. Today, she was the best version of herself, someone she'd almost forgotten she could be.

"But I do have ties and responsibilities," she said aloud to the empty room. "And children who I love, and a husband."

Maggie thought about Andrew and everything they'd been through the past couple of years. Their troubles hadn't started the day she'd found out he'd been cheating. They had started long before that, but Maggie hadn't let herself acknowledge them until that fateful day. Married couples disagreed, even argued at times.

Couples married as long as she and Andrew had been often fought about money, bills, and what was expected of each other. But their problems had grown deeper. Over the years, she'd lost respect for him and his dreams and goals, just as he'd lost respect for hers. They'd started drifting apart. She was left to care for the home and kids almost all alone while he pursued his own work and ambitions. Eventually, she'd become lost in being a mother, a wife, and an employee, and no longer looked forward to fulfilling her own dreams. And she had also lost the best part of herself in all of it.

Maggie lay in bed thinking about what had become of her life long after she'd turned the light out. She had always been the good mother and wife, the good daughter and sister, the good employee and volunteer. She'd always done what was expected of her, even when she was tired of maintaining the image that she had created for herself. Now, she no longer knew what she believed or cared about. Did she still love Andrew? Did she want to try to work things out with him? She didn't know. What she knew for certain was how Rob had made her feel when she thought he might kiss her. And it had felt good.

Maggie arose early in the morning, and showered and dressed for the day. She was about to head downstairs when her cell phone buzzed on the nightstand. Andrew. Sighing, she answered it. "Hello."

"Hi," Andrew said quietly. "I've been trying to call you, but you haven't answered. I talked to Cassie, and she said you went away for a few days. With some guy. Is that true?"

Maggie's defenses rose. "I didn't go away with 'some guy,' as you put it. I rode down the coast with Matt's former business partner, Robert. He has a nice place down here in the wine country, and he invited me along for the scenery and to take some pictures."

Andrew didn't reply right away, and Maggie could imagine him struggling to digest what she'd said.

"Oh, well, are you having a nice time?" Andrew finally asked, his voice calm.

"Yes, I am. It's beautiful here. The valley is ablaze with fall colors. Rob's home is practically a palace, and I can see for miles from my upstairs window. It's amazing."

"That's nice, I guess," Andrew said.

Maggie couldn't tell by Andrew's tone if he was fine or upset. "How are the kids? I got your text that Kyle was home."

"The kids are fine," Andrew said, sounding happy. "Kyle and I talked about him going to the tech college next semester, and we all had dinner together last night, including Ashley. She's a nice girl."

"That's wonderful," Maggie said, stunned but pleased. "I'm so happy that you and Kyle are talking about him changing schools. He thought you wouldn't want him to."

Andrew's voice softened. "I've realized it isn't really about what I want. It's what Kyle wants that counts. I don't know why I've been fighting with him about it all this time. It's time I stop thinking I know what's good for him and let him decide."

Maggie could hardly believe what Andrew had just said. Maybe he was changing after all.

"Someone came to the house yesterday, looking for you," Andrew said.

"Really? Who?"

"Cindi, your friend from the group home. She rode her bike all the way out here to see if you had come home yet."

Maggie's mouth dropped open. "She rode all the way to our house? Oh, my goodness. I can't believe it."

"She misses you," Andrew said. "She was disappointed to hear that you were still away. Kaia and I drove her home so she wouldn't ride her bike all the way back to town."

"Oh, that was nice of you. Cindi's a sweetie."

"I had a chance to meet some of the people you work with there. I guess it never really occurred to me exactly what you did at work," Andrew said.

Maggie frowned. "Why? What did you think I did?"

"I'm ashamed to say I never actually thought about what you did at work," Andrew said. "I didn't realize how attached everyone there is to you, or how important you are to them." Silence filled the miles between them. Andrew continued. "What I guess I'm trying to say is I didn't realize how important you are to so many people who count on you. You have a complete life I didn't know anything about, and I never took the time to ask you about it."

"I just assumed you didn't care," Maggie said honestly. "That it wasn't important to you."

"I'm sorry, Maggie. I didn't realize how much you really did, how important you are to every aspect of our family's life as well as the lives of so many others. Work, school, and home. You do so much more than I gave you credit for."

"What exactly are you trying to say, Andrew?"

"I'm sorry I took you for granted all these years. I'm sorry I only thought of myself and what I wanted, and didn't give any thought to whether you were happy or not. You were so involved with the kids and their lives, I blamed you for pulling away from me, but the truth is, I was the one pulling away. Instead of helping you, I just thought about how you weren't giving me the time *I* deserved. I made it about me, not about you or the kids. I made excuses to justify doing as I pleased, because you were too busy to pay attention to me. But now I know you were here all along. I was the one who checked out. I'm sorry."

Maggie was stunned. What would she give for him to have said that a year ago? But now, was it too little, too late? The fact was, there was more to be said, much more. One apology just couldn't wipe away all that had happened between them these past few years.

"Maggie? Are you still there?" Andrew asked.

"Thank you for what you said," Maggie said softly. "I do appreciate it. But there's so much more wrong between us. I don't know if we can fix it with just an apology."

Andrew sighed. "What more do you want me to say, Maggie? I've apologized for taking you for granted. I've apologized over and over for the affair. I've meant every word of it. What more can I possibly do?"

Maggie's heart felt heavy, and tears filled her eyes. "You'll never understand, will you, Andrew? Yes, you've apologized, and you ended your affair with that woman. You promised it wouldn't happen again. But that was it. How could you think everything would go back to normal between us again with a simple apology? You broke my trust, Andrew. You broke our vows, and you broke my heart. How can all that be fixed with just words?"

"Maggie, I don't understand what more I can do. I chose you. I chose our family. I stayed with you," Andrew said, exasperated.

"Yes, you chose to stay with your family. You chose to stay with me. But that was it. You stayed, and so did your resentment and your anger at having been caught and having to give up something you weren't ready to give up. You brought all that into our home, and things haven't been the same since."

"I never loved her, Maggie," Andrew said honestly. "I promise you, that's the truth. It was a stupid fling. Nothing more. I came back to you willingly. You have to let it go."

"But you never tried to win me back, did you, Andrew? You thought an apology was all you needed to find your way back into my heart. The affair hurt. It hurt me deeply. But do you know what hurt more? The fact that even after you'd made your choice, you didn't do anything to fix us. You didn't want me enough, or love me enough, to fight for me. If you'd really loved me, you'd have tried harder to bring me back to you. Your anger, resentment, and indifference are what hurt me the most."

"I'm sorry, Maggie. I truly am. At the time, I didn't realize I was doing any of that. I want us to start over and put this all behind us. I want us to feel like a family again. Please, Maggie. Give me one more chance. We were so good together once. We can be again."

Maggie wiped away the tears that streaked her face. She wanted so much to believe Andrew. He was her first love and the father of her children. She wanted to believe they could start again. But they'd been through so much, she was afraid it was too late.

"I'm not sure anymore that we can fix this," she said honestly. "Give me a little more time. I'll call you later. Good-bye, Andrew."

# CHAPTER TWENTY-THREE

Maggie composed herself, then walked downstairs and met up with Rob in the kitchen, with camera in hand. It was after ten o'clock by then, and she hoped she hadn't ruined his plans for the day by coming down so late.

"There you are," Rob said with a huge smile. He was freshly showered and dressed casually in a polo shirt and jeans. Maggie walked over to him and accepted a mug of coffee. Standing so close to him, she could smell the spicy scent of his aftershave.

"Sorry I'm late," Maggie said after sipping her coffee. "I had a call from home, and it took a little while."

"Everything's fine there, I hope," Rob said.

Maggie nodded. "Everything is fine, at least with the kids. Andrew . . . well, he's another story."

Rob cocked his head to one side and stared at Maggie. "Do you want to talk about it? I'm a good listener."

"Thanks, but no. I'll leave it for another time. Right now, it looks like a beautiful day outside, and I'd rather go enjoy that instead."

They sat at the table out on the veranda and enjoyed their coffee and the light, flaky croissants that Emma had made earlier that morning before Maggie was even awake. She couldn't help but let out a long sigh of contentment when she bit into the delectable treat smothered with butter.

"These are incredible," Maggie said as she buttered a second croissant. She looked up and saw Rob grinning at her, his eyes sparkling. "What?"

"It's nice to see a woman actually enjoy food," he said. "Most women I've known won't touch bread or butter, or anything that's the slightest bit fattening. You manage to not only enjoy it but continue to stay looking gorgeous."

"Don't be silly. I look like someone who eats bread and butter. But I don't care. I'm not going to insult Emma by not eating her croissants." Maggie looked around. "By the way, where is she? I didn't see her when I came down."

"She's already gone. She came early this morning, and then headed out. She's taking care of a little errand for me."

After breakfast, Rob led Maggie out to the garage. He entered a code and the garage door opened to reveal his motorcycle and a big ATV.

"I thought I'd drive you around the property today on the four-wheeler," Rob said. "There's too much land to cover on foot."

"That sounds like fun," Maggie said. As she walked into the garage, she saw four vehicles parked side by side: two convertibles, a black SUV, and a pickup. "Wow, look at all the cars. Your insurance bill must be a doozy."

Rob laughed. "What can I say? I love cars."

"Do you have a chauffeur hiding around here somewhere to drive you around in all these vehicles?" Maggie asked, teasing.

"Very funny," Rob said, grinning. "Hop on."

They drove down the driveway and then took off on a dirt road that wound around the many acres of vineyard. At intervals, he'd stop and point out the different types of grapes. One section held

grapes used to make Chardonnay, and another section was specifi-
cally for Pinot Noir. There were more grapes in different parts of the
vineyard for making a variety of other red and white wines. Most of
the vines had already been harvested. In one section where grapes
still hung on the vines, Rob explained that they were harvested last,
for the sweeter wines.

"For someone who doesn't make wine, you sure know a lot
about it," she told him.

"Well, you can't live around here and not learn something
about the wine business," he said, grinning again. "Tonight, we get
to sample some of the wines made from these very fields."

The day was gorgeous, with the temperature in the high seventies and a cooling breeze rolling off the ocean a few miles away.
Whenever they stopped, Maggie snapped pictures of the colorful
fields and rolling hills.

After a time, Rob drove up a hill to a gazebo that overlooked
the fields. In the gazebo was a picnic table with a cooler sitting on
it. "Emma left us some lunch up here," he told Maggie. He offered
his hand and she accepted it as she stepped off the four-wheeler.

They walked toward the gazebo and its welcoming shade.
Maggie was aware that Rob hadn't let go of her hand.

"Wow. Emma is everywhere, isn't she?" Maggie said. "I wish I
had an Emma of my own. Maybe if I'd had help at home, I wouldn't
have felt like running away." The words came out before Maggie
realized what she was saying, and she pulled her hand away from
Rob's and pursed her lips. "Sorry. Too much information."

"I don't mind," Rob said casually as he began to unpack the
cooler. Emma had packed sandwiches, strawberries, grapes, pasta
salad, a bottle of red wine, and two glasses. There were also two
bottles of water in the cooler.

"Wine?" Rob asked, looking over at Maggie.

Maggie nodded. "Sure. Why not?"

He opened the bottle and poured two glasses, and then they sat down at the table and began eating.

After a few quiet moments, Rob spoke up. "You can talk to me about anything," he said as he took a sip of the wine. "As I said earlier, I'm a good listener."

Maggie didn't doubt that he was a good listener, on top of all the other things he seemed so good at. He was kind, warmhearted, and caring—that much was certain. He'd already found a small place in her heart, but she had to be careful not to let him get too close, or she might find herself doing something she'd regret.

"It's not a very interesting story," she said, looking out over the fields at the tall pines in the distance. "In fact, it's probably the most clichéd story there is. Two people get married, have children, run into trouble, one cheats, and the other has a midlife crisis and runs off. I'd tell you the ending, but I don't know it yet."

Rob stood and walked over to Maggie's side of the table. He sat down beside her, lifted her hand, and placed a light kiss on the back of it. "It may be an old story, but it hurts just the same. I hope your story has a happy ending," he told her.

Maggie turned to face Rob. She cocked her head, eyes questioning his. "Why have you never married? You have everything a person could dream of, except someone to share it all with. I can't imagine why someone hasn't scooped you up yet."

Rob laughed. "You give me too much credit."

"Has there ever been anyone special?" Maggie wanted to know.

Rob looked up, then out into the horizon, his expression suggesting he was deep in thought. Finally, he turned back to Maggie. "There was someone once. It was a long time ago, before Matt and I sold our business. All those years I worked night and day, and I loved it. Work was my life. I had a girlfriend then, but she hated that I was married to my work. I couldn't help it—I loved what I did, and I just knew that Matt and I would succeed. Finally, she left.

A year later, we sold out. I think if she had just waited a little longer, we might have ended up married."

"Did you ever contact her again?" Maggie asked.

"No. I heard she was married and had a couple of kids. I'm sure she's happier with someone else."

"Now you have time for someone in your life," Maggie said softly.

Rob sat there, still holding Maggie's hand, unconsciously rubbing his thumb back and forth across her palm. He looked up, meeting Maggie's eyes. "Unfortunately, the right woman hasn't come along," he said.

The longing in Rob's eyes was too much for Maggie. She broke away from his touch and stood, turning to stare out at the vineyards. From behind her, Rob's words came through the air and landed softly on her heart. "I feel sorry for your husband. He doesn't truly understand what he's losing."

Andrew sat on the bed for a long time after his conversation with Maggie. She was right. He had been angry at being caught like a child with his hand in the cookie jar. He'd resented ending the affair and blamed Maggie for it. So instead of coming home and begging her forgiveness, as he should have done, he'd masked himself with his anger and gone about his daily life without acknowledging what he'd done and trying to fix it. But he hadn't done it on purpose. He hadn't realized his whole being was reflecting how he felt.

*"I'm not sure anymore that we can fix this,"* Maggie had told him. Had he already lost her? Could he blame her if he had? She'd waited a long time for him to apologize, and he finally did. But was he too late?

Andrew stood and walked over to the wall of family photos in their room. The one that stood out was the one of Maggie and him together on the beach at Lake Tahoe when they were still in college. They had been so young then and so much in love. What had happened? They'd grown so far apart over the years that he hadn't even noticed it had happened until he started looking at other women. But then he'd justified his actions by telling himself that Maggie wasn't paying enough attention to him, and he deserved attention.

"I'm an idiot," he said aloud in the empty room. "I sacrificed everything for a cheap affair."

Andrew lifted the framed photo off the wall and sat once more on the bed, staring at the picture. Maggie had stayed with him even after she'd found out about the affair. At the time, he hadn't realized how much she'd gone through to keep the family together. Now, he understood. It wasn't only to give the kids a stable home. She had stayed because she'd believed that he would eventually feel some remorse for his actions and ask for her forgiveness. She had stayed because she still believed in him, even after everything he'd done. But now, she was gone. And at this very moment, she was with another man. A man who might have so much more to offer than he ever would. A man who might see in Maggie everything that Andrew had ignored for years.

"It can't be over. Not yet," Andrew said to the photo in his hands. "I love Maggie. I've always loved Maggie. I was too blinded by my own ambitions to see how good I had it all along."

Suddenly, Andrew knew exactly what he had to do.

Downstairs, Kaia was eating breakfast and watching Saturday-morning cartoons that she was much too old for but enjoyed nonetheless. Andrew smiled at the sight of his daughter, sitting there in her pajamas, eating cereal and staring at the television. He wanted to remember this moment. The exact moment he'd decided he would do whatever it took to fix his family.

"What?" Kaia asked when she saw him staring at her.

Andrew walked over to the table and gave Kaia a hug from behind. She didn't resist, but she turned to him afterward and looked at him as if he'd lost his mind.

"What was that all about?" she asked.

"Do you think you could stay with your friend Megan for a few days?" Andrew asked her.

Kaia shrugged. "I don't know. I can ask. Why?"

Andrew grinned. "Because I'm going to go find your mother and bring her home."

Maggie and Rob rode home on the four-wheeler in the late afternoon after touring a large portion of the property. "I'm sorry if I made you uncomfortable back there," Rob said as they both slipped off of the ATV in front of the garage.

Maggie shook her head. "No. It's okay."

"I'd hate for you to miss the party tonight because I said something that upset you," Rob told her. "Do you still want to go?"

"Of course. I'll go clean up. What time does it start?"

Rob smiled. "I think the tourist bus comes around five o'clock, so we can go down anytime after that."

Maggie nodded, and then headed inside the house and up the stairs. When she entered her room, she was surprised to see a black sleeveless dress hanging by her closet. Below it was a pair of shiny red pumps. She slipped out of her sneakers and socks and tried on one of the shoes. It fit perfectly. She hoped the dress would, too.

Forty-five minutes later, Maggie headed back downstairs. The black dress fit like a glove. The bodice and waist were fitted, and the skirt flared out slightly from her hips down to just above her knees. The red shoes gave the outfit a pop of color, and were surprisingly comfortable. She didn't know how Emma knew her sizes, or where she'd found the dress and shoes, but she was grateful she had. Maggie had left her hair down, styling it the way Bobbi had taught her, and was careful to do her makeup just right. She felt beautiful as she entered the family room, and the look on Rob's face told her that he thought so, too.

"My goodness, you clean up nice," he said with a grin.

Maggie smiled up at him. Rob looked handsome in tan trousers, a blue shirt and striped tie, and a navy blazer. "You don't look so bad yourself," she told him.

They walked down the driveway to the small house below. The party was in full swing when they arrived. A string quartet played softly in the background while waitresses mingled among the guests, offering glasses of wine as well as trays of cheeses, meats, crackers, and a variety of hot hors d'oeuvres.

Maggie gazed around the lovely little building. Outside on the veranda, ivy grew up the posts and twinkle lights were strung all around, creating a romantic effect. Inside, the room was a soft mustard-yellow, with terra-cotta tile floors and a cozy brick fireplace that was crackling with an inviting fire. Against another wall stood a long curved bar of gleaming oak, with padded stools lined in front of it. Behind the bar was a wall-length mirror with rows of sparkling wine glasses on shelves. There were tables and chairs strewn about, with a space left clear in front of the band for dancing. The guests were already enjoying the food and wine, and laughter filled the room and veranda.

Rob picked up two glasses of red wine off a server's tray and handed one to Maggie. "We'll start with their Pinot Noir, and then try some lighter wines," he said. They clinked glasses and each took a small sip.

"Delicious," Maggie said. "I'm not a wine connoisseur—in fact, I rarely ever drink alcohol—but this is very nice."

"Then we'll just sip, so you can try a few different ones. We don't want you stumbling home, do we?" Rob asked, his eyes sparkling with mischief.

Rob looked around the room, and then his eyes lit up. "I see the owners," he said. "Let's say hello." Placing a hand on the small of Maggie's back, he guided her toward his friends.

"Maggie, these are the owners of the winery. Gino and Adrianna DeLuca, this is Maggie Harrison. She's staying with me for a few days."

Maggie shook Gino's and Adrianna's hands in turn. They were both definitely of Italian descent, with thick black hair and rich brown eyes. Adrianna was a beautiful woman, with a svelte figure and a mane of curly black hair that fell to the middle of her back. She wore a burgundy-colored dress that hugged every curve of her body, and tall black heels. Her husband, Gino, was as handsome as she was beautiful. His wavy hair curled around his face, and his eyes sparkled when he shook Maggie's hand. His light-colored suit fit him impeccably and accentuated his olive skin. They were a gorgeous pair, and it was difficult for Maggie to believe that either of these sophisticated-looking people spent any time in the vineyards or working in the winery.

"It's so nice to meet you both," Maggie said.

"It is so nice to meet *you*," Adrianna said, smiling at Maggie. "Emma told us that Roberto had a guest, but we could hardly believe it. He so rarely brings company home."

Maggie slid her gaze to Rob, just in time to see him blush. She tried not to laugh and embarrass him even more.

"Emma is Adrianna's aunt," Rob told Maggie. "It's a big area, but almost everyone is related in one way or another."

Maggie nodded. Having lived in a small town for over twenty years, she knew exactly what he meant.

"I hope you'll be staying here for a while," Gino said to Maggie. "It's so beautiful this time of year, and there's plenty for you and Rob to do."

The DeLucas were called away to attend to other guests, leaving Maggie free to mercilessly tease Rob. "*Roberto*, is it?" she asked, and Rob blushed again.

"Adrianna likes to put on a show for the tourists," Rob said. "She's a third-generation Italian American and has no accent. She just plays it up when guests are here."

Rob took two new glasses of wine from a tray on the bar and handed one to Maggie, taking the half-empty glass from her and setting it on the bar. "Try the rosé," he said. "It's wonderful."

Maggie and Rob sat by the fireplace for a while, eating their food and watching the guests dancing, talking, and tasting wines. Chatter, laughter, and music swirled around the room, and Maggie enjoyed every minute of it. She felt a million miles away from the woman she'd been just two weeks ago. The old Maggie would never have been sitting here, dressed up and sipping wine. She decided that she liked the new Maggie much better.

Rob brought them both a glass of Chardonnay to try next, and Maggie sipped it slowly. She was already feeling the effects of the alcohol, despite being careful. When Rob extended his hand to her as an invitation to dance, she accepted without any reservations. She felt happy and carefree as Rob placed his other hand on her waist and gently led her around the dance floor.

"You can dance, too?" she asked. "Are you good at everything you do?"

Rob raised his eyebrows, making Maggie laugh and shake her head. "Forget I asked that," she said.

As they danced, night fell and the stars twinkled high above. Inside, Maggie shone as she never had before. Dancing, joking, talking, and laughing, she forgot about the heaviness of her old life and embraced the best night she'd had in years.

# CHAPTER TWENTY-FOUR

Andrew took the noon flight out of Woodroe's small airport to Minneapolis, and then connected to a nonstop flight to Seattle. After having settled Kaia in at Megan's house and being assured once again by Megan's mother that she was happy to have Kaia there for as long as necessary, he'd packed a bag and headed out. He'd called Kyle at work from the airport to tell him where he was going, and Kyle cheered him on and wished him good luck. "Tell Mom we love her and really need her, okay?" Kyle had said. Andrew had smiled at his son's words. It made him proud that his grown son wasn't afraid to show affection for his family. He realized he could learn a thing or two from him.

Andrew's plane landed in Seattle at four o'clock in the afternoon. He grabbed his luggage and stepped into a waiting cab. Before he knew it, he was standing at Cassie's front door, hoping Maggie was back from her trip and that he'd be welcome in Cassie's home.

When Cassie opened the door, she stared at him in disbelief. "What are you doing here?"

"I'm here to see Maggie."

Cassie glanced from Andrew to his suitcase on the porch beside him and back again. "She's not here. I told you on the phone that she's gone with a friend to California."

Andrew took a deep breath and swallowed his pride. If he was going to do this right, he knew he'd be doing a lot of pride swallowing over the next few days. "I know she's with your friend Rob, at his house," he said. "Maggie told me. Would you mind if I stay a couple of days and wait for her to return?"

Cassie hesitated. Finally, Andrew said, "Please, Cassie. I know you don't like me. I know you've never liked me, for whatever reason. But despite what you may think, I love Maggie. I've always loved Maggie. And I just need a chance to tell her that in person. I promise I won't be any trouble. Heck, I won't even talk to you if you don't want me to."

His speech brought a smile to Cassie's lips. "Of course you can stay, Andrew. And I'll even let you talk to me if you'd like," she said with a sly grin.

Andrew followed her into the house and stopped in the entryway. "Can I ask you one more favor?"

Cassie turned, her eyebrows raised. "Okay."

"Please don't tell Maggie I'm here. I want her to come back on her own, because she wants to. I don't want her to come back just because she knows I'm here and she thinks she has to. Okay?"

Cassie nodded. Then she showed Andrew to his room.

Maggie and Rob danced one last slow dance as the party was winding down and the guests were preparing to leave. By this time, Maggie had tried several varieties of the DeLuca wines, and she felt a little tipsy and light-headed. With her arms around Rob's neck, and his around her waist, they swayed gently to the music, unaware and not caring if anyone was watching them.

"Thank you," Maggie whispered in Rob's ear as the music played on. Her face was so close to his, she felt the softness of his beard against her cheek.

"For what?" Rob asked, looking surprised.

"For making me feel alive again."

When the music ended, they thanked Gino and Adrianna for the lovely time. Adrianna gave Rob and Maggie each a hug good-bye. "Come again soon," she said, her thick, fake accent now gone. "I'd love getting to know you better," she said to Maggie.

Maggie and Rob stepped out into the clear, starlit night, happy that the damp fog hadn't rolled in. Maggie stumbled, and Rob caught her. She wrapped her arm around his for support as they slowly made their way up the hill.

"I think I drank more than I should have," she said, giggling. "You shouldn't have given me so many different wines to try."

"You really are a lightweight," he teased. "I'll make some coffee when we get back to the house."

When they reached the house, Rob started the coffeemaker and built a fire. Maggie sat in one of the cushy chairs and slipped off her heels.

"I have a surprise for you," Rob said, heading over to his stereo system. He turned it on and, a moment later, Bob Seger began singing "Roll Me Away."

Maggie laughed. "Nothing else could be more perfect."

Rob poured two mugs of coffee and handed one to Maggie. She held it tightly in both hands, savoring the warmth of the mug and the aroma of the coffee.

"Bob is quickly becoming my favorite person," Rob said with a smirk. "Without him, you might never have come here."

Maggie smiled at Rob. He was sweet and kind, and she'd enjoyed spending the last few days with him. "Thank you for such a nice time," she said. "This whole trip with you has been so relaxing and fun. I'll be sorry when I have to leave."

"Then don't leave," Rob said.

Maggie's eyes grew wide.

"What I meant is you're welcome to stay as long as you like. I have nowhere to be and no one needing me, so I'm happy for the company," Rob said.

Maggie stared down at her mug. "I do have somewhere to be, though," she said quietly. "I can't run forever. I'll have to go home eventually. Probably soon."

They both sat silently for a while, drinking their coffee and listening to the music. After a while, Rob spoke up. "You look beautiful tonight, Maggie. I was proud to have you with me at the party."

Maggie gazed into the fire. "If I look good at all, it's because Emma did a wonderful job picking out a dress for me."

Rob set down his mug and turned to Maggie. He placed his fingers lightly under her chin, turning her face toward his. "That was a compliment, Maggie. Don't downplay it and sell yourself short. You're a beautiful woman. Don't you know that?"

Maggie lowered her eyes. "I've never thought of myself that way. When you've been married as long as I have, compliments go by the wayside. I haven't thought of myself as pretty in a long time. But thank you."

Rob stood and reached for Maggie's hand. "Let's have one more dance, compliments of Bob."

Maggie stood and followed Rob to the open area between the family room and the kitchen. Bob was now singing "We've Got Tonight," a slow, mellow song. With her heels now off, Maggie was much shorter than Rob, but she fit in perfectly against him as he placed his arm around her waist and held her hand. They swayed slowly to the music in the dim light of the room, the fire giving off a soft glow.

Maggie moved in closer and placed her head on Rob's shoulder, enjoying his nearness. It had been a long time since anyone had held her close. A long time since she'd felt a caring touch. She cleared her mind of every worry and heartache she'd ever felt and just savored the nearness of this man she barely knew but felt she'd known for ages.

"If I were lucky enough to have someone like you in my life, I'd tell you every day how lovely you are. You deserve that, Maggie," Rob whispered in her ear as he held her tight.

Maggie lifted her head and gazed up into Rob's eyes. He lifted his hand and softly touched her face, running his thumb across her jawline, causing her body to feel weak from his touch. Slowly, he lowered his head and gently touched her lips with his. Maggie responded, wrapping her arms around his neck and rising up to meet his lips with her own. For one long moment, they kissed, but then the music ended, jarring Maggie out of her dreamlike state and back to reality. Reluctantly, she pulled away, taking a step back from Rob.

"I'm so sorry," she said softly, seeing the crestfallen look in Rob's eyes. "I just can't. I'm married, and I can't do to him what he did to me."

Rob stepped forward and grasped Maggie's hand in his. "Don't be sorry, Maggie. I'm not. I feel closer to you than I have to anyone else in a long time. But I understand. You made it perfectly clear that we are just friends, and I shouldn't have taken advantage of you. I'm afraid I couldn't help myself."

Maggie pulled away from his touch and moved back to the fireplace. Rob turned off the stereo and flicked on the overhead light in the kitchen, causing the magic of the evening to disappear. He walked over to where Maggie stood.

"I think I should go back to Cassie's tomorrow," Maggie said sadly. "It's time I go home and try to straighten out my life before I make an even bigger mess of it."

"Please don't go because of what just happened. I promise it won't happen again. I'd really love for you to stay a while longer," Rob told her.

Maggie gave Rob a small smile. "If I stay, it will happen again. I'm not going to lie. I'm attracted to you, and if I stay, it will just complicate my life further. I have to try to fix my marriage. I know things between Andrew and I have been bad for a while, but we used to be good together. I have to at least try one more time to fix things with him."

Rob looked at Maggie with soulful eyes. "Your husband is an idiot," he said, then smiled wanly. "But he's a very lucky man."

Maggie walked over and pulled Rob into a hug. She was grateful to him for the time they'd spent together, and she hoped they could still be good friends.

Maggie left early the next morning, driving Rob's black BMW convertible back to Seattle. She'd asked about taking a flight, but Rob insisted she take the car instead. He said he'd fly up the next time he visited Matt and Cassie and pick up his car then.

As she drove, Maggie thought about the past few days with Rob. She was surprised at the strong feelings she'd developed for him in such a short time. In all the years she'd been married, she'd never once looked at another man. But after such a long time of feeling alone and unloved, it had been easy to respond to Rob's attention. She wondered if that was what had happened to Andrew. Had he felt so disconnected from her that he'd searched for warmth from another woman? A part of her understood now how easy it would be to accept the affections of another in order to hide from your problems. That didn't excuse Andrew for what he'd done, but she understood his actions a little better.

She was relieved she hadn't done anything to make her situation even more complicated. She'd never had any intention of looking for love in another man's arms. She'd stayed with Andrew after the affair not only because of the children but also because she'd wanted to believe they could fix their marriage. And even now, she still wanted to believe it, despite everything.

It was time to go home and face up to their problems, whatever the outcome.

It was a twelve-hour drive from Rob's home to Cassie's, taking the main highway. Now that Maggie had made up her mind to go home, she just wanted to get back to Cassie's so tomorrow she could head for home. She'd spent enough time thinking about what she wanted, and she missed her children terribly. No matter what happened with Andrew, she needed to be home with her kids.

By the time she reached Cassie's house, it was after seven o'clock in the evening. The sun was just setting on the horizon as she entered the house, carrying a small bag Rob had loaned her for the few items of clothing she'd brought along.

Cassie was in the kitchen when she saw Maggie enter the house, and she rushed to her side. "You're already home!" she exclaimed. "I thought for sure you'd stay there a few more days. Why didn't you call me to pick you up at the airport?"

Maggie hugged her cousin, happy to be back after the long drive. "I drove one of Rob's cars instead. He insisted. He said he'd pick it up on his next visit."

Cassie seemed nervous and kept glancing toward the kitchen. Maggie was tired and just wanted to go up to her room and sleep. She knew she had a long drive ahead of her over the next couple of days to go home. But she couldn't help but notice that Cassie was acting strange.

"What's going on? You're acting weird," Maggie said.

Cassie sighed. "It's Andrew. He's here."

"*Here?* How long has he been here? Why didn't you call to tell me?"

"He showed up yesterday afternoon. I didn't call you because he asked me not to. He just wanted to wait for you." Cassie pulled Maggie toward the kitchen and pointed to the deck where the lights were now on as the sky darkened. "He's been moping around here the entire time. I kind of felt sorry for him."

"*You* felt sorry for *him*?"

"Oh, stop it. You'd better go out and talk to him before he jumps off the deck."

Maggie ran her hand through her hair to smooth it down and fidgeted with her T-shirt. She hoped she didn't look as terrible as she felt after a long day in the car. Taking a deep breath, she opened the patio door and stepped into the chilly night.

"Andrew?"

Andrew turned and his face lit up with surprise. "Maggie, you're back."

Maggie walked closer to him. They didn't embrace. They only stared at each other.

"Maggie. You look . . . wonderful," Andrew said, his eyes slowly surveying her. "Your hair looks really nice. You look beautiful."

Andrew's compliment unbalanced Maggie. She wasn't used to him noticing how she looked. "Why are you here?" she asked bluntly.

"Am I too late?" Andrew asked sadly.

Maggie frowned. "Too late for what?"

"To win you back."

Maggie stood there, stunned, as the ocean breeze caressed her skin and the damp air chilled her. But it wasn't the breeze or the damp air that caused the goose bumps to tingle down her spine. It was Andrew's words. The words she'd been waiting a long time to hear. She was so taken aback, she didn't know how to respond.

Andrew drew closer, taking her hands in his. He said softly, "You were right, Maggie. I didn't try hard enough to win you back. In fact, I didn't try at all. I just wanted to brush what I'd done under the rug and forget about it. But I was wrong. I'm so sorry. I'll do anything I can, anything you ask of me, if you'll give me another chance." He let go of one of her hands and pulled a folded piece of paper out of his back pocket.

"What's that?" Maggie asked.

Andrew slowly unfolded the paper. It was a copy of the photo of the two of them that hung on their bedroom wall. Before he'd left home, he'd asked Kaia to copy it so he could take it with him. Now, he handed the sheet of paper to Maggie.

"It's us," he said. "It's the couple we used to be, the happy couple I want us to be again."

Tears filled Maggie's eyes. She hadn't even realized he'd ever noticed this old photo on the wall, but he'd actually made a copy of it to bring to her. To remind her that he remembered how good they had once been together.

"I don't know what to say," she murmured. "I want to be like we were then, but can we? Is it possible to go back, after everything that's happened? You've changed, and so have I. I don't know if we can ever be like that again."

Andrew tilted her chin up so she could look into his eyes. She knew his eyes well, but she hadn't looked at him like this, so closely, so intimately, in a very long time.

"I mean it when I say I'll do whatever it takes for us to be happy again," Andrew said. "I know that somewhere along the way we both lost who we were. But I also know we can get it back. We can do whatever you want, Maggie. We can move somewhere else if you'd like and start over again. You can open an artists' shop, like you've always talked about, and work at your photography. And I'm going to quit all those committees that take up my free time so I can spend more time with you and the kids. The whole idea that I would run for mayor was ridiculous anyway. And it isn't as important as my relationship with you and the kids. Anything, Maggie, just say what you want me to do, and I'll do it."

Maggie's heart swelled. She was so happy to hear him say that she and the kids were important to him. She'd wanted to hear this for so long, and had been afraid she never would.

"Andrew, I never said I wanted to move. I like our town. We've planted roots there and raised the kids there. And I never meant for you to give up your committee work. You love doing all that. And running for mayor? That's your dream. I wouldn't ask you to not run if that's what you really want. All I've ever wanted was for you to balance your time better between family and volunteering. Even though the kids are getting older, they still need you. And *I* need you," Maggie said softly.

"Oh, Maggie. I'm so happy to hear you say that you still need me," Andrew said. He gently cupped her face with his hand. "I've missed you so much," he whispered.

Tears fell down Maggie's cheeks, and Andrew brushed them away with the side of his thumb. "To be honest, Maggie, I don't think it was ever my dream to become mayor. I was just fulfilling my parents' dreams. And as for all the committee work I do, if I'm completely honest, I only did it as a means to an end, not because I was so civic minded. Derrick pointed that out to me, and although it made me angry at the time, deep down, I knew he was right."

Maggie stared at Andrew, completely confused. "Derrick? Why would he say that to you?"

Andrew chuckled. "Apparently, he and the entire town think I'm a jerk. And you know what? They're all right. I am a jerk. I let my family fall by the wayside while I tried to act like a big shot. But I don't want to be a big shot, Maggie. I want to be your husband, and Kaia's and Kyle's dad. That's more than enough for me."

Maggie laughed with joy as more tears rolled down her cheeks. She reached out her arms and Andrew pulled her close. It felt so good to finally be in the arms of the man she was meant to be with. The man she'd chosen to be her partner many years ago and still, deep down, wanted to share her life with.

After a time, Maggie pulled away and looked at Andrew seriously. "It's not going to be easy," she told him. "We still have a lot to get through. A lot to talk about. Are you game for the long run?"

"I'm game," he said, smiling. "And we'll start by taking our time going home. I think a road trip sounds like fun, don't you?"

"Road trip? What about Kaia? What about work?"

"Kaia is fine at Megan's house, and her mother said to take our time. And my job can wait. I haven't taken a vacation in years. It's about time I did," Andrew said with a grin. "Besides, I can't wait to drive that Mustang across country. I was looking at it today. It's a great car."

Maggie laughed as they linked arms and walked inside. She knew it wasn't going to be easy and that all their problems weren't going to solve themselves. But she was happy they were going to try. It was all she'd ever asked for. And a few hundred miles on the highway together, with Bob as their soundtrack, might be exactly what they needed to bring them back together.

# EPILOGUE

Eight months later, Maggie stood in her charming little shop in downtown Woodroe as people milled about. It was the Northern Artists' Gallery's grand opening, and everyone in town was stopping by to wish Maggie well in her new venture. Even though the shop had been open for a month already, today was the day for everyone to celebrate.

Not long after returning home, Maggie had used some of her inheritance to rent an empty building right off Main Street. It was an old building like all the other downtown buildings, built in 1895, and had a main floor and a basement that Maggie currently used for storage. The feature that had drawn Maggie to this particular space was the large display window in front, perfect for showing off artwork. She'd fixed up the shop with shelving and glass cases. In addition to carrying local artists' paintings, photographs, and sculptures, she featured unique handmade pottery and jewelry. She also carried books written by local authors. Every piece was sold on consignment, so Maggie didn't have to invest much for inventory. So far, the sales had been good. Maggie knew that summertime, when the tourists came to town, would be her best months for sales, so that was why she'd hurried to open the shop by May.

Maggie's photography from her weeks on the road was displayed proudly beside the other artists' work. The walls of the shop were covered with her memories of the weeks she'd run away from home, and they were happy memories. That trip had helped her find her place in the world again, and had brought her closer to her children and Andrew than she'd ever thought possible.

Cassie made her way through the crowd to Maggie, carrying a large framed print of the curving mountain road that led up to Mount Rushmore. "I sold another print," she said, beaming.

Maggie smiled at her cousin. Cassie, Matt, and the kids had come for the grand opening, and Cassie had taken it upon herself to help out in the store. She was a natural salesperson and had already sold several prints that day as well as a few pieces of jewelry. Kaia, who'd turned fifteen over the winter, was also helping Maggie in the shop. She planned on working all summer with Maggie and also on weekends during the school year. She couldn't wait to turn sixteen and have a car of her own—preferably a small sports car like Maggie's Mustang—so she was saving all her money.

"Take it to Kaia to ring up," Maggie instructed Cassie, then walked over to where Cindi and a few of the other group-home residents stood with her former boss, Jan, admiring a photo of the vineyards around Rob's home.

"Your photos are beautiful," Jan told her, giving her a hug. "Congratulations."

Maggie hugged all her friends in turn, thanking each for coming. She and Cindi hugged the longest. Maggie knew that Cindi still missed her, but she invited her to come visit her at the shop anytime.

Across the room, Maggie caught Kyle's eye as he and Ashley talked to friends in front of the local photos she'd taken over the winter and spring. Kyle smiled and nodded, then turned his attention back to his friends. He'd finished his fall college classes but hadn't gone to school that past spring. Instead, he'd worked full-time at the motorcycle shop. He planned to go to the technical college in the fall for a degree in automotive service technology. Maggie was happy that he was finally doing what he loved, and they'd just have to wait and see where it led him.

Derrick Weis and his wife stopped by to say hello, as did a few of the kids' past teachers who Maggie had assisted as a room mother. Russ from the pub and Charles Larson from the bank also popped in. Everyone in town was dropping by, and it warmed Maggie's heart that they were all so supportive of her new business.

Andrew walked over to Maggie and draped his arm around her waist. "Amazing, isn't it? This town can really come together and support one of its own when it wants to."

Maggie glanced over to the corner of the room where Andrew's mother was standing in the center of a group of older women. Her lips were pursed tightly, and her expression was sour. "What about your mother? She doesn't look pleased to be here."

Andrew's face broke out in a smile. He bent his head toward Maggie so only she could hear. "I don't think she's very happy at how successful your shop is, but her friends all love it, so she has to pretend she does, too."

Maggie laughed along with Andrew. He looked relaxed and happy, and for that, she was thankful. As promised, he'd resigned from most of his committees, and surprisingly enough, when it came time to nominate someone to run for mayor, many of his former committee colleagues had asked him to run. Andrew had been ready to decline, but it was Maggie who had told him to reconsider. After much thought, he finally realized that being mayor was something he did want to do, so he was now in the midst of running for office. Maggie didn't mind. She wanted him to be as happy as she was with her shop. Over the past few months, Andrew had immersed himself in family life. He now helped her when she cooked dinner and even did a load or two of laundry each week. On weekends, he was right there when she and Kaia went bowling or to the arcade. Surprisingly, he and Kaia joined a Sunday-afternoon family bowling league and had a blast competing against the other teams. Kyle, and sometimes Ashley, too, joined the fun whenever they could, and dinnertime had once again become family time. Maggie could tell that Andrew was actually enjoying his time with the kids, as he had years ago.

As a couple, they were healing as well. It took time, but the trust grew as the weeks and months passed, and they were slowly becoming exactly as Andrew had hoped—like the happy couple they had once been. Older, yes, and no longer naive about the ups and downs of marriage, definitely—but they were finding their way back to happiness.

As Maggie surveyed the photos on the wall, she was reminded of her trip last fall, and of the people she'd met. She'd kept in touch with Robert "Wild Bill" Prescott as well as Bobbi, and sent each a print of a photo she'd taken of them. Wild Bill told her he was going back to teach middle school in the fall, but he planned to use his acting talents to help with the school plays. Bobbi had met a man and told Maggie that she hoped she'd be inviting her to her wedding very soon.

The one person she hadn't contacted was Rob. She heard about him through Cassie and was sure he heard what she was up to as well. But Maggie decided it was best to just let their friendship go. She didn't want anything to get in the way of healing her relationship with Andrew. Rob would always be a sweet memory that she'd leave tucked away like a photo in a scrapbook.

As Maggie started to walk up to the counter to help Cassie and Kaia wrap and ring up purchases, a familiar song began playing on the overhead speakers in the shop. It was the song that had enticed her to run away, "Roll Me Away" by Bob Seger. Maggie smiled.

She was no longer lost, no longer angry, and she finally knew her place in the world. It had taken a rock 'n' roll singer, miles of highway, hundreds of photos, a gunslinger, a hairstylist, and a man in a vineyard to help her become her true self again. She sent up a silent thank-you to all her new friends who had helped her find her way back, and then made her way, smiling and chatting, through the crowd.

# AUTHOR'S NOTE

*Maggie's Turn* is a work of fiction. Woodroe, Minnesota, is a fictional town that I created for this novel, and it portrays a typical small town in Minnesota but does not reflect any one town in particular. All the characters depicted in this novel are fictional. Well, except for Bob Seger, a famous, talented, old-time rock 'n' roller whose music I mention throughout the novel. If you haven't had the pleasure of listening to Seger's music, then be sure to pick up his first *Greatest Hits* album, the one I mention in the story. If you love rock 'n' roll, you'll love his music.

One final note. In Deadwood, South Dakota, at Old Saloon #10, Wild Bill Hickok is shot daily. There is a gentleman who has been portraying Wild Bill there for many years, and he does such an excellent job of it that you forget he's not the real thing. My Wild Bill in this novel is not that talented gentleman. He is a product of my imagination, created to fit the story.

# ABOUT THE AUTHOR

 Bestselling author Deanna Lynn Sletten writes heartwarming women's fiction and romance novels. Sletten has two grown children and lives with her husband in northern Minnesota. When not writing, she enjoys walking the wooded trails around her home with her dog.

For more information, please visit www.deannalynnsletten.com.